THE LUMENOTS

THE LUMENOTS

NORBERT STEWART

LOWELL
STEWART
PUBLISHING

Published in Canada in 2015 by
Lowell Stewart Pubishing
lowellstewartpublishing@gmail.com

3 4 5 6 7   18 17 16 15

The Lumenots
ISBN Number 978-0-9920433-0-8
EPub ISBN Number 978-0-9920433-3-9
Mobi ISBN Number 978-0-9920433-4-6

Printed by CreateSpace
An Amazon.com Company

ACKNOWLEDGEMENTS

I would like to express a sincere thank you to my wife Theresa for her on-going encouragement and support and boundless patience in the writing of this book, my children, Monique and Sean for their encouragement and prodding to "get on with it" and to Heather English for her support, encouragement, cover elements and reviewing activities. Without the help of these magnificent individuals, the story would have remained part of my "didn't get around to it bucket list".

I also express my gratitude to Stephen and Emily Farquharson and Yvonne MacPhee for the design of the cover, proof reading and valuable suggestions regarding the layout of the text.

PROLOGUE

VANAVARA - SATURDAY, JANUARY 7, 1905

It was a clear Siberian night; crystal clear with not a cloud in the sky. Though the moon was not visible through the small window in the loft, Stepan saw that its light coloured almost everything in the modest space a warm blue. On the opposite side of the room, his younger brother Yakov, completely oblivious to what Stepan was seeing, was sound asleep, a well deserved sleep after a long, cold and arduous day helping his brother and parents with the endless routine of farm chores. But for Stepan, tired as he was, the sight was magnetic and more powerful than the need to sleep. He wondered just how many stars there were, those white, often twinkling specks of light so clear against the dark sky, not realizing that he was staring directly into his own future and that of his yet unborn family.

Thousands of kilometers to the west Miroslav was also pondering the infinite heavens from the window of his flat, but for entirely different, yet oddly related reasons. Dr. Miroslav Oborski, a theoretical physicist, academically brilliant, well published and a well respected, enormously popular dissident resided unfortunately in a political environment rife with amorphous top-to-bottom paranoia. These were not qualities consistent with personal longevity. While somewhat oblivious to his political naivety, Miroslav held fast to his belief in humanity, that all things were possible and that the history of planet Earth may not be entirely of its own making.

EARTH DATE - JANUARY 7, 1905

By traditional standards, the ship was small, less than one hundred metres in length with a breadth that varied from five to ten metres. Most of it was an exo-skeleton with only three areas covered with a silvery, super smooth skin. It did not have to be large or conventional in construction. In fact, the ship was highly unconventional. It carried no living beings and, therefore, required no environmental control systems, save the experimental fuel housed in a super cooled cell located at the trailing end of the ship. 2,4 Dinitrophysium was one of a group of metal organo compounds developed specifically for the new warp drive. Although totally stable within a wide range of temperatures, at elevated pressures or temperatures, even a small amount rapidly destabilized, resulting in an explosion of near nuclear proportions. The ship was carrying slightly more than two hundred fifty kilograms of 2,4 Dinitrophysium.

Almost all computer systems on the ship possessed redundancy. Captained by a set of three identical computer systems, the ship automatically transmitted operational updates upon entering and leaving warp, signals that would eventually be picked up by way stations located at strategic points throughout the universe. The intercepted data would then be transmitted by gravitational wave communication techniques to the home base.

The last report indicated small but measurable power anomalies that were confirmed by both ComSys1 and 2 as well as an increase in the frequency of the anomalies. The command to exit warp was authorized by CompSys3, bringing the antiproton initiated micro-fusion sub-warp drive on line until such time as the source of the problem could be identified and rectified, perhaps requiring the deployment of repair robots. An update was transmitted in the normal fashion, stating only the coordinates of the ship; approaching the third planet from a yellow dwarf star well known to the base and that systems analyses were being conducted.

The exit from went smoothly. However, the root cause of the power fluctuation problem could not be precisely identified by the analysis process, complexed in part by the unavailability of access to the complete array of computing power. Other systems, primarily CompSys3 were busily engaged in attempting to calculate risk assessments of alternative measures:

1. Re-establish warp and continue on the programmed flight path

2. Re-establish flight path at sub-warp speed

3. Establish geo-stationery orbit over nearest planet and await repairs or instructions

Although problem identification was not halted, CompSys3 initiated the command to accept alternative three and the ship reoriented its flight path to intercept the orbital path of the small blue planet, timing its run to make an apogee intercept, thereby marginalizing the requirement for anti-gravity assistance, a wonderful devise but a power sponge of mammoth proportions! Once the geo-stationery orbit was established, with the 2,4 Dinitrophysium compartment pointed toward the planet's surface to minimize heating and reduce power requirement. A message to that effect was transmitted to base and the ship automatically shut down all non essential systems.

All transmissions were sent to Waystation MW417-9, an unmanned retransmitter located approximately 2.47 earth LY's from earth. From this point, the transmissions were forwarded by gravitational wave links to the home base.

Authors Axiom No. 1 – *That which is totally unexpected, is totally inevitable!*

Authors Axiom No. 2 – *Gravity sucks!*

Authors Axiom No. 3 – *Calculated results and reality are frequently total strangers!*

EARTH DATE - AUGUST 17, 1906

Orbital decay was detected within the first 65 revolutions, requiring a draw-down on the limited fuel reserves considerably greater than estimated. CompSys1 calculated that, at the present rate, orbital decay would become irreversible in another 300 to 350 revolutions, barring interception by a rescue from home base or Aqualarus 7.

EARTH DATE - JUNE 30, 1908

As the distant star cast its last rays of the day over the blue-green landscape far below the ship, on revolution 314, the craft had fallen to within 1,200 kilometers of the surface and well beyond the point of no return. The inevitable had arrived. It would now be only a matter of time until the ship, totally out of control, slammed into the atmosphere.

At six thousand meters above the surface of the planet, the recorders were launched. The blinding flash of exploding 2,4 Dinitrophysium was only 15 microseconds long; the time it takes a bullet to travel a scant two centimeters down a rifle barrel and in that 15 microseconds, the temperature of the ship shot to more than 20,000 deg. C. The ship and everything in it, was instantly vaporized; reduced to countless trillions of free atoms, charged ions and molecular bundles, spread throughout the rapidly expanding fireball.

VANAVARA - TUESDAY, JUNE 30, 1908

Stepan Semjonov had little reason to think that this day would be any different than any other June day in this area of Siberia. Farming in the Tunguska Region was hard work every day, including today, but his tall, lean frame, topped with a head full of midnight black hair and friendly dark eyes meant survival, but not much else. Yet he, his parents and his younger brother Yakov, carried on the tradition handed to them by previous generations. Yakov was a head shorter than his older brother, a head that was also awash with scraggly black hair and dark, piercing eyes. Like their father, they were only mildly interested in the politics of Russia and the so-called "leadership" of Czar Nicholas II. There was little incentive to be otherwise than passive and, besides, there were many other, far important matters with which to be concerned, not the least of which was survival in this richly wooded but environmentally harsh and unforgiving land.

The last day of June was most pleasant, clear with a light breeze, a little cooler than he would liked to have seen it, but a nice day just the same. It wasn't far for him and his fifteen year old brother to go, since the farm was less than ten kilometers from Vanavara Station and, with considerable urging by Stepan, he and his still bleary eyed brother left the house at around 5:45 AM. The purpose of the trip was to pick up much needed supplies at the Vanavara Station and Stepan had insisted on going instead of his father. Yakov also sort of insisted on going (although he wasn't all that keen on rising so early) and, between the two, that surprised their father. Not so much with their mother who, being a woman after all, suspected Stepan's real motive although mystery still surrounded Yakov's reasoning.

Stepan loved the farm as did Yakov. The only difference being that Stepan also loved farming. Yakov, on the other hand, loved the farm but hated farming. Working dawn to dusk for little more than what he saw as a subsistence survival held no appeal for him. Stepan saw the world in a different light. He felt an attachment to the land; land that had been worked by their family for... well, longer than he, his father and his father's father could remember. Stepan also carried a torch for the lovely Polina Zukanova, the only daughter of the managers of the Vanavara Post store that so fascinated Yakov. The vision of her long brown hair and eyes that could calm the most ferocious of beasts was burned in Stepan's mind. Stepan was in love!

And to complicate matters, so also was Polina in love with Stepan. But neither could inform their parents, at least not for a few years yet since Polina was only 16 and Stepan, 18 years of age.

Yakov was also in love but it was a love of a different kind. He loved Polina's parents business; how it functioned, how they obtained supplies, the ever changing inventory, their access to news from, well, everywhere and, most importantly, the art of trade and barter and it was business that he knew would be his life. Without realizing it, he was a burgeoning Capitalist.

The trip to Vanavara was not so much an adventure as it was a re-acquaintance with the land they both loved. The sun was just starting to awaken shadows of the seemingly endless forest of tall spruce and juniper trees that lined the road. The only betrayal of wind was the tops of the trees swaying in perfect unison as if by music unheard by human ears.

The horse kept a steady, easy lope as it moved along the dirt road. The steel rims and wooden spokes of the little two wheeled wagon loaded with constantly shifting burlap bags of grain, explored each and every rut, assuring that the two passengers spent at least half the trip airborne. They finally arrived at Vanavara Station, quickly dismounted, tethered the horse with others to a wooden hitch next to the veranda and went inside. It was 7:15 A.M.

They both spotted it at much the same time; off to the northeast, a glowing ball of fire trailing a long plume of grey black smoke. Yakov and Stepan had seen meteorites several times before but this time, there was a difference. The fireball was not so much round as oblong with sparks filling the smoky trail as it rushed along at a shallow angle.

Without warning, the fireball disappeared and was instantly replaced with an enormous white glare that filled much of the sky and bathed everything in white light so intense that nothing could be seen in its brilliance. Although it was clear that there had been an explosion, no sound was heard for almost three minutes.

Then it came; first the heat. It arrived on the front of a compression wave that slammed into the post store at almost 100 metres per second. It ripped through Stepan's clothes and Yakov's ears felt like they were about to explode. So intense was the heat that they thought the store, everything and everybody in it would catch fire. The startled and half blinded horses ripped from their tethers and began running in all directions, crashing through wood rail fences, turning Stepan's cart into kindling and tossing burlap bags through the air as if they were feathers.

Then came the wind and its mind numbing sound, like a hundred locomotives all passing through at the same time. A low rumble that filled the dust laden air with fear the like of which none had ever experienced. There was no hiding from it; no place of shelter or safety. Stepan, Yakov, Polina and her parents were all thrown to the floor of the building and windows popped out as if driven by an unseen fist and the building itself swayed back and forth but held its ground though nothing inside did. Then came the wind again, from the exact opposite direction, but not as strong as before, filling the vacuum created by the explosion.

The object had exploded over the Tunguska forest, more than seventy kilometers away. As Stepan, Yakov, Polina and her parents started to get up and regain their composure and the ground under them stopped trembling, a dust filled mushroom shaped cloud boiled steadily upward into the cloudless sky above the horizon.

MOSCOW

THURSDAY, APRIL 23, 1925

It was raining; not just a gentle rain that growing plants love so much. This was a downpour that would have made Noah's neighbours instant believers! It was just a little past 7 PM when Dr. Miroslav Oborski emerged from the front entrance of his workplace, the Institute for Scientific Research Building No. 14, a non-descript, grey concrete structure, designed by an imagination less architect, but it fit well with the other non-descript buildings in this non-descript part of the city. The pouring rain actually enhanced the look of the area, that gave it an almost pristine, motion picture setting. But, for Miroslav, this was no make believe motion picture script. This was his reality and reality had not been all that kind to him, at least until recently.

The shadeless dim lamp over the doorway cast Miroslav in a near full length shadow, made all the more eerie by the wide brimmed fedora he was wearing. Although in his late forties, he looked somewhat older, tall, relatively slim, a full head of graying hair atop a face that most women would find somewhat attractive, perhaps enhanced by the grey moustache and deep set black eyes. Still, he had never married.

He gave little notice to the black car parked on the opposite side of the street about a hundred meters to his left, made almost invisible by the torrential rain striking the cobbled street so hard as to cast a ghostly fog like mist. Nor did he notice the taillights flash briefly and another car eased around the corner and onto the street, a taxi with its yellow and black sign on the roof.

It pulled to a stop in front of the Institute, Dr. Oborski rushed to the car, protecting his beloved, although well worn fedora as best he could with his equally well worn brown leather briefcase.

"Where to sir," inquired the driver, a man Miroslav guessed to be in his mid thirties and well dressed for a Moscow taxi driver. It was dry and comfortable in the taxi and that was all he wanted for the time being and, besides, it gave him a chance to collect his thoughts as they drove along, traffic becoming thicker as they approached a section of the city filled with small shops and restaurants.

Time to collect his thoughts! Indeed, there wasn't much else that occupied his days other than the collection of thoughts, reviewing and re-reviewing reams of data. Dr. Miroslav Oborski had graduated at the top of his class but the Russian administration under Lenin and now Stalin, while cognizant of his academic qualifications, was less that appreciative of his public soapbox orations. Under circumstances that passed for 'normal' in 1920's Russia, Miroslav would have simply been made to disappear. But unwittingly or not, Miroslav had become something of a pop culture icon to a growing number of every day Russians with his 'coffee-shop' talks on the deafness of the Russian hierarchy.

Miroslav was not totally oblivious to what was clearly going on around him, although somewhat naïve when it came to judging its impact. His mid-town office and lab had been removed from him, his budget had been sliced to near zero, paydays were getting fewer and far between and his workstation was little more than an empty space in the corner of the basement of the Institute. They were trying to get rid of him alright; they hoped to bore him to death!

"2357 Rubstovsk Blvd. please," said Miroslav.

"Did you have a good day, Dr. Oborski," asked the driver.

Miroslav started to respond but before the words could be formed he replied, "How do you know me? You don't look familiar."

"You're not unknown in Moscow, Doctor or perhaps in much of central Russia for that matter I expect," responded the driver. "I don't wish to alarm you Doctor, but I don't have a great deal of time so perhaps I should get right to the point."

"I don't know who you are or what you want," said Miroslav, now clearly annoyed, confused and somewhat worried, "but I want you to pull to the curb and I will hail another cab. I will pay the fare of course."

Miroslav tried his best to remain calm and at least give the outward impression of being in control while seated in the back seat of a moving automobile and with a heart rate approaching critical levels, believing that the Politburo had decided that he had reached the end of his shelf life!

"I'm sorry, Doctor. I cannot do that and believe me sir, you have nothing to fear from me", said the driver. "We are on our way to your street as directly as possible and yet, I have much to tell you. All I ask is that you listen. By the way, my name is Yermac Janeskanov. I know that means nothing to you. My employer is Mr. Viktor Treschev who is Chairman of the National Science and Development Foundation. You may be familiar with Mr. Treschev or his Foundation."

Miroslav recognized both but had never met Mr. Treschev although his philanthropic ventures were quite familiar to him. Although visibly ill at ease and unsure if he had become the victim of a kidnapping and a cleaver plot by those who sought to keep him quiet, Miroslav realized that listening, at least until an alternative plan could be formulated, was his only option for the time being.

"Doctor, "allow me to review some of your recent history and perhaps that will help ease your mind," continued the driver. "You are a career scientist, an outstanding Physicist with an abiding interest in, shall we say, the science of space and things of the future. You also have a strong love for mother Russia and you have made no secret of your less than kindly views of the morals and actions of some top ranking politicians," he continued, glancing briefly at the rear view mirror. "While these views have struck a positive chord with many of the general public who are sick to death of the corruption, lies and outright thievery by officials, they see no alternative and fear the worst for themselves and their families if they attempt to do anything about it. You have moved from being a minor irritant to a major pain that won't simply go away. To that end, you have long since lost favour with those who control project funding and, as you know, you have been moved from the prestigious central location to a basement cubical in the outskirts of nowhere and a enough project rejection letters to wallpaper a good sized room. Am I on track Doctor," he concluded, checking Miroslav's expression in the mirror.

The view outside the taxi became even more blurred as Miroslav re-lived his fall from grace and the path he had created for himself, something he had realized for many years but simply refused to dwell on. Lightning flashes lit up the night sky, silhouetting the city skyline and the rumble of distant thunder was almost constant. But, it all went virtually unnoticed by Miroslav, now lost in contemplative thought. In spite of hearing that the driver was in the employee of the NSDF, which he wasn't at all certain he actually believed, the conversation provided little to ease his concerns and growing state of confusion.

"Yes, of course you're quite correct and I know it's now far too late to try and redeem myself to my overlords... nor would I want to at this stage," admitted Miroslav, spoken quietly as if not to be overheard by prying ears.

"I'm glad to hear you say that Doctor and I will explain why in a moment. About a month ago, you were visited by a Mr. Kazamin Barkov. Isn't that correct?"

"Yes... yes. That's correct. But... how? And you are Cossack. Am I correct?" Immediately upon asking the question, Miroslav realized he had just succumbed to a lapse of control and his mouth was in gear while his brain was momentarily stuck in neutral.

"Yes, Doctor, I am Cossack. I compliment you on your powers of observation and unique knowledge of Russian people, although I'm not sure what inference you can draw from that. But to your question, how we know is, at this point, unimportant. What is important is that you know who these people are, Doctor," responded Yermac.

"People? There was only Mr. Barkov", said Miroslav. "A very well spoken, obviously well educated Russian gentleman."

"True, Kazamin is well educated and an articulate speaker. But he has a brother, Slava, and believe me, Slava is neither well educated nor well spoken. Both he and his brother, in spite of their seemingly gentile appearance, are little more than very dangerous, opportunistic thugs," said Yermac. "Kazamin was educated in the UK and was with the Russian diplomatic corps for several years and that's where he built up his political clout and rightfully earned political enemies, most of whom have since, shall we say... retired," continued Yermac. "Both he and Slava are labor camp honour graduates and that's where they learned their nasty skills. Slava was always a street fighter and, with his brothers smarts and their combined insatiable greed, are busily eliminating competition in Russia's underworld. But you don't have to believe me. Just check the newspaper archives and see how many times the Barkov name crops up."

"I find all this very hard to believe," stated Miroslav. "How do I know you're telling me the truth? Mr. Barkov, as I'm sure you know since you seem to know everything else about the Barkovs and me, made a very generous offer; to fund a project that I have been collecting data on for years and his interest was sincere, I assure you."

"Doctor, you may believe what you wish. But I ask you to consider this. Your project proposal is not new. You have submitted it at least five times to the Central Government in as many years and each time it was soundly rejected, and we both know that's the truth," said Yermac.

Miroslav sat back into the seat and had to admit that the driver was, regrettably, correct.

"And consider this Doctor; all of a sudden, one of the Barkov brothers shows up, ready to fund your project. Why do you think that is? Because of their community spirit or out of scientific interest? Not likely! If it is, it will be the first time," said Yermac. "There is only one reason that makes any sense at all. If you don't know what motivates the Barkovs, It's money and power and lots of it! So, again I ask you to do your own research, something you know far more about than me. But I will tell you why you received a visit. The Barkovs aren't funding anything. They never do. They are takers, not givers. The money is coming from their partners, those very rats in a nest that you piss off on a frequent basis. And the money isn't to fund your research project; it's to pay for your disappearance."

The pause was far more than 'pregnant' unless elephants are considered. It was downright apocalyptic. It took time for Miroslav to digest what had just been said – his disappearance, his demise, termination his... death! "This cannot be. It just cannot be. You must be mistaken. I have done nothing to cause this level of aggression."

"Doctor, give your head a shake. Wake up and smell the coffee while there's still time. Indeed you have. I don't mean to be cruel about this but, if you want to survive, you had better start seeing the world in Russia as it really is and not what you imagine it could be," said Yermac. "The powerful individuals you have targeted and the kind of information you have made public, places them in very delicate positions, especially given the paranoia that is so prevalent in Russia today. Please don't get me wrong. I'm not suggesting that your information was not true. There is every reason to believe it is very true; after all, you are not one to broadcast lies. They have everything to lose and nothing to gain by keeping you alive."

Yermac again checked the rear view mirror, not simply to gauge Miroslav's reaction but to see if they were being followed. Satisfied that Miroslav was still in a receptive mood and that a tail had been verified, he continued.

"These are extremely ambitious and totally corrupt people who have gained positions of authority by intimidation, extortion and outright murder. The only thing that keeps you from being the target of an assassination is your popularity with the general public. The cure could be worse than the disease," continued Yermac. "So, enter the Barkov brothers. Combine that with your project that would transport you far away from Red Square and, voila, the perfect setting for an 'unfortunate' accident, your corpse never to be found. Am I getting through, Doctor?"

Miroslav's head felt as though it would lift off his shoulders and explode. Endless thoughts, mostly re-runs of talks he had given, conversations with friends and colleagues, articles he had written (although few had been published in the so-called legitimate press), disassociation from working comrades, isolation and the ever increasing loneliness all came crashing through his brain like a runaway steam locomotive. He was no longer aware of where he was, the rain dancing off the engine bonnet and the paved street, the traffic or even the driver; there was just him and the feeling of free falling to oblivion.

"You must understand that I have great difficulty in absorbing everything you have told me" continued Miroslav, hardly hearing or understanding what he was saying. "I'm not completely oblivious to the impact of my letters and discussions, and I have always known that certain bureaucrats were uncomfortable with my commentaries and dissertations but I had no idea they would go to such extremes. I have never had a visit from anyone concerning it although I realized some time ago that my passion for mother Russia was, ah … hindering my career. But do I believe you? I don't know. I just don't know. I will have to think on our conversation."

"Doctor, I understand your confusion, but consider this. What benefit would it be for me or the NSDF to tell you all of this if it was simply a pack of lies? And also consider this. We have been tailed by another car almost from the time I picked you up at your office," said Yermac

Miroslav started to re-position himself in the back seat to get a view out the rear window.

"No, no, no Doctor, please don't do that," said Yermac. "I don't want our follower to know that we have been in conversation or to know that I have spotted them. It would only increase your vulnerability. I would suggest you take a short, very short glance up the street when I pull over to let you out, but, please, don't make it obvious. I will make a u-turn so that I can let you out at the door to the apartment building. Just look down the street before going into the building."

"For the Barkov's part," continued Yermac, "they believe they can't lose. They get very well paid to dispose of you and, as a possible bonus, if you do actually find whatever it is you will be looking for, that becomes the property of the Barkovs who would have no hesitation in selling it to the highest bidder regardless of origin. They won't do the deed before you get to Tunguska. Who knows, you may find what you are looking for. In all probability, they may try between Tunguska and Krasnoyarsk, along the river perhaps, if they do it at all, because, let's face it, you are a well known and highly respected and that makes you a commodity of interest to, oh, I don't know, the Japanese, the Chinese or the Germans perhaps. So the money the Barkovs are getting for your 'disposal' may be only a drop in the bucket to other income streams," explained Yermac. "I don't say this to alarm you, it's just fact and a reason to be cautious. Very, very cautious. And, a couple more things. Although the Barkovs are not to be trusted, they don't even trust each other. There is little honour among those thieves. We expect that both brothers are hatching plots against the other."

A horse, startled by the sharp crack of a lightning strike near-by, suddenly bolted into the street directly in front of Miroslav's taxi, dragging a cart and driver with it. Yermac quickly swerved the vehicle to the left, avoiding a collision by the narrowest of margins, all of which went almost totally unnoticed by Miroslav, his head still swimming in an ocean of confusion.

"You are not alone in this venture," continued Yermac, trying to instill confidence and calm Miroslav's concerns. He again checked the rear view mirror. "We will be watching out for you as best we can..

The Barkovs, in spite of their sleaziness, aren't stupid. They are aware of the Foundation and so we have to assume that they are watching us too. If you want to meet with us again, you can send a message in two ways. You have two coffee cups on your desk in your office, one is white. If you want a meeting, turn that cup upside down and a meeting will be arranged. If you feel you are in danger in your flat, stand in the window facing the street holding an open book in your left hand. Your NSDF contact will use the word '*outcome*' as an identifier," explained Yermac

"Well, here we are," concluded Yermac as the taxi came to a stop at the front door to Miroslav's apartment building. "I have probably not made your evening but better to know now than when it's too late. Good evening Doctor. We will be in touch, and that's a promise, and please, please, don't forget the identifier word."

The rain hadn't let up even a little bit. Drops bounced off the car, the pavement and the sidewalk like bullets being sprayed from a machine gun with an endless belt. Gutters ran full and many overflowed and the rain created its own impenetrability. Still, Miroslav spotted the 'tail' about fifty metres down the street, stationary but its running lights still on. It was impossible to see who or how many passengers it carried. His taxi was just pulling away by the time Miroslav got to his second floor flat and the taxi's headlights, for a split second, picked up the black fender of the other car parked at the curb.

He was right about that anyway; if it was a tail, thought Miroslav.

The rain beat heavily on the old glass panes of the even older windows of Miroslav's flat but the sills and frame, sealed by countless coats of paint over countless years of creeping rot, amazingly held against the torrential onslaught. Unencumbered by an overabundance of space, with only a living-dining-bedroom, a washroom not much larger than a moderate sized closet and a few antique, rustic closets and a time tested ceramic stove.

The flat was cold both in its décor and environment; cold and damp. But what it lacked in elaborateness, it made up for in its unadorned qualities . No pictures adorned the walls, not even photographs of his brothers, sisters or any of his relatives, not even the obligatory photograph of Stalin. Instead, there were shelves piled to the brim with papers, journals and magazines and maps, mostly northern and eastern Russia as well as the north west part of North America and central and northern China. It offered Miroslav respite from his less than exhilarating professional life.

Sleepless nights, tonnes of questions and micrograms of answers filled Miroslav's days and nights. He quickly realized that he had to devise a plan to acquire answers he so urgently needed, even if only to get more sleep. But sleep had not come easy for the past several years for he was alone, no contact with the few relatives he had in a world full of used-to-be friends and colleagues. The discussion with the taxi driver did not lessen his burden. Miroslav's mind told him he was ensnared in a trap of his own making; an exitless room that was growing smaller with each passing day.

If Yermac was right, he thought, then time is surely not on my side and there isn't much of it left and I have to verify something, anything! But was Yermac right and was he who he said he was, thought Miroslav. He recalled what Yermac had said: check it out and if it's even partially true, the time to act must be now! *So, could there be an escape from this impossible situation?* he thought. But, eventually, each and every night, his body said *Miroslav, enough is enough. Give it up. What will be, will be* and merciful, if not restless sleep, came his way.

MOSCOW

INSTITUTE FOR SCIENTIFIC RESEARCH BUILDING NO. 14
FRIDAY, APRIL 24, 1925

Miroslav's office, as he flippantly referred to it, consisted of four unpainted concrete, windowless walls that had been leaking water for so many years that evaporation had left thick deposits of white calcium salts all over their exterior and weakened structural integrity. It was not scheduled for repair until Hades opened as a skating rink. Consistent with the bucolic theme, the concrete floor was untarnished by paint or any other western Imperialistic covering. A very old wooden desk, complete with four legs that were more or less the same length (more less than more), supported a telephone that even worked from time to time. A lamp, a swivel chair that complained loudly with each and every minuscule movement and had a tendency to wobble a bit.

One straight back wooden chair completely devoid of even the slightest appreciation of ergonomics, one bookcase completely filled to the top with several layers deep of books and just about everywhere, every paper he had read, authored or co-authored in his years with the Institute completed the inventory of furnishings. The ambiance was topped off by two coffee cups, one red and the other white, and the unmistakable odors of coal dust mixed with more than a hint of aged cigarette smoke.

Miroslav had grown used to his cost-conscious surroundings (as he frequently referred to it, mostly to himself) in the full realization that he was the architect of his own demise. He was even getting accustomed to the aura of avoidance and isolation that permeated each and every day. To associate with Miroslav on any level was to risk being noticed and that could be hazardous to one's health. He was on an island surrounded by hundreds of other islands all governed by fear of being viewed as the long necked turkey at Thanksgiving time. This was his own personal Bastille!

The man filling the doorway was no stranger to Miroslav. He was tall, dressed to the nines in a black pin-striped tailored suit, carrying what was obviously a very expensive overcoat draped over his left arm, very broad shoulders, square jaw, slightly pock-marked face, clean shaven, thick coal black hair, narrow deep set, black eyes under eyebrows thick enough to hide a nest of robins and a large, noticeable scar running down the left cheek.

"Good morning Dr. Oborski," he said cheerfully, seating himself in the only other chair in the room, not letting the overcoat from its resting place on his arm. "Are you well, sir? You look a bit, how shall I say it … fatigued? Are you not sleeping well? Perhaps I should have you visit my personal Physician; very professional you know; excellent Physician." A heartless pseudo grin and forceful eyes were welded to Dr. Oborski.

"No, no, Mr. Barkov, I'm perfectly fine," responded Moroslav. "I've Just been spending a lot of time doing some very interesting but very tedious research, nothing serious, I can assure you."

"Ah, then I am glad to hear that. So, may I ask what you think of my proposal? Good news I trust."

Kazamin removed his long coat from his arm, folded it gently over the arm of the chair (exposing nothing but an arm, much to the Miroslav's relief), and pulled his chair closer to the desk, never taking his unblinking, cold eyes off Miroslav. Miroslav's heart was in sprint mode and he was certain that Kazamin could hear it or, at the very least, detect Miroslav's nervousness that he was desperately trying to disguise. Miroslav was calmed slightly by the fact that he was not covered in a flood of sweat. His plan was,… well, going according to plan and he felt closer to at least a few answer, if the wheels didn't come off in the next few moments!

Miroslav grabbed the red coffee cup, "May I pour you a coffee, or perhaps something a little more bracing" offered Miroslav, (remembering he still had a part bottle of Vodka somewhere in the room).

"I'm fine Doctor. I am sorry to rush our meeting, but I am already late for another appointment. Perhaps we can get down to business, shall we?"

"Yes, yes, of course," said Miroslav, clearing his throat and getting ready for the next statement, the most critical part of his plan and the outcome of which he had dire thoughts. "I have gone over my data again, several times actually, Mr. Barkov and, while I recognize the generosity of your offer and the effort that you have devoted to this project to date, I regret to say that the data is far too inconclusive to justify a venture of this magnitude and cost. The risk of failure is far and away too great. It is my recommendation that we wait until considerably more data has been collected and analyzed; perhaps in a year or so." *There, I said it and it didn't come out in blurts and my head is attached to my shoulders,* thought Miroslav.

Strange, Miroslav was thought. There was no immediate reaction from Barkov, no eye twitch, no shifting in his chair, just the unrelenting, cold, cold stare into Miroslav's own eyes, intimidation honed to an art form. Miroslav found it difficult to keep his own facade expressionless: difficult not to remove himself from the unrelenting cold stare; difficult to maintain composure in a situation that surely demanded total composure to assure even a modicum of success to say nothing of self preservation.

"Dr. Oborski," stated Kazamin, clearing his throat, a slight smile pasted on otherwise chiseled lips, glanced momentarily to the ceiling before returning to his arrow straight gaze at Miroslav, "what you are telling me is that you are not interested in my financial support or my assistance in this project. This is not an opportunity that will present itself again, Doctor,... ever. Do you understand that?" His poise openly showed signs of increasing impatience.

Miroslav nodded his head slightly in the affirmative.

"Doctor, I think what we have here is a failure to communicate." By this time, Kazamin was standing, leaning over the desk toward Miroslav with his left hand supporting him on the desk, his face slightly red and his eyes flashing in obvious irritation-overdrive. "You have told me on numerous occasions that your research is as complete as it is ever likely to be, that the area is and has been for quite some time, to all intents and purposes, closed to visitors and so no other data is forthcoming. Isn't that true Doctor Oborski?"

Regaining his composure, Kazamin returned to his chair, shook his head, raised both arms , hands flat up, head slightly down, but otherwise, looked little different than when he entered the office. He was clearly not someone who took rejection lightly.

"Doctor, I apologize for my outburst. Very unbecoming of me. However, I do not concur that the current research is inadequate. I think you are simply suffering from anxiety, perhaps even fear of failure. But I assure you I have complete faith in your expertise and I look forward to working with you on the project. This project is important to mother Russia and will be going ahead as planned, Doctor. Now, I must beg your indulgence and be on my way to my next appointment. I will be in touch as plans progress." He picked up his coat, draped it over his shoulders and partially turned to face Miroslav. "Good day Dr. Oborski."

Clearly, thought Miroslav, *things did not go quite as hoped but at least I now have some of the answers I needed.* He felt cautiously relieved as he found the half full bottle of Vodka and turned the white coffee cup upside down.

WEST OF
VANAVARA

MONDAY, AUGUST 24, 1925

The few homes that existed in the area, although not clustered together, showed no immediately discernible signs of orderly development or planning, suggesting that the lots were possibly laid out by a surveyor who had apparently missed a few key classes. But, what the area lacked in urban planning, it more than made up for in astonishing rural beauty. Situated on a slight rise that overlooked a dark green, glacial valley with a small, clear blue stream that meandered back and forth for its entire length, it was bordered by mixed conifers along the valley that gave way to deciduous forests on the high ridges and the occasional clearing. A golf course designer would have viewed it as going to Heaven without the disagreeable inconvenience of dying.

Compared to other houses in the region, it was somewhat larger and in better condition than most. The owner, Tanya Kirshnova, was taller than average and grey haired. A slightly plump lady of 50 plus years, she managed the small farm with her 30 something son, Alex, a monumental task under conditions that were far from ideal. Miroslav well understood that the money she had received from Slava in payment for the stay was a God-send.

In spite of the relative affluence of the farm, comforts were modest. Furnished with an ancient ceramic stove, that also served as a home heat source, a large but very sturdy wooden table, six or eight solid chairs, a wash basin, wood box and cabinet, it gave the word 'Spartan' complete meaning.

The four sat around the large wooden table covered with pots of borscht, pelmeni, boiled potatoes, black bread and a half bottle of vodka. Slava Barkov, seated at one end if the table and the clear leader of the group, was average height with an average build for a man in his mid forties, a mop of coal black unkempt hair, deep set, slightly blood-shot eyes and a well scared face that said a mean attitude resided within. At the other end of the table sat Anton Pavlovski, as tall as Slava but a bit younger in appearance. He had a solid well muscled frame, smooth black hair but a more kindly demeanor than Slava. Miroslav was seated on the side to Slava's right, facing Alex seated across from him while Tanya, arms folded, stood next to the old iron stove.

Dinner was over and it was almost dark. Slava got up from the table, grabbed the bottle of vodka and motioned for Anton to follow him to the barn with Alex to make sure the wrangler, who had just arrived from Yarkino, was prepared for the journey, leaving Miroslav alone to review his voluminous pile of notes.

About a half hour later, the four of them came back to the house: Slava, Anton, Alex and the wrangler (a female, much to Miroslav's surprise). Miroslav guessed the wrangler to be in her mid to late thirties. She was plainly the outdoors type with a stocky build, a warm smile under a head of brownish-black hair tied in a bun behind her head and sparkling grayish-blue eyes. Slava, a consummate creature of habit, immediately showered Miroslav with the usual tirade of vodka stimulated, less than complimentary, remarks designed more as a gesture to solidify the fact that he, and only he, was in-charge than a slam at Miroslav. But Miroslav, although not entirely immune to it by now, was learning to live with Slava's self-assumed righteousness. Anton said nothing, maintaining his expressionless demeanor as he seated himself directly across the table from Miroslav.

Tanya stared out the window for a long time, watching large flocks of crows line the picket fence that surrounded the farmstead. Finally, she turned from the window, moved around the table and stopped

behind Anton. "You should think more on this trip for I do not see..."
Her voice trailed off, then she continued. "The signs are not good,
not good at all. You must not go to the Devils Home. It's cursed and
so is he." When it was clear that her ravings were falling on deaf ears,
she turned toward the stairs to the loft and pointed to an adjacent
room. "Your beds are in the next room, and I will prepare breakfast
at dawn." Tanya's comments seemed to slip off Slava and Anton like
water off a greased pan, but for Miroslav, who was not ready to sack-
out, the remarks were disturbing and he knew he had to ask Tanya
questions. But they would have to wait for another day.

"I will be staying in the barn with the horses in case there is a
thunderstorm tonight," said the wrangler, and she got up from the
table and left the house.

Tanya came down to the kitchen an hour later and was surprised to
see Miroslav still seated at the table, very much as he was when she
retired for the night.

"Уважаемая Kirshnova, may I ask you a few questions?" inquired
Miroslav. Tanya offered no response which Miroslav did not take
as a refusal. "What did you mean by the 'Devil's Home' and who is
cursed?"

She stood by the basin, motionless and stared straight ahead at
a blank wall. Tanya said nothing and Miroslav grew increasingly
uncomfortable with the dead air. Suddenly, with no fore-warning,
Tanya turned around and came to the table, looked about the room as
if to check for other, perhaps unwanted listeners.

"The house of that cursed Joakim Gersuan. He has sold his soul to
the Devil. Mark my words, everyone knows that he and that place are
cursed. Stay away from him and that unholy place."

Miroslav realized that Tanya meant this as no idle warning. There
was overpowering sincerity in each and every word; her eyes burned
with deep-seated fear and it shook Miroslav to the core. He had never
heard of Joakim Gersuan until the other day when he overheard Slava

and Anton mention the name as a possible guide on the venture.

If he is in league with the Devil, thought Miroslav, *then he is in good company with Slava.*

Recognizing the risk of pushing too far, Miroslav asked, "why is the place cursed?"

To his surprise, Tanya volunteered immediately.

"You are not from here so you have no way of knowing. It's the lights. They started about two years ago, the Devils lanterns, I tell you. Ask me no more. I value my soul and that of my son."

Miroslav didn't need to ask any more questions and he wasn't sure if he should laugh or cry but he knew he was vindicated but he could tell no one. He felt like one who had just committed the perfect crime and the physiological dilemma that it ensues. All he had to do now was live long enough to enjoy it!

WEST OF VANAVARA

TUESDAY, AUGUST 25, 1925

An old, small house looked more like a log cabin, set back from the well worn, narrow dirt lane that, following a day of heavy rain, was more slippery slush that solid earth,. There was a low, unpainted picket fence surrounded the house; well, some of it anyway. Both it and the house had seen better days but, clearly, real estate renovation was not high a priority item on the 'to do list' of the owner, one Joakim Gersuan.

Joakim lived alone and he never wondered why; his lifestyle was not one that had any degree of magnetism with local bride wannabes. It wasn't his appearance. He was average height, lean but not thin, a full head of long brown hair and a well trimmed beard and clear steel-grey eyes, a combination that many women would find attractive. Nor was it that he was a slob, because he wasn't. His living quarters were… modest, to say the least. But now approaching the age of forty, he had given up any hope of marriage and family. But where he failed as a homemaker and property manager, he excelled in his skills as a hunter, trapper and guide, and these skills were not unknown to the local population, although rebuked by the community and tarnished by a number of events that even he was at a loss to fully explain.

Joakim saw them coming. There were two of them and they both exhibited the impacts of street life that screamed a complete lack of gentile humor. Still, they were reasonably well attired and obviously not from this area. They came on a horse drawn two wheeled cart, common to the area, a contrivance not built with the comfort of the traveller as priority one.

"Are you Joakim Gersuan", asked Slava. Anton stood a little behind and off to one side, arms folded across his chest, saying nothing; just staring.

"I am," replied Joakim, somewhat hesitantly, mauling over the limited options he had in this situation and believing at first that these two goons had been hired by the paranoid riddled community to accelerate his departure. "Why do you ask?"

"My name is Slava Barkov and this is my… assistant, Anton. You are a guide, yes?"

"Yes. Is there something you wish of me?" asked Joakim, as the pair pushed past the open door requiring Joakim to back-step into the kitchen.

Joakim closed the door behind them as the two visitors surveyed their surroundings. Joakim's home décor may best be described as late Jurassic. The house consisted of one room, almost square, perhaps eighty square metres or so, completely devoid of furnishings with the exception of an iron and ceramic wood burning stove (which was pumping out enough calories to smelt iron), a small but extremely sturdy wooden table with four equally sturdy chairs, a cot covered with a horse blanket fresh off the horse, a kitchen counter with the compulsory calico curtain covering whatever was under the sink area, a hand pump and some well stocked shelving.

Three windows covered with burlap 'curtains', a gun rack, several trophies from past wood lore ventures, two well oiled and cared-for saddles, three kerosene lamps (all lit) and a back door that surely led to the outdoor plumbing completed the decor. Behind the house, not far from the 'restroom', was a pyramidal stack of cord wood, a small corral and barn somewhat larger than the house and one fine looking stallion (which seemed out of place amid such surroundings).

"We wish to employ your services. We want you to guide us to the

Tunguska Valley. You will be well paid," said Slava, sliding a small leather case toward Joakim.

Joakim took the case, opened it and swallowed hard at the sight of more cash that he would see in a year.

"What? Why Tunguska? It's a very large place, hundreds of kilometres in diameter," stammered Joakim with a bit of a smirk. "The closest part is only eighty kilometres or so away and not all that hard to find. Just travel northeast but when you get there, there's nothing to see. Just a whole lot of grassland, dead trees and swamps. I know. I have been their many times. The place is,… well, dead." ended Joakim, regretting the choice of the final word. "Why do you want to go to such a place?"

"We want to do some hunting. We need you to be our guide us and help set up our camps during the trip. Your celebrated hunting skills will be most useful. And besides," continued Slava, "the area we want to visit is, as you said, only eighty kilometres away."

The tag-along Anton cracked something closely akin to a smile at this point, glancing briefly at his partner.

"Hunting skills? Hunting what? Deer? Bear? What is it that you are after? And how long do you figure this trip will take. It's only about three days to get there and another three to come back. We can carry enough food for that long. That area of the valley doesn't have much for wildlife. Why there?" At this point, Joakim thought he may just have pushed a bit too hard and he was right!

Slamming his fists down onto the table, Slava screamed, "Listen you overblown excuse for a guide. It's not your job to tell us where we want to go. We will tell you where we want to go and you will guide us," Slava's face was not five centimetres from a visibly shaken Jaokim. "Now, we will be gone for at least two weeks, perhaps a month and there will be four of us and you. You will provide the horses and pack animals for our food and supplies. After that, all you have to do is guide, is that clear? As for hunting, what do you think Anton? Bear perhaps?"

Anton responded with a pursed lip shrug of approval.

"I think we will hunt for... bear. Yes, it will be bear," ended Slava with a sardonic smile. "We will start in two days. You have the horses, mules and supplies ready."

"If I choose to guide you and your... friend here, you understand that everything must be carried by mules. It has been very wet and it could get a lot wetter and colder soon, by the way. The mules may even get bogged down in the swamps and marshes. We may never be able to get them out. And besides, I really don't think I'm all that interested in being your guide. I can suggest others in the region who might be if you wish," sliding the packet of cash in Slava's direction.

Slava's hands gripped the table like two steel vises, his face swelled with anger, was far more red than before and his eyes generated a stare that could bore holes in concrete, but he made no move to retrieve the packet.

Anton's hands that he had rested on the table top, quickly became fists the size of bowling balls and by his quick and abrupt stare at Slava, he made no effort to disguise the fact that he was ready for whatever action Slava requested of him.

This reaction did not go unnoticed by Joakim who now saw his whole life flash before his eyes. He realized, perhaps too late, that Slava was not one to take the word 'no' nonchalantly.

Slava raised his arm slightly, signaling Anton to cool his heels, at least for the time being, and that's when Joakim caught a glimpse of the seven shot Nagant revolver nestled in a shoulder holster and figured correctly that Anton was also packing. Slava, eyes closed, hands now flat on the table top, leaned back in his chair, head back as if getting ready to inspect the ceiling. Slowly, he leaned slightly forward, rose from his chair and turned toward Anton.

"As my brother is so fond of saying, my friend, what we have here is a failure to communicate!"

As fast as a bolt of greased lightning, Slava whipped around to face Joakim and in one, smooth, well practiced motion, withdrew the revolver, cocked the hammer and shoved the barrel of the gun a good 2 cm up Joakim's left nostril. Joakim's eyes popped open to their max, grunted something unintelligible and started sweating like a roofer in mid August.

"Now you listen to me, you brainless piece of backwoods crap. The honeymoon is over! You accepted my money and that, my friend, means we have a contract and here's what that means. First, I'm not asking you to be our guide; I'm telling you! If I had wanted anyone else, I wouldn't be here in this outhouse you call a home! Second, you will be ready at 5 AM the day after tomorrow! Is that clear, hayseed?"

Joakim's brain, as the rest of his body, went paralytic and he was unable to even think of what to say, so he slightly, ever so slightly, nodded his head in the affirmative, expecting the nod to be his final act on Earth.

With the Nagant removed from Joakim's nose and returned to the holster, Slava turned toward the door. Anton followed. As Slava threw open the door with enough force to break one of the hinges, Anton turned toward Joakim with a parting gesture, thumb of the right hand vertical, forefinger pointed toward Joakim with the other three fingers folded, mouthed 'pow', gave a wink and left.

Joakim took several minutes before he could move a muscle and his breathing was restored to something approaching normal then rose from his chair, closed the front door and secured it as best he could, then promptly made a beeline for the back door.

WEST OF VANAVARA

By 4:30 AM the mules and horses were ready and tethered to the fence in front of Joakim's house. It was still dark and it was cool, but the ever present mist made it seem colder than it actually was. A slight breeze was coming in from the south west and that, Joakim knew, was usually a precursor to more rain. The wind blew a few leaves from the proliferation of hardwoods that characterized the area and the wet mass dropped quickly to the ground and, but for the wind, there was a disquieting silence. Off in the distance, a horse whinnied and, shortly after could be heard the unmistakable sound of steel clad hooves sloshing along the muck spattered lane. To his disappointment, this was not going to be a no-show and Joakim's anxiety level rose to amber alert status!

Now would be a good time to get out of here; to run and not look back. Actually, the other night may have been a better time, he was thinking out loud, But… run from what?

To where was no problem. Joakim was uniquely familiar with every nook and cranny in the hilly, heavily wooded area and certainly had the skills necessary to survive indefinitely as well as all the required gear, including his favourite hunting rifle, a Mosin-Nagent five shot bolt action with a scope with which he could take out a moose at 500 meters.

This is just panic, Joakim. Stay calm, he continued to think to himself. *If this bunch are an execution squad, they don't need me to show them a good spot; we are in the middle of nowhere right now. And why Tunguska? Perhaps they know or maybe that snake Pyotr has been telling stories again.*

Not two, as a few nights ago, but now four people. A female, slightly muscular build but very easy on the eyes never the less. Joakim guessed that she was probably from northern Siberia where he had spent a good deal of time in years past. Bringing up the rear were the two that visited Joakim a few nights back: Slava and Anton. Following them a tall, lean gentleman, with a full grey beard and dressed for an arctic expedition.

Definitely not a hunter, Joakim said to himself and, in his mind, gave him the name 'Professor.' Then added quietly to himself, if any of this collection of odd-balls is a hunter, except maybe the female, then I am probably the Emperor of Japan!

Few words were spoken except by Slava who insisted that Joakim part with his hunting rifle which would be 'cared for' by the Siberian until needed.

The one from northern Siberia, who Joakim correctly guessed to be the wrangler, took the rifle and packed it into the saddle of her horse. For Joakim, the thought of running or escape had evaporated with the loss of his prized rifle.

It was shortly after sun-up when the eclectic troupe got underway. Lead by Joakim on his horse, followed by the Professor, then Slava and Anton with the Siberian bringing up the rear with the two mules in tow. They headed northeast along a trail that would only be recognizable as such by an experienced guide. In spite of the almost overwhelming sense of foreboding felt by Joakim, the unrivalled beauty of the area never ceased to sooth his inner soul and tell him that all was right with the world.

Before them, running left to right, the glacial valley and beyond stretched a gently undulating sea of spectacular forest growth and small, open plains, rocky outcrops and small cliffs, traversed with literally hundreds of small clear, blue water streams, the entire canvas painted with greens, yellows, oranges and reds of every hue. Mother nature's wares, completely unspoiled by war and untainted by the hands of man.

TUNGUSKA
VALLEY

TUESDAY, SEPTEMBER 1, 1925

By mid afternoon on the fifth day, they arrived close to the southern edge of the Tunguska Valley. If not for Slava and Anton's nightly love affair with their favourite tipple and the morning-long curative process (spiced with Slava's profusion of verbal abuse on the other 'team' members), they would have arrived on schedule several days earlier. None of this seemed to bother the Professor all that much who seemed more concerned about other things. The Siberian wrangler displayed not the slightest sign of an emotion, one way or the other. It was only Joakim who soaked it all up and lugged it around like a tonne of baggage.

Over the past few days, Joakim had a couple of opportunities to ride briefly next to the Professor and they talked as best they could. Although he was quite certain that Slava and Anton realized they were talking, no move was made to promptly discourage it. He learned that the Professor actually had a name; Miroslav Oborski, actually, Dr. Miroslav Oborski – and that they had nothing to fear from the Siberian but to keep a watchful eye out for Anton.

"I feel that there's more to him than you might think," warned Miroslav. "He could be far more dangerous than Slava, his boss for now."

"What's the real reason we are going to Tunguska," inquired Joakim. "I know this trip has nothing to do with hunting game, so why are we going at all? There's nothing there to see but dead trees, foxes and rabbits!"

"I want to find… an object. I can't tell you much about it because I'm unsure myself. It's probably metallic but not large and probably unlike anything you've ever seen before, or should I say, I've seen before," said Miroslav with an uncharacteristic grin that caused a bit of a geologic quake in Joakim.

After a lengthy pause, while Joakim was trying to fathom his way through what the Professor had just said, Joakim asked "but how do you know it's in the Tunguska Valley."

There was a long, quizzical stare from Miroslav before he answered Joakim's question. "The last piece of evidence I have pretty much confirms its location, at least within a few kilometres or so. Do you have evidence to the contrary Joakim?"

"No, no," said Joakim. "It's just that… well, I've heard the stories from hunters and guides about lights in that area for years and years, but that's about it," prefacing his comments with a shrug of his shoulders.

Miroslav chose not to pursue the topic farther… for now.

It was clear that they were approaching a devastated area. The incidence of tree-fall increased as they closed in on the valley. Although Joakim had seen it many times, the enormity of the devastation never failed to amaze him. As far as the eye could see, every tree lay flat on the ground, with the exception of an area several kilometers distant where a small group of trees were still standing, burned and dead as the ones laying on the ground. Still, the area also showed clear signs of the renewal of life – short, healthy second growth fir, pine and spruce shrubs where everywhere. And green remained the hope giving constant.

On Joakim's suggestion, they stopped to make camp about two kilometers south of the valley rim, not far from a small stream. To venture into the valley at that time of the day, would put both

people and animals at unnecessary risk due to the preponderance
of fallen trees. Given that they were all hungry, tired, wet and cold,
the suggestion didn't garner a lot of resistance. Tents were erected, a
cooking fire started and, when all had eaten, the horses were bedded
down.

The Miroslav suddenly broke into a loud rant. "… one of my best
blankets is missing," he screamed at Slava who, at first, couldn't care
less. But Miroslav was persistent. "What do you expect me to do –
sleep under my saddle?," he continued, grimaced face and pointing an
angry finger at his saddle sitting on the ground next to his little tent.
Turning and glancing at Joakim and giving him a barely noticeable
grin.

"Look," Miroslav continued, "I just want another blanket and I don't
care if it's the missing one. It's too cold for me and I'm too big to fit
under my saddle."

At this point, both Slava and Anton were looking at each other
with expressions that, to say the least, were dazed and left them both
speechless.

"Under my saddle it is then," said the Miroslav.

"Here, take this one and quit your stupid complaining," said Slava,
throwing an old horse blanket at Miroslav, grabbing Anton and
headed for their tents, leaving the wrangler trying to comprehend
what had just happened.

But Joakim thought he knew what had just happened, *under the
saddle*, he thought. *The Professor said it a couple of times and looked
directly at me.*

Totally out of curiosity, Joakim lifted the saddle from his horse and
there it was; a wad of torn, white paper, wedged between the saddle
and the blanket.

There is something very wrong. We need to talk but not in camp. I will propose a search system tomorrow. Please agree with it.

Evening came and, as per their usual routine, the passing-out exercise began. Slava was the first to pass out, followed soon after by his cohort. But, even though he knew that Slava was out of the picture, Miroslav dared not meet with Joakim since Anton was still showed signs of some mobility and stumbled about the camp site at infrequent intervals.

TUNGUSKA
VALLEY

WEDNESDAY, SEPTEMBER 2, 1925

The troupe broke camp in the early afternoon. Cloudy, cold and the air hanging with dampness, they made their way to the valley rim. The valley had a way of leaving all its viewers with a state of awe and wonderment, enhanced this day by the mists that shielded the on-lookers from the massive devastation, save for the moss covered deadfalls that lay everywhere and disappeared into the haze below.

Green. It's even more green than the last time, Joakim was thinking.

In its million shades, even though the brown and black that characterized the area for years after the event was still very evident in the rotting trees along the upper slope on which they were standing. It would be a few months yet before a blanket of snow would paint the valley and, at least in part, hide what had happened here.

Completely unappreciated by Slava and Anton, the group made base camp just below the rim. The wrangler busied herself with setting up tents, preparing food, making leans for the horses and mules and bedding them down, leaving Joakim and Miroslav to erect their small tents (a task with which Joakim was most familiar but was not in a position to provide assistance to Miroslav even though he discernibly needed it even now, after a week on the trail).

Joakim noted that Miroslav had left his tent and followed Anton to Slava's tent. A half hour went by and Anton emerged and came over to Joakim.

"Slava wants to see you. Now"!

Joakim quit what he was doing and followed Anton. Inside the tent, Anton took his place to Slava's left at a small collapsible table on which two revolvers laid, in parts. Both Slava and Anton continued with their cleaning operations. Without looking up, Slava motioned for Joakim to sit on the canvas floor next to a somber Miroslav.

Joakim's thoughts were of something not too good about to happen but it didn't matter to him at this stage, thinking, *how much worse can it get?*

Again, without looking up, Slava continued cleaning his weapon, and with a slight hand gesture only, granted Miroslav the right to speak.

"My name is Miroslav Oborski," turning to face Joakim who wisely maintained his appearance of ignorance. "I am from the Institute for Scientific Research in Moscow."

"Get on with it," barked Anton. "We have more important things to do than listen to a history lesson," a comment that caught a mild grin from Slava who still continued cleaning the gun.

"Everybody knows about the explosion, Joakim, but what we don't know is what caused it. Over the past decade or so, I have interviewed well over 50 people who have visited this site and I am convinced that it was caused by some kind of hereto unknown airship, from where, I don't know. I hope to find solid evidence to support my theory, and that's why we are here."

"Well, I had it figured that this was no hunting trip," muttered Joakim, that solicited no perceptible response from any of the other three.

"Doctor, it's a very large valley. If all those people couldn't find anything, what makes you think you can find something?" asked Joakim.

Slava calmly finished cleaning the gun, placed a full load into the cylinder, snapped it in place, cocked the hammer and pointed it directly at Joakim's forehead. Joakim was paralyzed. This was his second encounter with Slava's deadly toy and one that he was relatively certain he may not survive.

"Hayseed," said Slava, "how did you know he was 'Doctor' Oborski, hmmm? He didn't introduce himself as 'Doctor'. Perhaps you're a mind-reader and we don't like mind-readers, do we Anton?"

Anton, now clearly fascinated by the rapid turn of events, fully agreed.

"You told me," blurted Joakim without thinking, desperate for any quick answer and amazed by his relative calmness, secretly almost hoping the trigger would be pulled and this nightmare to come to a quick end; almost!

"Back on the first day, when you told Doctor Oborski to get down from his horse," continued Joakim, knowing full well that it was an outright lie, hoping he was not digging himself even deeper into a hole but counting on the fuzzying effects of a constant diet of high octane vodka over the past week and, to his quasi-enormous relief, it worked.

He would live to experience another miserable day. It was obvious that Anton was searching his memory of that day as an apparently satisfied Slava raised the gun, set the hammer and placed the weapon in the leather holster on the table without taking his stare off Joakim who, to his credit, returned it in kind. It was also clear, however, to both Joakim and Miroslav, that Anton was not so well satisfied by the answer, probably disappointed by the action that didn't happen… this time.

"The search will begin tomorrow," continued Miroslav. "Unlike others who have searched the valley at random, my research suggests that our best chance of success lies in exploring about 1,000 hectares near the south end of the north-west quadrant, the area immediately in front of us."

Joakim was trying to visualize the location in his mind with reasonable success.

"I suggest that we start the search tomorrow morning. The sooner we all get on with it, the sooner we will be able to go home", ended the Professor.

Slava shot a quick glance to Anton.

"We? Who are 'we'? Not 'we' Professor; you and that overpriced guide. Forget 'we'. I have better things to do than go on a nature hike, thanks anyway!"

This garnered a round of hearty laughter from both Slava and Anton. Outwardly disappointed but inwardly happy as a clam, Miroslav pursued the topic no farther.

"Then it's Joakim and I tomorrow morning. Evening all", and, with that he and Joakim got up to leave the tent.

"Just a moment, you two", said Anton and Miroslav's heart skipped more than one beat. "How do you plan to carry out the search?"

Miroslav was the first to answer. "We will take one of the horses, both of us on the same horse. Is that what you're concerned about? That we will attempt to leave without so much as a hug or saying bon voyage?"

Anton shrugged his shoulders suggesting that Miroslav had hit the nail on the head. Slava was still in the recuperative stage and not fully appreciative of what was being discussed.

"We will take one of the tents and enough food for, say two days.

Would that be okay?" asked Miroslav.

After a very long pause with Anton studying every square centimetre of the walls of the tent, clearly mauling over the possibilities and calculating that he was smarter than those two combined.

"Yeah, go ahead. But if you two don't show up here the day after tomorrow, I will be doing some hunting with that rifle and scope of yours, Joakim! You get the picture?"

They both got the picture and it wasn't pretty.

TUNGUSKA VALLEY

THURSDAY, SEPTEMBER 3, 1925

At first light, the trio assembled for the trek: two trekkers, one horse. one tent and enough food for two days, all checked for accuracy by Anton. It was slow going, over and around countless dead trees and rotting stumps, swampy land in many places but they moved steadily northward under the direction of Miroslav. Joakim chose to walk most of the time, something he was quite used to and actually enjoyed.

"Where should we start the search and set up our own base camp," inquired Joakim when they stopped for a lunch of beans and bread.

"Doesn't matter," replied Miroslav in a cheery yet disturbingly withdrawn tone, "any place that is out of sight of Slava and Anton works for me. "

"When do you want to have our talk," responded Joakim.

"Doesn't matter. Perhaps when we make camp this evening," said Miroslav.

The afternoon wore on with little to no conversation.

"Over there," said Joakim, pointing to a stand of spruce that bordered a small stream that meandered through the area, flowing with clear, cold water over a bed of well rounded pebbles.

"No problem with me," replied the Professor, checking in the direction of the base camp, dismounting his horse and unpacking the saddle bags and tent.

While Miroslav may have seemed satisfied, Joakim sensed that something was clearly not right.

He wants to talk with me but he won't talk with me, he wondered.

After dinner, which was somewhat of a repeat of lunch, Joakim started the ice-breaking process.

"Professor, let's cut the crap and get serious. You have been acting really strange from the minute we left Slava and Anton at the base camp. What's going on?"

"You're right Joakim, and I apologize," said Miroslav. "However, I didn't want to have our talk until we were well away from that camp. Up until a few days ago, I was certain that what we are looking for would be in this valley, but not anymore."

"Professor, if what we are looking for isn't here" swinging his arm is a wide arc, "then where is it and why in the name of all that's holy, are we in this awful place?"

"Good enough Joakim. You asked that we get down to business, so here it is, straight up as they say in the west," answered Miroslav, looking sternly at Joakim. "All my evidence points to you. I'm certain you already have this thing we are searching for and have had it possibly a couple of years or so."

Joakim's mouth flew open as if a jaw hinge had broke.

"I am also convinced that the thing you have, Joakim, is not mine, nor is it yours, but I cannot tell you to whom it belongs nor what it's purpose is," continued Miroslav. "If it eventually gets to its rightful owner will almost certainly be your decision. As to why we are here? What do you think would have happened to you and probably me had I told that liquor sodden crook of my suspicions? I'll give you a hint: an unexplained house fire and two charred bodies. Believe me, I have been around the Barkovs long enough to know what they are capable of."

"Yeah, especially that Anton. When he gets liquored up, he scares the pants off me. I think he can be worse than Slava."

"Possibly, except for one thing; Anton doesn't drink! His drunken stooper routine is a well rehearsed act. He's here for other reasons that I only half suspect," said Miroslav. "So, Joakim, are my suspicions correct? I think you have what we are supposed to be looking for, perhaps not with you but you know where it is."

After a very lengthy pause during which he searched the sky and everything around him for a possible escape route. Starring straight ahead Joakim said, "how did you know?"

"Simple. The lady at the farmhouse, Tanya Kirshnova where we stayed before setting out on this venture, provided the second piece of evidence and, on the trip to the valley, you filled in the missing pieces."

"I told you? Second piece? What was the first piece?" inquired Joakim.

At this point, Miroslav was all smiles and truly enjoying the proceedings. "My interviews stopped a couple of years ago when the sightings of the mysterious lights moved away from the valley southward and then just about ceased altogether. I say just about because they tended to be more erratic but centred south of Vanavara along the Tetere River," explained Miroslav.

"At first, I thought the appearance of the mysterious lights were random occurrences. But, when I reviewed the data more closely, I discovered that, far from being random, they were very much ordered, only on an extremely high plain. Then when Уважаемая Kirshnova told me why she called your place the Devils House and spoke about the Devils Lanterns and what they looked like, that cinched it for me. And on the trip to the valley, you started to ask a question about the item we were supposed to be looking for and you just about answered your own question. So, how did you come to have it - and by the way, what is it and where is it?"

Joakim rubbed his chin, looked at Miroslav then at the sky as if searching for the right words. He took a deep breath. "I don't know what it is and I wish now I had never seen the thing," began Joakim. "A couple of years ago, another guide, Petyr Kovlun, dropped into my place on his way to Ayava. We played durak most of the night and he ended up owing me about a hundred Rubles. He had no money left and so he gave me this... thing. It was inside a piece of lead pipe. He said that was the only way to keep it calm and it could be worth a fortune but it was cursed. I told him I would rather have the money and I would take his horse instead. What do I want with a piece of lead pipe, I told him. He got mad and when I went to claim his horse, he drew his pistol on me, threw the pipe onto the floor and left. And that's the last time I saw him."

"Where did he get it? In this valley," asked Miroslav.

"That's what he said. Said he came across it laying on a stream bed about six months before he came to my place," answered Joakim. "I don't know how he came to keep it in the lead pipe; he never said."

"So, what was inside the pipe?"

"A little piece of metal, kind of soft but still metal. It's about ten centimetres long and maybe a couple centimetres wide; really thin though, and that was it."

"Any markings on it?"

"No, none that I could see; feels like tiny ridges or something on the surface, almost like a powder. The metal's too soft for steel though. But I think he was right about one thing – it is cursed. I kept it in the lead pipe because every time I took it out, those cursed Devils

Lanterns show up and they stick around for a long time afterward. I think they are the ones that burned the numbers on the back door of my house and near scared my horse to death. Broke a couple of the railings in the barn and almost got away on me before I got him calmed down."

"Wait a minute, wait a minute; numbers? What numbers? What are you talking about," inquired Miroslav.

"Oh, a day or so after I got the thing, I woke up one night when the lights were going crazy. I went out the back door and there, on the door, were these numbers – a whole bunch of them. I kept the bloody thing for a month or so after that. Don't ask me why, I don't know; curiosity, I guess, and then I buried it near the shed one night. I should have taken into the woods a kilometre or so and buried it and I don't know why I didn't."

"Can you recall the number?" asked Miroslav.

"Some of them but there were a lot, ten or twelve or so. I remember a few of them; 1025726… that's about all I remember. When we get back, or if we get back, I'll show them to you. The door is still there, at least I think it is if the good people in the area haven't burned my place down in the meanwhile."

Miroslav was absolutely beside himself with the joy of the moment. More than twelve years of research and the null hypothesis was all but proven in less than five minutes. *At last,* he was thinking, *at long last, the search was almost over,* but first he knew he had to tackle another issue. Miroslav was so close yet, in every sense, a universe away from closing the book on the mystery. The news was his and Joakims alone – no one to tell, no one to talk to, and the probability of ever telling anybody was getting slimmer by the hour. It wasn't the least bit comforting to Miroslav to ponder if they should ever tell anybody even if the opportunity presented itself.

Obviously, an organized search was pointless so they decided that they may as well act like tourists for a few days.

But after that, what will become of us when we go back to camp empty handed? thought Miroslav. *Something to sleep on and not the time to burden poor Joakim with more worries.*

TUNGUSKA VALLEY

FRIDAY, SEPTEMBER 4, 1925

The start of the day was cold. Both Miroslav and Joakim felt better after the discussion of the night before and Miroslav did not broach the question of their future; there would be little point. It was a clear sky day with a breeze coming from the north. He and Joakim sat around their camp site passing the hours in relaxed talk, about family, work, and politics and, of course, the weather.

It was mid afternoon when Joakim dropped his cup of tea, sat bolt upright, looking quickly to the south and the base camp.

"Did you hear that Professor?"

"Hear what Joakim?, responded Miroslav.

"Pop Pop. Didn't you hear it?" asked Joakim. "Sounded for all the world like gun fire; a pistol, not a rifle."

"There's no one here but us, Joakim. So who would be firing at us?"

"I don't think the shots were fired at us. I think they came from the base camp. Something has happened up there."

Both men peered as much as they could toward the base camp some four kilometres to the south but they could discern nothing.

"I think we should pack up and get back to the base camp, Joakim, and find out what's going on up there."

"I think we should wait a while. If someone's up their firing off live rounds, I don't think it would be a good idea to waltz into the middle of it. Let's wait a while and see if any more shots are fired."

Miroslav wasn't sure what to do but relying on Joakim's superior survival skills, he opted in favour of a wait. After about an hour, when no more shots were heard, they decided to pack it up and head to the base camp. About a half hour later, Joakim looked at Miroslav.

"Listen. Do you hear that, Professor?"

This time Miroslav could hear it; the sounds of a horse coming their way in a hurry.

"I think it may be a good idea to take shelter in the trees until we see who's coming and why," suggested Miroslav.

Both men took off like a pair of jack rabbits and hightailed it for the grove of thick spruce, hitting the ground just before the rider with another horse in tow ripped into their partially dismantled campsite, the rider jumping from the saddle, even before the horse came to a stop.

Lying prone on soggy wet ground was not Miroslav's idea of something to do when there's nothing to do, but, given the uncertainty of the occasion, it seemed like a good idea for the time being. Getting off the horse and coming into the view of Miroslav and Joakim, they were surprised to see that it was Oksana Mukhina, the wrangler. After inspecting the little campsite and noting that the coals in the fire pit were still hot but finding no one, she put her hands to her mouth in megaphone fashion.

"Miroslav, Joakim. Come on out. You can change the outcome of this situation."

"Right; by getting shot as well?" whispered Joakim.

Both men stayed rock solid in place, hardly breathing and certainly not moving for fear of revealing their location but, at the same time, realizing that eventually, they would be out of options unless she left. They were puzzled by the fact that she had brought another horse with her. Apparently she intended that all three would ride back to the base camp.

"Miroslav, the outcome is in your hands."

Then it hit Miroslav. He tapped Joakim on the shoulder.

"Get up Joakim, it's okay. We are in friendly hands."

"Are you crazy Professor", whispered Joakim as Miroslav rose to his feet and gave a hearty wave to Oksana. Joakim also got up, but with a great deal more trepidation.

"It's all right Joakim. We have nothing to fear. Oksana here is a member of the Foundation. Isn't that so Oksana?"

"Yes, yes I am," she said. "But we have no time to waste. Pack up your gear as quickly as you can. We have to get back to the base camp as soon as possible. We have a serious problem. I'll fill you in while you get ready"

Both Miroslav and Joakim scurried around the camp site like two frenzied scavenger hunters, picking up anything and everything they had brought and packed it away as quickly as they could without saying as much as a word.

"Please listen carefully because I don't have time for questions and I don't have time to repeat myself. Slava hasn't put the bottle down since you two left and he and Anton got into an argument. Apparently Slava was rummaging through Anton's gear and came across a piece of metal with strange marks etched on the surface. He figured that Anton had found what you two are looking for and accused Anton of trying to cheat him. There was a lot of screaming and I saw Anton storm out of Slava's tent and the next thing Slava comes out and fires two shots at Anton, catching him in the thigh and right side. Anton went down, I came over to see what was going on and Slava came over, pointed the pistol at Anton and I thought he was going to finish him off as well as me. He told him that's what you get for trying to cheat and then went back to his tent. I patched up Anton as best I could but the bullet that went into his thigh is still there. The other one went clean through but I don't know how much damage it did along the way. He's in a lot of pain. Slava commandeered all the weapons, including your gun Joakim and now he wants you back here because he's leaving and needs you as his guide to get back to Vanavara. C'mon, Professor. Speed it up! Never mind trying to be neat about it! Joakim, show him how to ram stuff away so we can get out of here and back to base. God only knows. Slava may yet decide to get rid of Anton for good."

The main camp site was a mess. In fact, in order to qualify as a 'mess' it would require a significant clean-up! It was a war zone: belongings and rucksacks were scattered all over the place and all the tents had been slashed to bits, pots and pans were everywhere as well as saddles, bridles and other horse gear. Anton, only semi-conscious, with bandages soaked in blood, was propped up against a large boulder and Slava, mumbling something totally unintelligible and cradling a half empty bottle of Vodka, was busy stumbling around an untethered mule trying to get the last of his belongings packed onto the animal without dropping Joakim's rifle slung over his shoulder. Clearly, this was not family day at the park!

"Stay on your horse hayseed", screamed Slava. "You and I are taking a trip. The rest of you bunch of traitors can stay here and rot for all I care. You're getting what you deserve! Did you think I was stupid? That I wouldn't find out what you were planning? Well, I have some sad news for all of you. I'm on my way to fame and fortune and the rest of you are about to lose a lot of weight!" With a contemptuous grin that would make Jack the Ripper cringe, "Hey, you can always eat your horses. Oh! Oh! But I've got the guns. Too bad! Let's get going hayseed. Now!"

"Not a good idea, Slava. That mule wouldn't make it a kilometre before he would start kicking and we would be picking stuff off the trail and out of the trees. What packed it anyway? A blind drunk monkey?," said Joakim.

Although it elicited partially concealed laughter from the others, right then, Joakim realized too late that his choice of words would probably not be well received by Slava. They were less well received than Joakim imagined. Slava brought up the rifle, aimed it directly at Joakim's knees.

"One more word from you and you will be walking funny for the rest of your life! Now, get off that horse, re-pack that mule and do it now. You have two minutes and not a second longer!"

Silence ruled the next two minutes as Joakim quickly evened up the load, not pretty but adequate, got back on his horse and lead the way out of the campsite, leaving the others to but stand and watch. Before disappearing into the trees, Joakim turned in his saddle and waved, his hand arcing from north to the northwest and he was gone from sight.

Miroslav and Oksana stood motionless for a few moments, both pondering their future which, at present, was not filled with boundless hope and aspiration. All about them was mindless devastation and little to salvage from it. Miroslav, probably for no other reason than to do something, anything, started cleaning up the well strewn mess. It wasn't long before Oksana joined in after checking on Anton's state.

"I found a half bottle of vodka and used a bit of that to disinfect Anton's wounds. You're a Doctor. Is there anything that can be done for him? " asked Oksana.

"Wrong kind of Doctor I'm afraid; Ph.D., not MD. He doesn't look that great. Still losing blood by the look of things."

Miroslav and Oksana inspected Anton's dressing and made him

as comfortable as possible, covering him with some of the horse blankets, but, unfortunately, no tent.

"If we don't get him to a hospital reasonably soon, it will be hard to say what his chances of survival will be, if not from blood loss and internal bleeding but the probability of infection," observed Miroslav. "But I doubt he could take riding on one of the horses for very long without doing even more damage."

They both proceeded with the clean-up that took the best part of an hour. I nothing else, it gave them time to calm down and take stock of their situation. They had three horses, one mule, three saddles, matches, three water canteens, lots of pots, pans and bowls, one hatchet, one Dietz oil lantern still in working order, one first aid kit, a bunch of blankets, no usable tents and a smashed compass. As well, when the ruckus started, Oksana had the presence of mind to hide as much food as she could, which wasn't much, unfortunately.

"Well Doctor. What would you like for supper this evening," said Oksana jokingly.

"You know Oksana, I think this evening we should go American. What do you think?"

"Go for it Doc."

"Right," and looking skyward in contemplative thought, "I'm thinking sirloin steak, medium well, smothered in mushrooms and onions with baked potato, sour cream and a Greek salad with Feta cheese. Perhaps after dinner, a bowl of chocolate ice cream and cap it off with a snifter of Ararat Brandy."

"Excellent choice, Doctor. How about a bowl of Ukrainian Borscht?"

"Close enough. If we had some!"

"We do. When the fight broke out, I was taking stock of our food supplies. So, I squirreled away enough to keep us going for three or four days if we take it easy. We're lucky that Slava didn't think to check beyond the campsite."

"You, my dear Oksana, are a miracle woman. The Foundation is certainly in good stead with people such as you on its staff."

He wanted to lean over and kiss her on the cheek but lack of experience in that department cancelled the effort, so she did it for him!

After dinner, neither eating very much considering their meager rations, it was time to review their situation. The temperature dropped markedly as the sun set and the only recourse they had was to bundle up with the remaining horse blankets and make sure that the fire was well stoked.

"Oksana, you say that we only have enough food for a few days. Is that correct?"

"Three or four, if we don't eat much. Water shouldn't be a problem, but food and shelter will be big problems that will probably get worse. And then we have Anton to take care of as well."

Nothing was said for the next few moments as both digested the true nature of the position they were in.

"Well, one thing's for certain Doc," said Oksana, "we can't stay here and the chances of a rescue is remote at best, if at all. Who would rescue us? Only the Barkovs know exactly where we are and the only thing the Foundation knows is that we are in the Tunguska Valley. We must be the proverbial needle in the haystack. And what about Anton? If he doesn't get treatment, well… who knows?"

"It doesn't look good, that's a certainty." replied Miroslav. "But Anton or no Anton, you're right. We can't stay here."

"I wouldn't suggest that we go south."

To their utter surprise, that comment came from Anton who was now apparently fully conscious.

"You know how long it took us to get here, and why," said Anton. "Well, I wouldn't expect Slava to be any quicker heading south, certainly slower than we would travel. So the chances of meeting up with him would be pretty good. And besides, I'm not sure exactly what he has already planned; perhaps to meet his buyer along the trail. I don't know."

"Buyer? What buyer? Of what?" asked Oksana.

"That piece of metal he found in my tent," groaned Anton, trying to change his sitting position.

"What is it anyway, the piece of metal I mean," continued Oksana, with Miroslav paying extremely close attention.

Anton turned his head to look directly at Miroslav.

"Tell me Professor, did you find what you were looking for?" asked Anton.

Not wishing to lie (something he was never very good at anyway), "No, no I didn't" and that was the truthful answer to the question as it was phrased; he had not found it.

Somebody named Pytre did.

"So, Anton," interrupted Oksana. "what is the story with the piece of metal that was worth getting shot for?"

Anton gave the other two a long and quizzical gaze before responding.

"Well, I suppose at this stage, it really doesn't matter anymore. That piece of metal is just that – a piece of metal – a useless piece of junk. It wasn't worth getting shot for, but I had no control over that. But

Slava thinks it's what the professor was searching for and believes the professor found it and that I took it off him and was going to sell it on my own without cutting him in on the deal or give it to his brother without telling him. Slava has always been jealous of Kazamin and Kazamin knew that Slava was plotting against him. Kazamin is a smart cookie. Would it surprise you to know, Professor, that Kazamin was at Oxford for two years?"

"Anything that Oxford does wouldn't surprise me," said Miroslav, gaining a poker face expression from Anton but a broad smile from Oksana. "But how could Slava think the object had been found when we hadn't even begun the search?" asked Miroslav.

"I don't know. Slava's mind isn't working a hundred percent," replied Anton."Anyway, Kazamin suspected a double cross from Slava so he had a machinist make that metal thing. The plan was that if you and Joakim found what you were looking for, I was to 'relieve' you of it at some point in time, hide the real one, hand the fake over to Slava for 'safe keeping' then let nature takes its course, as it were. Slava would probably want to cut a deal with me, which of course I would never get, sell it to a buyer, cut me out, possibly get rid of me, and that would be that and Kazamin would have the real one."

"But you said it's a piece of junk? How will Slava sell a piece of junk to any buyer?" asked Miroslav and Oksana, almost in unison.

"Slava's got street smarts but he's not cut out for a deal like this. What he doesn't realize is that the buyer will want to verify the authenticity of the item before any money changes hands. I have no idea just how they would do that but when they find out that he's trying to sell them a bill of goods, he's history, immediately, or back to a labor camp if he's unlucky. And my job, for the most part, would have been done!"

There was a long, lingering period of deep thought, chin scratching, head rubbing by both Oksana and Miroslav. Finally, Miroslav was composed enough to continue.

"You know Anton, the out-and-out deviousness of you and the Barkovs defies imagination. And mix that with apparently a very high degree of astounding greed for the sake of greed… I'm at a total loss for words."

Anton responded with only a slight shrug of the shoulders and raised eyebrows.

"So let me get this straight," continued Miroslav. "It wasn't the plan to get rid of me at some point in this adventure? The plan was to dispose of Slava"

Anton drew a long deep breath, even though the act clearly caused significant pain.

"Professor, I like you. I can't say that I did at first, but, if it's any consolation, I do like you. But… had things gone as planned, yes, it was our intention to get rid of you and I was to make sure it was done. Sorry!" he concluded with another shoulder shrug and a half grin.

Oksana looked at Miroslav, expecting to see a depressed man immersed deep in thought, perhaps even shock. But that's not what she saw. Miroslav was smiling, calm as calm can be, smiling, totally at ease, relaxed and apparently feeling right with the world.

"Miroslav, are you alright?" asked Oksana.

Without hesitation, Miroslav answered.

"I haven't felt this good Oksana, in months. What I had up to this point in time were half answers. Now I have all the answers to all those questions that have been ruining my life and plaguing me for more than a decade. Yes, Oksana, I feel great. Just great. Tell me Anton," continued Miroslav, "If Joakim and I had returned to camp with the real object, would you have taken it from us if you knew we had it?"

"Yes, one way or another, yes," was Anton's instant reply, shaking his head and staring at Miroslav with those cold, unrelenting piercing eyes, warning Miroslav that the game was still afoot as far as Anton was concerned, in spite of a dramatic change to the game plan.

It grew dark quickly and the only light was that cast by the fire, sparks flying high as chunks of damp wood exploded in the heat of the flames. Although Anton was made as comfortable as they could, it was clear that he was in some agony and was not going to have a comfortable night. After about a half hour, Miroslav spoke, not looking at Oksana, but rather in the direction that Slava and Joakim had taken earlier that day.

"You know Oksana, one of the odd things about this afternoon was that wave from Joakim as he left the campsite. Do you remember it?"

"Yes. Why? What about it?"

"Well, his hand swept from about the north over to the northwest, away from where we were standing at the time. He's a guide and he told me that he knows this region very well. I think he may have been trying to send us a message – to leave this place but go northwest. I think he realized that following him and Slava would be a potentially dangerous option. The question is, why northwest? What's in that direction?"

"I'm not totally familiar with the country north of here but, as I recall there is a river. I think it's part of the Chunka River system. It leads to Mutoray and there is probably a hospital there. If we could make it to the river… but it's still, I don't know, forty or fifty kilometres or so. I know we can't stay here but even if we make it to the river, then what? Mutoray is still another… fifty kilometres or so west at least!"

"Whether we go north or south, doesn't make much difference to you or I, Oksana, but it can make a big difference for Anton. In as much as I most assuredly don't count him as a friend, he is still a human being and I believe that every human is basically good;

yes, even Anton and perhaps even Slava given the right set of circumstances although, I have to admit, he has strained the limits of my beliefs in humanity!"

"Okay, we head toward the river, a fifty kilometre trek or it could be less, I'm not sure. I think Anton could make the trip on horseback that far anyway. He's going to have to! That's all there is to it," said Oksana. "So, are we in agreement then? We head northwest to the river? I'm not certain what we do after that but it can't be worse than staying here. Tomorrow morning? Might as well stay here for the night. I'll tell you this, I'm not ready to cash in my chips just because Slava decides to get in a snit," concluded Oksana.

Oksana's comment prompted both of them to consciously step back from their situation and have a mentally healing, well deserved laugh.

"You know, you're right Oksana," observed Miroslav. "True, we have a bit of a situation on our hands but, as my father used to say, 'it's never so bad that it can't get worse!' Sorry, that just came to mind. But look around: beautiful country, we're still alive and healthy, except for poor Anton over there, we still have our sense of humor and it's not winter. Things really could be worse."

"And if we need it, we have a gun and some ammo," replied Oksana to Miroslav's complete dismay.

"A gun. You have a gun," stammered Miroslav.

"Yep; it's no artillery piece but it is a gun: 25 caliber actually, and 2 clips of ammo. I keep it in my boot. It won't put moose meat on the table but if you like rabbit, it should do the job."

"Amazing. You're absolutely amazing Oksana. Wow. Things are getting better all the time."

TUNGUSKA VALLEY

SATURDAY, SEPTEMBER 5, 1925

The morning was less than merciful. The air felt as though it would explode any minute with a deluge. The valley shallow below was completely hidden in a layer of thick, white, undulating ground fog. At least, there was little or no wind, just the awful dampness from which there was no relief. Anton, now fully conscious, did not seem any better but no worse either. At least the external bleeding seemed to be under control. They all ate a light breakfast of beans and black bread and, when everything they needed was packed onto the mule and they were about to set out, Miroslav noticed that most of the shredded tent pieces were left behind.

"I think we should take those with us Oksana. Don't ask me why but, as my father used to say, 'better to have it and not need it than need it and not have it.'"

"What did your father do other than say things, Miroslav? Sure. Pack them in somewhere. I don't know why either but we can ask your father later on."

The trio descended into the valley in a direction they guessed to be north to northwest, more or less! Without a compass they could not check their direction, not that it really mattered so long as it wasn't south. Although Miroslav had a pocket watch, there was no clear view of the sun to provide a more exact reference.

It took less than a half hour for them to become completely

swallowed up by fog so thick it seemed it could be cut into blocks. It was far from comfortable for all of them but it was Anton who suffered the most. The ride on the horse was anything but smooth and every step was followed by a groan from Anton but nothing could be done that hadn't already been done.

By late morning, the fog started to burn away and they got glimpses of a valley literally covered with grass greener than anything they had ever witnessed before and small streams, many less than a metre deep and ten to forty meters wide, with so many with trout, one would almost be forced to bait the hook behind a tree. Food was no longer a great concern for themselves or the horses.

By noon, the unspoiled beauty of the area hit them like a tsunami. The sun became visible in spurts but long enough for Oksana, using Miroslav's watch, to get a reasonably accurate bearing on their intended track. Directly in front of them was a long, fairly high, partially wooded ridge and one that would have to be crossed if they were to get to the river.

Miroslav prodded his horse until he was beside Oksana. "Tell me something Oksana," asked Miroslav, "wouldn't it have been shorter for us to simply head directly to Mutoray rather than go north to the river then west?"

"Well, yes… and no. Suppose we went that way, more toward the north west, and we get to the river sooner or later and we don't see the town? I have no idea how long that ridge is," she continued, pointing to the ridge ahead of them, "so I don't know if we could spot the town or not and if we miss it, would we then go west or east?"

"But this way," said Miroslav, "we get to the river and we know that Mutoray is to the west. I take it you have something in mind, right?"

"Sort of," she responded. "I have no intentions of riding all the way to Mutoray with Anton in tow. Once we get to the river, we can build a raft. There's lots of trees around, we have a couple of axes, of a sort, and you packed those shredded leather harness pieces. Should do the job, don't you think Miroslav?"

"No problem for us and Anton, but what about the horses and the mule?"

"Yeah… the horses. Well, we will just have to release them. They won't starve, that's for sure. I expect they will survive all right and maybe someone will find them," she concluded. "I think it's better for us if we take our chances and head as quickly as we can to the river."

"Well, Oksana, chance usually favours the prepared mind," said Miroslav with a broad smile of satisfaction, borrowing an expression coined by Louis Pasteur.

"Oh please, don't tell me; another Oborski-ism, right?" With that, Oksana spurred her horse to pull somewhat ahead of Miroslav, looking back with a grin that said "enough dogmatism for one day, Doc!"

By mid afternoon, Anton's groans had increased in frequency, peaking, Miroslav calculated, at about three hundred per hour, the obsessive scientist musing to himself, and since there wasn't much else to do seated atop his horse! Although they calculated that they had only travelled about ten kilometres, it was decided to make camp near the foot of the ridge in a grove of mixed conifer and deciduous trees.

TUNGUSKA VALLEY

SUNDAY, SEPTEMBER 6, 1925

An early rise that morning didn't present much of a problem. The accommodations, that consisted of a lean-to constructed of sodden spruce boughs over a birch frame partially covered with pieces of canvas, even facing away from a cold westerly, offered little comfort from the wind or the frequent showers and constant dripping from surrounding trees. The only one to complain was Anton, a near constant rant until Oksana decided that enough was enough and strongly suggested he *"...suck it up or run the risk of being the sites only human occupant when they broke camp in the morning."* He sucked it up.

Mercifully, the day broke clear but cool with little or no wind. In spite of their weariness, both Miroslav and Oksana could not help gaze in awe at the beauty of the valley they were about to depart, a testament to the miracle of Mother Nature. With the exception of Anton, who to this point in the day, remained uncharacteristically silent, they began the ascent to the ridge top on foot, leading the horses and the mule as they maneuvered between rocks, outcrops and boulders the size of small houses. It was steeper than they had at first envisioned and the footing was not made easy by the ruff that consisted of pea-sized pebbles that frequently rolled under foot. Still, by noon, they made it to the top.

What lay before them was a large, relatively flat, partially wooded plateau about eight or ten kilometres or so wide. After a brief lunch and a check of Anton's bandages, they continued on course, making good time without the obstacles encountered during their climb to the top.

Oksana said little but she was clearly worried about Joakim's fate although Miroslav tried his best to assure her that Joakim, with his wilderness knowledge and experience, would come away from this probably far better than his capture.

The plateau on the north side, fell off into a large, wooded plain, the terminus of which they hoped (and prayed) would be the Chunku River. They calculated that they had covered about twenty to twenty-five kilometres this day and, if correct, should be less than twenty kilometres from the river and so made camp near the north slope of the plateau.

It did not take long for exhaustion to catch up with all three of them and, in spite of less than comfortable conditions, sleep came quickly.

Miroslav had remembered experiencing blackness years before when exploring a cave in Czechoslovakia but then there were sounds, droplets of water hitting unseen ponds somewhere in the distance, bats and, now and then, the feel of cold air in motion and the comforting feel of the rock floor beneath his shoes. But this was different and far more dreadful and terrifying than anything in the recesses of his memory. There was light; more accurately, lights, small, tiny pin points of light; thousands if not millions of them, everywhere, in every direction, but they cast no shadow nor gave any warmth; they were just there, far, far away and totally unreachable. His was the feeling of cold, absolute entrapment from which, he knew, there could be no rescue - no escape. The sound came from somewhere, away in the distance but he couldn't figure out where, but it became clearer and unmistakable.

"Miroslav, Miroslav."

He recognized it and he sensed the urgency.

"Miroslav, wake up, wake up."

It took a moment to focus his eyes before realizing that he had been rescued; that it was Oksana.

"Miroslav! Look! Over there, to the south! Do you see it?" she asked.

Miroslav stared hard in the direction she was pointing, but saw nothing other than the blue endless forest in the distance, painted by the near full moon.

"There it is again," she said, still pointing.

This time Miroslav saw it as well. Just a brief, orangish flicker, but he saw it.

"What do make of it," asked Miroslav, sitting upright and unsure of what it might be.

"A campfire, I'm pretty certain. But whose? I didn't see any trails in the last couple of days so it isn't as though this place sees a lot of travel. I don't know."

They both came to the same conclusion at the same time.

"Slava! But how... how did he find us," stopping in mid sentence, noticing that *are you on drugs?* stare from Oksana. "Right! Stupid question. Ours is the only trail," said Miroslav, answering his own question. "So, what do we do now, Oksana?"

"Not much we can do if he turned back to find us. We're still at least a day ahead of him right now but he's apparently travelling faster than us. What about Joakim? You don't suppose... Av?" The unthinkable question trailed off to an unthinkable thought.

"Joakim will be fine, Oksana. He's a very resourceful man," said Miroslav. "As for Slava catching up with us, that may not be so if he still has his love affair with Vodka."

"True. So, my suggestion is that we get a good night's sleep, head out early in the morning and stay the course, Okay? Really, there isn't much else we can do unless one of us wants to head back and intercept him, a man with a gun, by the way."

"Not something I would relish," replied Miroslav as he crawled back under his horse blanket.

TUNGUSKA
VALLEY

MONDAY, SEPTEMBER 7, 1925

Early came early. Anton wasn't all that happy about the earlier than usual start and the other two weren't about to reveal their observations from the night before. Travelling slightly downhill was a whole lot easier than travelling considerably uphill, and they made good time in spite of the relatively dense forest growth. But it was old growth and the bottom most branches of many of the trees had long since become part of the forest floor. The day was cloudy and cool but it did not rain and, from one of several low hills, they eventually caught glimpses of the river in late afternoon, a bit off to their right and they guessed about five or six kilometres distant, and they breathed a lot easier. Given the grueling day, through which Anton moaned on occasion but said nothing, they decided to make camp and keep a watchful eye to their south, sleeping in shifts.

Miroslav took the first watch, and there wasn't much to watch, just the bright white moon as it swam it's way though an endless loop of dark clouds. He felt alone, so very alone in the middle of nowhere. He was on watch and he hoped strongly that his would be a watch marked by constant nothingness.

I'll take the loneliness' he said to himself, *'at least this time.*

Immersed in his thoughts, he almost missed it. He had heard that sound hundreds of time during the day; the snap of a dry branch under a horses hoof. There it was again and this time the faint, muffled sound of a horses snort. Covered in a cold sweat, he ran quickly and as quietly as he could to the lean-to and woke Oksana.

"It can't be my turn yet. Go away," she said, half sitting up from her blanket.

"Quiet," said Miroslav, holding a finger to his mouth. "Listen… I heard something. A horse coming our way. It has to be Slava. He's been riding long and he's caught up with us."

"Get Anton'" said Oksana. "I will put out the campfire. Get him to that bunch of spruce over there," pointing to her left.

Miroslav hauled the half-conscious Anton as gently as he could into the shadows of the grove of spruce trees then came back, grabbed Oksana by the sleeve and they both ran in a crouched position toward the trees.

It didn't take long for the rider to appear, perhaps less than five minutes. By this time, Oksana and Miroslav were laying prone on the ground about twenty meters from the campsite, the smoking fire pit between them and the approaching rider. He wasn't all that tall, dressed in black with a brimmed hat pulled low over his brow.

"That's Joakim's gun in the saddle holster," whispered Oksana and both went stone still.

What happened to Joakim was not something they wanted to think about but it was clear that whatever happened, wasn't good and there seemed a good chance for a repeat.

The rider dismounted, drew the rifle from the holster and walked over to the lean-to, stopping momentarily. Turning around, he strode lazily over to the dying fire, then grabbed a cup and poured himself some coffee from the pot, still slung above the coals, and sat in a squat next to the fire pit, with the rifle laying across his lap. He looked around the site again, stood up and rested the rifle against a dead tree stump before tossing the contents of the coffee cup on the ground, put the empty cup down and walked slowly to his horse.

"What's he up to," whispered Miroslav, and Oksana shook her head as if to say.

"I have no idea. Perhaps getting his vodka bottle."

"Well, we can't stay here all night. A bit of déjà vu though, wouldn't you say?"

Oksana gave him a wondering look.

"He's got a pistol too, remember Miroslav," she whispered back.

To Oksana's complete surprise, Miroslav began to slowly crawl toward the rifle, making not a sound. The distance seemed infinite as he avoided anything that would produce sound but, finally, he was within reach and with cold, sweaty hands trembling like a feather in a hurricane, snared the rifle and quickly took aim, realizing that the shot would probably have little or no chance of hitting the target but at least they will have gained some small advantage, as temporary as it might be.

"Professor, the coffee you two have is awful; tastes like a mix of gunpowder and horse bedding."

Miroslav was even more shaken in spite of the fact that Oksana was now at his side. To his utter confusion, she gently pushed the barrel of the rifle away from the intended target. Miroslav looked at Oksana. Oksana was all smiles.

"One of the first things you should know Professor, is that you have to put a bullet into the breach with the bolt then release the safety catch in order to have that gun fire."

The rider, with hands raised in submission, slowly turned around to face his captures and walked slowly toward the dying embers of the campfire and doffed his hat.

"What's the matter with you two? Don't you like me anymore?"

"It's Joakim, it's Joakim," screamed Oksana, racing from Miroslav's side, nearly bowling him over in her headlong onslaught toward Joakim who was now standing, hat off and weathered, tired features clearly visible in the moon light.

Oksana broke out in a flood of tears as she virtually crushed Joakim with a hug while Miroslav stood, rifle arm limp by his side, mouth open and no longer covered with cold sweat.

Their salvation, he hoped, had arrived.

He brought food and water and, after getting the fire re-started, partied as best they could without waking Anton.

Joakim answered the obvious question.

"Slava didn't stop drinking the whole day and into the night and finally passed out," he said. "So getting away wasn't that much of a problem. I went back to the Tunguska and found your trail. Going south wasn't an option for me either. I knew that Slava would get to my house sooner or later and I heard him mumble something about his buyers meeting him there. I doubt that the house even exists now. The good folks in my village would see to that, I'm sure. It wouldn't take long for the buyers to discover that all Slava had was not the real item and it's not likely they would let him walk away. So being followed by Slava didn't concern me. So what are your plans when we get to the river?"

"To make a raft," replied Oksana, "and sail down the river to Mutoray. I don't think Anton can take much more on horseback."

"Well frankly, I don't give a rats behind about Anton's condition but the raft idea is faster than getting there on horseback. But it may not be necessary anyway. Yesterday, I caught sight of a small boat upriver from us and I think it may be headed our way. Whoever is on the boat I think camped west of where I saw it on the river so I'm quite certain the boat is headed west. Still, it's nice to see that you two were prepared."

Oksana cast a quick glance at Miroslav who didn't return the look but simply grinned the grin of an I-told-you-so.

Early didn't bother any of them except Anton again who did not seem as excited as the others over Joakim return, but he said nothing.

By the time they reached the river bank, it was well past four in the afternoon and a light rain began and, from the look of the sky and haze, there was little doubt that they were in for a very wet and totally uncomfortable night. There was no sign of a boat and they feared that they had arrived too late. Still, there was little else to do than wait to see what the next morning would bring.

"I was thinking something," said Miroslav. "If the boat does arrive, there is nothing to say that we will be allowed aboard. Look at us. We don't paint a very pretty picture. And then what do we do with the horses and the mule?"

"Don't worry about the horses," answered Joakim. "You know as well as I do Oksana that they will not starve and will probably go back the way we came. Someone will find them."

TUNGUSKA VALLEY

TUESDAY, SEPTEMBER 8, 1925

They were up early to a grey overcast day that promised more rain. It was only Anton that got any amount of sleep. The others wanted to be very sure that, as the saying goes, they didn't miss the boat.

They all heard it at more or less the same time; at about 7 AM; the unmistakable chug-chug-chug of a one cylinder gasoline engine, missing as many beats as it fired. But, with such an engine, the steady power comes as much from the over-sized flywheel as the engine itself. It came into sight, coming around the bend to their right, dead down the centre channel, plowing through the water at a breathtaking three knots or so. When it got within earshot, they lined the bank and shouted.

"Привет лодки, Привет лодки" (hello the boat).

The boat slowed immediately as the driver slipped the transmission into neutral and looking toward the assemblage on the embankment.

"How can I help you?"

They all looked at one another and it was Joakim who finally said, "I think he's speaking English; an American. Does anyone speak the language?"

Both Miroslav and Oksana volunteered a "yes" but Oksana continued, "not well. How about you Miroslav?"

"Yes, I speak English; spent a couple of years in the UK." Turning toward the boat and using his hands as a megaphone, "Can you give us a lift? We have an injured man with us. How far are you going?"

By this time, the boat pilot engaged the transmission and, to their gleeful surprise, brought the bow around, heading for their location, causing an enormous sigh of relief from the collective. The boat was about eight or ten metres in length and one and a half metre beam with a canopy erected near the bow. The engine, pilot and tiller were at the stern. As the boat gently touched the shoreline, Joakim was the first to jump into the cold water and bring the craft to a gentle halt, swinging the boat parallel to the shoreline. He held out his hand to the pilot and told him how happy we were to see him but, of course, the pilot had no idea what was said. Miroslav acted as translator. After introductions, Miroslav told the pilot of the circumstances and he agreed to take Anton and the others aboard for the trip downriver.

Turing to the others, Miroslav translated what had transpired.

"His name is Daniel Buchanan and he's not American; he's a Canadian. He's here on a government project to evaluate the forest industry in this region. Seems genuine. What do you think? Take him up on his offer?"

"You mean there's a choice," asked Oksana. "Of course. It's the only chance that Anton, for one, will have. What do you think Joakim?"

"Listen. We hailed this guy down, he has a boat, and we don't. I don't know what the problem is? Kind of a no-brainer don't you think? But I think I will stay with the horses and take them down river. I was thinking about this last night."

"I will stay with Joakim as well. Both of us are, well, horse people and we will be fine. We will meet you in Mutoray in a couple of days or so," Oksana said.

With that, Anton, now fully conscious and alert, was loaded onto the boat and placed comfortably under the canopy, followed by

Miroslav. Joakim and Oksana pushed the craft into the channel and away they went, both parties waving as they departed. Parting was, as the saying goes, truly sweet sorrow.

"I think we should backtrack a bit, Oksana, and follow the ridges west. The trail will be a lot easier; better than fighting a losing battle with those dense woods." With that, he and Oksana packed the animals and headed up, toward the ridge.

Joakim was, of course, correct. The going was a lot easier; a whole lot easier. Now and again, they even caught sight of the little boat as it chugged its way down the river.

"Joakim, can I ask you a question?"

"Sure. What is it?"

"When you left Slava's campsite to find us, did you think about retrieving the metal object that Anton had? I learned that it's a useless piece of junk but Slava didn't know that."

"Nope. If I did that, Slava may have got the idea to track me down."

"So, is there a real object? I mean, what the Professor has been trying to find. Is it real?"

"Oh it's real alright but the professor doesn't have it; at least not yet."

"How do you know that Joakim?"

"Because I have it. I've had it all along – for a couple of years now, but I didn't know it. At least not for sure, until you and the Professor came by."

Several kilometres went by while Oksana tried her best to digest what she had just learned. It annoyed her feeling that the trip may have been a total waste of time.

"Joakim, what you're telling me is that this whole venture was fruitless right from the start. Here we are, in the middle of nowhere, cold, wet and miserable and, on that boat down there is a disillusioned Professor and Anton with two bullet holes in him, and you're okay with that! Not to mention the fact that Slava thinks he has an item of great value that is really worth nothing and could cost him his life."

"Oksana, most of what you say is true. But think of this. Yes, I have what the Professor has been looking for and he now knows that I have it. In fact, I didn't have to tell him. He figured it out for himself. When I get back, he can have it or you can have it. I really don't want it. it's brought nothing but misery to my so called life. What do you think would have happened had I told Slava and Anton I had it? They would take it for sure but they would probably have disposed of both me and the Professor and possibly you as well. When I learned of the real purpose of the trip and then Anton came up with the fake, that was a fantastic stroke of pure luck. The fight between the two was unforeseeable and unfortunate. I'm not sure when Anton planned to spring the fake on Slava but my guess would have been the day of the shooting, after the Professor and I returned to the camp empty handed. This was part of the plan to get rid of both the Professor and Slava."

The remainder of the days that followed rarely included much discussion of the Tunguska Valley adventure. The boat plied its way peacefully down the river, easily taking the many turns and twists. Although the sky remained an ominous grey, the mist had cleared, there was little wind and it was the picture of serenity.

The little boat was the epitome of comfort in relative terms as it chugged its way toward Mutoray and both Miroslav and Anton experienced total relaxation that had been foreign to them for several weeks.

"May I ask you a question, Mr. Buchanan?" said Miroslav.

"Shoot, but my name isn't Mister; it's Daniel. Daniel, all right?"

"Yes, yes, I apologize. I thought that it was proper to address you as mister. My most humble apologies."

Dan was slightly embarrassed by Miroslav's interpretation and tried to backtrack.

"Miroslav, please, no need for apologies. I was actually making a bit of a joke. At home, folks just call me Dan or Daniel. It's just that I'm not used to something as formal as Mister. So, what would you like to know?"

"Yes. I understand. You know, you are the very first Canadian I have met inside Russia and where do we meet; in a boat on a long forgotten river in north central Russia. Odd wouldn't you say?"

"When I first arrived in this country from British Columbia, and I would guess a hundred times since, I have been asked to produce my papers to prove that I am here with the blessings of your government. I guess it is kinda unusual for a Canadian to be here, doing nothing but looking at trees. But the constant displays of suspicion gets a little tough to handle from time to time. But Miroslav, put your mind at rest. As we say in Canada, I'm here for a good time, not a long time. okay?"

"Yes, Quite so. I understand completely. And you are right in your observations. Very sad for my country. Very sad. And, you are having a good time, may I inquire? Did I ask that correctly?"

"I'm havin' a great time. Look around my friend: lots and lots of quiet country, beautiful scenery, a little weather now and again to make it even more enjoyable. Am I having a good time? Jimminee pelt, you bettcha I am! Oh, I don't know where my manners have gone but can I offer you and your friend their a drink of rye? It will have to be straight up."

"Anton doesn't drink but I would appreciate a small glass of rye."

"A Russian that doesn't drink? Perhaps he would like a coffee or tea.

I have both. Would you mind asking him Miroslav?"

Miroslav moved toward the bow, and asked Anton for Dan.

"He said that would be most kind. Tea if you wouldn't mind"

"Great. You take the tiller and I will go and make it."

"You want me to steer the boat?"

"That would be the idea, Miroslav. Just keep an eye peeled for dead heads. We don't want to sink this sixty year old beauty."

"What is a dead head and what should I do if I see one?"

"A dead head is a partially submerged log, could rip a hole in the hull. Perhaps steering around it might be a good plan wouldn't you say?"

When Dan finished making the tea over a small kerosene stove, he poured it into a large cup and handed it to Anton.

"Спасибо. Спасибо так очень," spoke Anton.

"What did he say, Miroslav?"

"He said 'thank you. Thank you so very much.'"

Dan reached down and gave Anton a warm pat on the shoulder that was returned with a very uncharacteristically sincere smile.

"Miroslav – may I ask you a question?"

"Yes, of course. Discharge."

Seeing Dan's look of amusement, Miroslav knew that the choice of words may not have been entirely correct.

"Fire? Explode? No, no ….ah yes, shoot, yes?"

"Yeah, that's it. Tell me something. How did Anton happen to catch a couple of bullets?"

Miroslav related as much as he could to Dan, starting with the trip to the valley but omitting the part about a hunt for a mysterious object, the alcohol fuelled fight, the shots and the trip to the river on which they now found themselves, and hoped that Dan would not pry any deeper, and he didn't, much to Miroslav's relief.

"Hmmm, very interesting," said Dan, shaking his head slightly from side to side not looking at either one of them but eyes welded on the river ahead.

"Dan, you say this is an old boat," hoping that the question would elicit a change in conversational direction. "Where did you get it?"

"It's called a Schliupka in Russia; very sturdy and easily maneuverable. This one was built about a half century ago; no engine then, just oars and lots of them. In Canada, we have something similar called a whaler. A friend of mine from Zelenograd near Moscow made arrangements for me to pick it up in Mutoray and I will be leaving it in Bayk where the owner lives, probably in a few weeks. From there, I will take a steamer to the railhead, back to Leningrad and a ship home; a trip of a lifetime, wouldn't you say?"

"Yes, for sure. I hope you will take back good memories and perhaps we may meet again someday only under better conditions."

"Miroslav, these are great conditions. You're relaxed, our friend up front is comfortable and moving around a bit, the weather is cooperating, we have lots a food, and rye. Enjoy the moment Miroslav. Remember, none of us are passing through more than once."

FRIDAY, SEPTEMBER 11, 1925

The little craft dropped Miroslav and Anton off at a wharf late in the afternoon of the third day after their rescue. With a sincere wish for a safe and happy journey, they watched the boat ease its way out into the channel and disappear around the bend in the river. With the assistance of some men dockside, Anton, in the company of Miroslav, was taken to a local hospital; small but more than adequate. A few days later, Joakim and Oksana arrived, very tired but otherwise in good health and spirits.

Anton's room was small but clean. The air was thick with the odor of a mixture of disinfectant, chloroform and lye soap but the room was warm and while not the comforts of home, the bed was infinitely better than laying on wet spruce needles under a leaking canopy of boughs.

"Anton, we have to ask the question and you can answer it or not. What's the story with the metal object that caused Slava to shoot you," asked Joakim.

For what seemed like a mini eternity, Anton simply stared at the ceiling, a thumbnail rubbing his upper teeth and shaking his head, he was clearly thinking about alternatives and just how deep the questioning would go, and just where his loyalties were.

"Okay," he said finally. "I've already told this to Oksana. The metal was a just a piece of junk that Kazamin had engraved with weird, meaningless markings. If the Professor there", pointing to Miroslav, "didn't find the object, I was to give that thing to him and tell Slava that he had found it in the valley. Since none of us knew what the object is supposed to look like, even if there was such a thing, Slava would probably believe it. Kazamin found out that Slava was going to double-cross him, take the find and sell it the highest bidder, probably some Russian officials. Apparently a deal had already been made."

"But the buyers would know it's a fake in a minute. What good would that do," asked Joakim.

"Exactly. Beautiful, isn't it? Kazamin wants to get rid of Slava, the buyers realize they have been had and poor dumb Slava ends up in a Russian jail."

"But what about me, Anton?" asked Miroslav.

Anton simply opened up his hands, head slightly cocked to one side, looked straight at Miroslav with a slight grin and a wink.

"Doesn't matter now, does it Professor! By the way, do you know where Slava is? Did he head south after the fight?"

"Not certain," answered Joakim. "Probably making his way to Vanavara would be my guess."

Anton continued, "Hate to say it Joakim, but it doesn't look good for your house. You know what kind of temper Slava has and since he can't beat the crap out of you, I would say he will target the house."

This time, there was no grin of satisfaction from Anton, just a nonchalant expression that Joakim interpreted as a vast improvement in relations.

A couple of nurses came by and Oksana asked one of them if there was a telegraph office in the town. There was and she gave Oksana directions.

NEAR VANAVARA

TUESDAY, JUNE 8, 1926

She heard it more than saw it; a whine, something like a child only rising and falling in almost timed intervals and it wasn't a child. It was an automobile making its way over a rut-riddled road that hadn't seen any form of maintenance since the end of the last Ice Age.

It was a beautiful day, partially cloudy sky with no hint that rain might be in the offing. A great day for farm work, a great day to hang clothes out to dry. Just a great day for anything, and she felt good about it. The damp clothes lay in the wicker basket at her feet waiting their turn to be draped over the clothes line that ran between two cedar poles in the farm yard, adjacent to the small but sturdy house. She loved this time of the year. The crops were in and growing and everything seemed to be alive. All around, for as far as she could see, it was an ocean awash in countless shades of green that, in the distant waves, turned almost to black near the densely forested foothills. There was almost no wind but still, there was enough to move a thin cloud of reddish-brown dust from the road and, filtered by the tall black spruce trees that lined both sides of the road, quickly dissipated over the field of greenish-yellow ripening wheat next to the road and she silently prayed, that the clothesline would be spared.

Indeed, it was an automobile, bouncing, slipping and sliding with jarring motions from one rut to another, the driver engaged in a futile effort to keep the contraption on the ridges between them, ruts formed by countless decades of wagon travel on a narrow road that barely qualified as such. Automobiles were not a common site in this area of Russia, but not entirely unknown. A truck would come to their farm once or twice a year, a military vehicle, to collect 'levy', a much dreaded time that invariably raised the bar on hardship for her, Stepan and their family and, eventually, all the other families in the region.

Polina had seen lots of automobiles once on a short visit to Krasnoyarsk with her father years ago. She even had the opportunity to ride in one, an experience well remembered. But this was an automobile, not a truck, and to her surprise, and cautious delight, it turned into the drive that lead from the road to their home, barely missing a thick wooden post at the entrance before sliding into a rut that thankfully dragged them back on course, sans the dust cloud.

It was a Ford. The only reason she correctly identified its make was from the word emblazoned across its steam puffing radiator. She was spellbound by the sight of the automobile as it bounced, burped and whined its way toward the barnyard, the passengers looking more like popcorn than people. The sound of a car wasn't that common so it didn't take long for Stepan to come out of the barn to see what all the racket was about, thinking that it was far too early for the military vehicle. The crops had yet to be harvested. But, almost instantly, his fears were quelled for he thought he knew who it was, at least he hoped it was who he thought it was; and it was!

Even before the car came to a grinding, steam shrouded halt, Stepan grabbed the figure emerging from the right front seat and gave him a bear hug that would take the wind out of a Sumo wrestler.

"Yakov, Yakov my brother. My God Yakov, how good it is to see you again. What's it been, eight, ten years or so? And you look great."

Without hardly drawing a breath, Stepan ran over to Polina who was now standing by the back door of their little home and fairly yanked her off her feet as they flew back to the car.

"Remember Polina?"

"Your husband, Polina, doesn't leave much time for others to speak," said Yakov. Polina was noticeably impressed by Yakov; the kid she remembered from years back who had more interest in her parents business than just about anything else, and look at him now, tall, handsome, dressed like a king and yes, with an automobile!

"Yakov, it's so good to see you again. But, let's not stand out here. Please come inside and bring the other gentleman with you."

The driver had exited the car and stood, almost at attention in front of the vehicle. He was also well dressed. Somewhat taller than Yakov, broad shoulders, square jawed, short black hair, thick, black eyebrows, slightly pock-marked face and cool demeanor. He was clearly not one that you would want to have as an enemy unless you carried a considerable amount of health insurance!

"My sincere apologies", said Yakov. "Please, may I introduce Ivan Kozinsky. Not only is Ivan my driver, he's my bodyguard, my teacher and one of my very best friends."

With that, Ivan nodded, extended his bear paw sized hand into which Polina's hand virtually disappeared. He followed the three into the house. Ivan's 1.9 metre frame meant that he had to stoop so as not to hit the top of the jam.

The house was small, not unlike most farm houses common to the area. Built from rough hewn timbers on a rock wall basement that served as vegetable storage for the long, cold winter months, it could clearly withstand anything that Siberian weather Gods could to throw at it. The immaculate cleanliness of the house did not escape the attention of either Yakov or Ivan, even to the top of the small wood stove that looked as though it was purchased yesterday, although Yakov knew that it had been in the family for generations. The house consisted of a small entrance foyer and open closet, an unusually large kitchen with lots of storage space and two bedrooms with two small beds in the loft.

The atmosphere was one of family contentment, made more so

with and the unmistakable odor of something really good cooking on the little stove. Stepan and Polina's youngest son and daughter, Yuri and Katrina, came in about an hour after Yakov and Ivan arrived and, following introductions and went to the loft to read. Both were fascinated more so by Ivan than Yakov and kept him under careful scrutiny.

"And Griggory," asked Yakov. "Is he not around?"

"He's on a fishing trip about a day's ride from here. He should be back tomorrow with a lot of fish… we hope."

NEAR
VANAVARA

WEDNESDAY, JUNE 9, 1926

The next day passed quickly as both Stepan and Yakov filled in the years since they last saw each other. Polina, as a welcome to the guests, baked several loaves of bread in the outdoor oven, a delicacy loved and enjoyed by all. Late in the day, Griggory arrived home. The fact that he had fewer gutted fish than expected to show for the extended period he was away, surprised no one; no one, that is, except Yakov who, until now, was not aware of the duality of the venture. While it may have been Yakov and Polina's hope that the catch was good, that was somewhat secondary for Griggory who was far more interested in a number of ancient, long forgotten and unrecorded human habitations sites in the same area. So, what he had to show for his adventure was a bunch of drawings, a map, notes and about fifty or so brook trout.

Depending on who was the observer and who was the observed, time did not fly by over the next few weeks. For Stepan, Polina and Griggory, it was work as usual: long, hard days of hand labor, weeding vegetable plots and cutting, yarding, sawing and splitting fire wood in preparation for the inevitable onslaught of winter and even more hardship with little to show for it than an ongoing testament to survival and stamina.

Griggory rarely complained of the hard work. Tall, lean and muscular, with a head full of dark brown hair that matched the colour of his friendly intelligent eyes, he well understood that hard summers were a necessity if hard winters were to be survived.

For Yakov, the days were even longer and provided confirmation that he had made the right decision for himself years ago. On the other side of the coin, it gave him time to ponder what he knew to be the unraised question harboured by Stepan and Polina; why was he here after so many years?

For Ivan, it was a time of unanticipated metamorphosis. The work didn't wear on him as it did the others and, by nightfall, he still had lots of energy reserves that he devoted almost entirely to the two younger children in the household. Katrina and Yuri took to him as to a long lost grandfather. Children have a unique and uncanny ability to see through a physiological shell and peer deep into the very soul to discover the real person. Without realizing it, what they discovered in Ivan was an empty childhood with countless destroyed and buried dreams and hopes suddenly awakened and, at least in part, Ivan realized that it was good, for all three of them.

The charade of avoidance came to an end in early July, a combination of having had enough of the very thing he wanted to escape, the need to move ahead on his plans and the feeling that the question was becoming stronger as each day passed. No further time could pass.

"Stepan, Polina, may we talk?" began Yakov.

Dinner was over, dishes washed and put away and the two youngest, in bed for the night. Ivan sat at the table as well, his chiseled features catching every flickering shadow cast by the lone kerosene lamp on a shelf next to him. A slight breeze had come up and whistled through the old spruce and hemlock trees that stood guard next to the house as if to say, *'beware, beware.'* There was deafening silence even though Stepan and Polina had patiently waited for this time to arrive but not having any clue whatsoever what to expect.

"Of course, Yakov. We are all ears. I'm sure it's no surprise that we wonder why you have chosen now to pay us a visit. But please, do not take that as an offence. Nothing of the kind is intended for we are so very delighted to see you and to meet Ivan and have you both as our guests for as long as you wish to stay. We are indeed humbled."

"I thank you brother. Two years ago, when our parents passed away, you know that I could not be here," said Yakov." It was one of the worst winters in our country's history and my train barely made it to Chelyabinsk and it was from there I sent the telegram."

"I understand that, Yakov. There was nothing anyone could have done. It was a horrible winter for us as well. As you know, they had had pneumonia once before and it almost killed them. But this time, it was too much and no doctor was available and unfortunately, they passed away within a week of each other. But it was good that you visited the grave site. I go there often to think and, yes, even plan although there really isn't much to plan for these days. We had hoped that things would improve with the death of Lenin but, under Stalin, it's probably worse. The trucks come more often, take more, leaves us less and the school; well it only runs a few days each week, whenever a teacher is available."

"Sad memories Stepan, and a guilt that will follow me to my grave. I am more familiar with the hardships than you probably realize."

There was a long silence punctuated only by the crackling of wood in the old, cast iron stove and the sound of the north wind in the tree tops.

"Stepan, I will come to the purpose of my visit as quickly as possible and I assure you that, first of all, I am not in trouble or running away from the OGPU," explained Yakov. "I come here mostly out of concern for you, Polina, Griggory and the other two children. A few years after I left here, I was taken in by a gentleman from Sevastopol, Victor Treschev, who owned a highly successful import–export company. I will not go into details of how that acquaintance developed, that's another story, but suffice to say that he was unmarried and had no heirs. Over time, he and Ivan tutored me in the nuances of doing business, not only in Russia, but with the west as well that would be, shall we say, both profitable and sustainable in a country not openly fond of capitalism. In a real sense, I became his protégé. But Mr. Treschev, my adopted father, if you will, looks forward to enjoying life a little more than he has been and so I have been given more and more responsibility. The consequence Stepan, is that I have acquired a very comfortable lifestyle, so to speak."

"Earned," added Ivan who, to this point, sat in the shadows in stone-faced silence.

Stepan and Polina said nothing, hardly blinking an eye and in complete awe of what they were hearing but not sure if any of it was true or simply bravado or a nice bedtime story. Sensing a growing mood of disbelief in both Polina and Stepan, Ivan intervened.

"It's all true. But someday, you must get Yakov to tell you of his adventures in Moscow before Mr. Treschev rescued him," concluded Ivan, putting his arm around Yakov, easing a growing sense of tension in the room.

"Stepan," continued Yakov, "Ivan and I came by airplane. Even so, it was a long trip and a good many fuelling stops along the way but faster, far faster than taking a train. The plane is a Moskalyev SAM5. There are only a handful of them in Russia and my employer owns five, all obtained for prospective buyers. That's the kind of business the NSDF is. The Foundation gets what people want, not necessarily what they need. But Stepan, for those that have wealth, and believe me Stepan, I have learned there are a great many in Russia who have accumulated enormous wealth, want is a far stronger driving force than need."

"But we really want for nothing, Yakov", interjected Stepan, at the same time catching a *what are you saying* look from Polina with eyes that at that moment could bore holes in an iron rail.

"Stepan, I'm not here to dump money in your lap as if you were some kind of medieval serf. But, as I said before, I am here to help you and your family. So, if I may continue, things will become quite clear," continued Yakov. "All is not well in mother Russia. You know that when Vladimir Lenin died, he was succeeded by Josef Stalin, and

I tell you, Stepan," said Yakov, bending over the table and pointing alternately to both his brother and Polina, "a man with less moral fibre and a greater penchant for human cruelty has never lived," he concluded, sitting back in his chair. You have said yourself how things have got worse recently and I believe you. I won't pretend that I have not done things that I am not proud of."

At this point Ivan shot a glance at Yakov that said *put the brakes on, my friend.*

"Even as we speak, Stalin is gathering up all those who oppose him or who he even thinks could oppose him and they simply disappear. His total focus is on industrialization with little concern of its impacts on rural populations. He certainly has not made any attempt to hide that fact. So far, he has had more than ten thousand military generals executed because he *'suspected'* that they might offer some kind of resistance to his plans. Can you imagine? And I expect this paranoid driven purge will continue for a long time to come. I fear that Russia will suffer greatly at his hands."

"Yakov," said Stepan, "are you sure there isn't something else you're not telling us? I know what you said earlier, but are you one of those being hunted?"

"No, no, no Stepan. Stalin poses no threat or danger to me, Ivan or Mr. Treschev. We make a habit of being publically inconspicuous. Stalin's regime needs us in the same manner as those before him. That's not to say that his personal devils could not get the best of him someday, but if we continue practicing our... art, as it were, and with other events unfolding, we will be fine."

"But there are other even less pleasant things happening that you may not be aware of," continued Yakov. "The NSDF believes that Russia will be involved in another war in Europe in the not too distant future and then, of course, as I mentioned, there is Stalin and his plans for mother Russia."

"Yakov," interrupted Stepan, "the last war, even Conscription and

The Revolution had little effect on us except that life was a little more harsh in that period. Why would it be worse this time, even if it happens? And as far as Stalin is concerned, these are games played out in Moscow and, remember our father; he couldn't have cared less about Czar Nicholas, or Lenin, so why should we care about Stalin? They will do what they do and I don't care so long as they leave us be! Granted, they sometimes don't leave us much but the farm has always provided what we need and what we don't need and the military don't take, we sell in the marketplace. Isn't that so Polina?"

The look on Polina's face and the silent response spoke volumes to all of them; *yes, but is there something better? Isn't that the real reason for your visit?*

"The situation is different now, Stepan. I wouldn't put it past Stalin to start seriously conscripting boys and men into his armies and don't think your isolation here in Siberia will protect you. The Trans Siberian Railway stretches crosses the country, the tentacles of the Politburo reach everywhere, even here. Are there not labor camps near here? Believe me, if he wants to conscript Griggory, he will. Opposition could get you shot, or worse, sent to one if those camps."

Silence and an almost comatose atmosphere broke out, long, eerie and broken only by the glances bouncing back and forth between Stepan, Griggory and Polina. Stepan, placing his arm around Polina's shoulders, broke the uneasy stillness.

"Yakov, what you say is most interesting and fascinating. And we are happy that you are doing well and have taken the time to visit us. As I have already said, you know as well as me that our parents expected nothing from the Russian Central Government and they weren't disappointed. Leaders have come and gone and nothing much has changed. Life in this area is hard but we are tough enough to survive it. We produce crops, we have chickens and pigs, we sell what we don't need and we survive, we have friends in the area to help us when we need help. You have your fancy airplane, that automobile and fine clothes and…," his voice trailing off.

Yakov's eyes widened, he became red from the neck up. He was visibly furious at those words and in mid sentence, half jumping to his feet, he slammed his fist onto the table and leaned as close to his brothers face as he could.

"Stepan, you idiot, have you not understood a word I have said? You're not surviving, you're subsisting in the same way as did our parents. Nothing, absolutely nothing has changed! Doesn't that raise any red flags for you, your future, for Polina's future and the future of your children?" Ivan got up and eased Yakov back into his chair. "Do you really think I came all this way just to give you a history lesson? Do you have any idea what we went through to get here? This desolate, God forsaken place isn't just down the street, Stepan," screamed Yakov. "It took almost a week just to get to Krasnoyarsk, then repairs to the aircraft, bad weather and every delay imaginable. We were on the road for almost a month, Stepan! Does that sound like a vacation trip to you?"

Yakov was beginning to cool, slumped back in his chair, starring at the table top, Ivan's hand still on his shoulder. Polina had got up from her chair when Yakov started into his screaming rant and stood behind Stepan and Griggory, a look of shock and fear in her eyes, glancing at the loft but the youngest were still in blissful sleep. Stepan, recovering from the unexpected verbal avalanche, was about to deliver an equally animated response when Polina derailed his intent with a gentle squeeze to his shoulder.

Removing Ivan's hand and thanking him for not allowing the spirited discussion to go farther, Yakov spoke in a much more controlled manner.

"I apologize to all of you. I did not mean to speak so harshly. You have welcomed me into your home and we have been treated royally. Please accept my apology. But I am worried, very worried about your future, Griggoy's future and the two children."

Polina resumed her place at the table and stared at Yakov, almost in wonderment but certainly with no small amount of trepidation.

"Yakov, no apology is necessary. We understand that the journey was long and tiring and will take some time for you to get back to being yourself. We all have those times. I know you have something to say, something to tell us, so please go on."

Yakov gave a long, lingering look at the assembly, moving his head in almost a half arc, staring above their heads, trying desperately to regain his composure and placed his slightly trembling hands palms up on the table.

"Stepan, Polina, Griggory; it wasn't the journey. Your kind hospitality has provided us with more than enough rest. This visit is very complicated. To be honest, I was not the one first asked to undertake the trip but I insisted on coming because we have been apart far too long. But, I will be truthful, there is also another reason, totally unrelated to the primary reason for being here."

At this point, all around the table, except Ivan, had looks that screamed confusion.

"If it's alright with you Stepan, Polina, Griggory, I would like to continue and tell you why I am concerned about you. I promise, I will fill you in on the other reason. Who knows – you may find it exciting."

They glanced at each other and quietly gave nods of approval.

"It's the Russia of today; it's not the Russia of twenty or thirty years ago; it is not the Russia of our parents Stepan. It has changed, some good things, some not so good things. How do I know? Our business is to acquire information and knowledge before others have it. Knowledge is power, Stepan, it's a new era. As I said, we are here because we fear for your future and the future of your wonderful family if you do not listen and understand. It was actually the NSDF that first alerted me and encouraged me to undertake this trip."

"But why fear for us, Yakov? We are all well. Yes, we have little by way of wealth but we are comfortable, the crops are good and we have good friends all around us. Our farm is small I'm sure by standards you know but it is sufficient and, most of all, we are happy? Isn't that so,

Polina?" looking at her and prompting a positive response, that he received, if not reservedly.

"Stepan, my dearest brother, the world is changing and you and your family and this farm and every farm in the nation are about to feel that change, Let me explain."

By this time, he had the full attention of Stepan, Polina and especially Griggory.

"I fear for you because of what I know, of what Ivan and the NSDF know and the most important reason for our visit."

By now, they were all ears and leaning into the table to make sure that no word was left unheard.

"The Central Government will soon be instituting a policy of land reform called Collectivization that will not be good news for any farmer in Russia. Stepan, you are proud of this farm, and rightly so. It is one of the largest and most productive in the area. But Stepan, you have lost sight of something… the farm isn't yours. It never has been, nor did it belong to our parents!"

"I know this, Yakov. We tend to forget it much of the time, but we know you are right. We pay tribute to the Central Government each year."

"Twice a year now, Stepan," interrupted Polina.

"True Polina, but we usually have enough to survive. We have heard of the new policy and, what are they called," looking to both Polina and Griggory.

"Communal farms, father", prompted Griggory.

"Ah yes", continued Stepan. "Communal farms. The farmers here will never tolerate such madness. They will protest and government must listen."

"There have already been many, many protests all over Russia, Stepan," said Yakov, "and Government has not listened to any of them – none! And each and every protest has been brutally crushed by the military. The deaths have been in the thousands. I told you Stepan, this Stalin is totally without scruples and more ruthless than either of us can imagine. Murder by the hundreds or thousands to him means nothing. Farmers protesting means nothing. The first thing that happens is that most if not all your food and grain stores will be confiscated and transported for distribution or export. If you're left with anything, it probably won't be enough to sustain you. You can count on that. The evidence is everywhere in Russia. Check it out for yourself."

There was a long pause and Yakov wasn't sure if they believed him or not. The communication between the three of them was totally non-verbal but confusion, fear and disbelief was written all over their faces.

"You say this will happen here. To this area. To this farm?"

"Yes it will, with one hundred percent certainty I'm afraid."

"When?"

"I can't answer that Stepan but my best guess would be within a year or less. Would you agree Ivan?"

Ivan shook his head in agreement, but said not a word.

"Is there nothing we can do to prepare?"

"No! What will happen is that troops will arrive along with government officials whose job it is to implement the transition. Farm houses, land and buildings will be confiscated as well stores of crops and animals, most of which will be sent to Moscow. This house and all the others will become little more than overcrowded dormitories and everyone, without exception, will work at whatever you are told to work at by the appointed manager, and believe me Stepan, you should pray you are not that person. It's a one-way ticket to a labor camp or the cemetery if you fail or even if there is a hint of failure."

The outbreak of total silence and expressionless faces seemed to last for hours. Nothing was said and the only sound, other than the crackle of a dying fire in the hearth, was Polina's muted sobbing.

Yakov was clearly shaken. It was not his intent to cause such mental devastation but, as diplomatically as possible, to present facts. It was also his intent to present what he deeply hoped would be good news. He felt like the proverbial drowning man watching his life play out before his eyes.

"I know what I have just said is like a knife to your heart, Stepan. Everything our parents dreamed about and everything you and Polina and your family have accomplished seems about to drift into nothingness. But we didn't come here to destroy what you have built nor did we come here simply to inform you of what your future holds if you stay. I could have sent that information to you in a letter or a telegram. We came here to offer you a new life, far different than the one you have, but a life worth living and a life of safety and freedom from the inescapable drudgery that is about to befall this place."

There was no response, just looks that conveyed extreme worry mixed with tears and the shock that comes from having the rug pulled from under you. Polina lifted her head from Stepan's shoulder as he removed his arm from around her and motioned for Yakov to go on.

"I want you to leave this farm and the community as soon as possible."

Nothing was said by any of them for more than a minute

that seemed to Yakov and Ivan to be more like an hour; a very uncomfortable hour of seeing the blank expressions on the faces of his brother, his nephew and Polina, the look of fear mixed with the enormous weight of anxiety.

"And go where, Yakov? This is our life! You say all that will end but I don't know whether to believe you or not. I don't know, I just don't know. I don't know what to do."

And Yakov saw tears in his brothers' eyes for the very first time. Polina now became the comforter.

"Listen to his plan Stepan. What do we have to lose? He has no reason to lie to us."

"Polina is right, Stepan. As you know, on our way to your farm, we stopped in Krasnoyarsk, yes, to make arrangements to have the aircraft repaired, but for something else as well." He could tell that the pain was lessening and that the mood to listen had just taken the high road.

"Stepan, did you know that Krasnoyarsk is reputed to be one of the most beautiful cities in all of Russia? I didn't realize that either, but it is, and it is just as beautiful as people say it is."

"Yes, it is," said Polina excitedly. "I was there many years ago, Yakov, with my father and it truly is a beautiful city."

"Thank you Polina. Yes… it is a very beautiful place," continued Yakov. "Stepan, I can't say this any other way. I have purchased a home, in your name, for you and your family just on the outskirts of the city. It's not a large home but well constructed and very comfortable, and Polina, it's got a very beautiful flower garden and a large vegetable plot."

"Yakov… Yakov, I… we…"

Stepan, looking first at Polina, then Yakov and Ivan, all the time searching but the right words and the right questions were not coming quickly. Polina's tears faded as the morning fog and that brilliant smile came to life.

"Did you hear that Stepan, a real flower garden."

"Yes, Polina, I heard. Yakov, it must have cost you a fortune. But we have no way to move. And what would I do, what would any of us do. I can't buy the house. You know that Yakov."

Stepan brain was a mass of confused thoughts as he stammered and stumbled from one sentence to another, not really knowing where he was going with any thought or even why, realizing that his mouth had become disengaged from his brain.

"Stepan, the cost was nothing. Do you remember all those times when you covered for me on the farm when I was off to the village and you did your chores and mine as well?" And this brought a broad smile to Stepan's face, for he did remember and he also remembered how badly Yakov hated farm work. "Stepan, you, Polina and the children are my family also. I have no other family, so I am doing this for myself as well."

"But the cost, Yakov. How could you purchase such a wondrous place?"

"Yakov, my dear friends, is a very wealthy man'" offered Ivan. "But he has worked hard for many years and he has learned the business of business and the responsibilities that come with wealth. He is generous, yes, and believe me, you are not the first to be aided by Yakov. He and Mr. Treschev have the same philosophy; help others get what they need and eventually, you will get what you need. Mr. Treschev has said this to me many times and he would not have it any other way."

Polina was not really in the room, only physically. She was in her new home, with the garden and the children were at school. She was away from the endless drudgery of life on a Siberian farm, the constant fear and the not-knowing what would befall them tomorrow and life was good for she and Stepan and the children.

"Stepan, you asked what would you do? Simple, my brother. You have a love of the land and of growing plants and people with those skills are rare indeed. To have not only survived in a land that has killed so many, you have not only survived but prospered. The NSDF has donated a sizeable tract of land in Krasnoyarsk to the city to be developed into botanical gardens for the city, the most beautiful botanical gardens in all of Russia, and you, my hard working brother, are to be its manager. So you will not be giving up farming, just relocating your skills and to a use that will be much more appreciated and rewarding."

Stepan was clearly moved and, just for an instant, Polina thought she saw a tear exit for one of his eyes. As if prompted by an off-stage director, Stepan and Yakov rose from their chairs, met and embraced.

"As for moving. Stepan, Polina? If you decide to leave the farm, I will leave Ivan and the automobile with you to help. The auto is mine. I purchased it from a local merchant after we arrived here. Oh yes… one other thing, and I do not need your decision now but I do ask you to think seriously about what I have said but also this."

Both Stepan and Polina felt a mood of devastation sweep over them, as if what they had been offered was now going to be taken away.

"In short, I would like Griggory to return to Sevastopol with me whether you decide to move to Krasnoyarsk or not."

There was silence that could be cut with a knife; *loss of the farm and now our eldest son*. Stepan and Polina thinking in unison.

"I suggest this for a couple of reasons. It's the only way to keep him from getting swept into Stalin's army but, more importantly, to provide him with the opportunity to pursue a university education. In some ways, Stepan, Griggory is a bit like me. He really doesn't have the passion for farming that you do. You know that as well as I do. He is so much like you and Polina in his patience, in his great intelligence, tough and the guts to pursue what he wants and that needs to be fostered. I have taken the liberty of setting aside enough funds to provide all your children with a good education – a trust fund as the Americans call it. Education opens doors to the future, Stepan, not just to the right people but to the right opportunities. I read somewhere that you cannot see the future seated backward in the saddle."

Stepan , Polina and Griggory sat almost motionless, trying their level best to digest all that had been said and deeply engrossed in non-verbal communication. "Yakov, there are many things to think about. Surely you don't expect an answer tonight. Polina, Griggory and I must think hard on what you have proposed, and we must talk to Yuri and Katrina as well. These are not things to be taken lightly and I hope you understand."

"Of course Stepan, take whatever time you need. However, I would prefer that you not mention any of this to the two youngest. I fear that if word gets out too quickly, it could raise alarms locally and you would be inundated with, well… others seeking assistance that I am not empowered to give."

"Yakov," asked Stepan, "you mentioned a second reason for your visit. What might that be? Hopefully not as, how shall I say this… as overwhelming as the first reason."

"Not at all, Stepan, but I think you will be intrigued by it – especially Griggory. But it will take some time to explain. The hour is growing late and you, Polina and Griggory have much to think about and to discuss among yourselves. Perhaps in a day or so – whenever you feel you are ready."

NEAR VANAVARA

THURSDAY, JUNE 10, 1926

Farming is not a part time occupation and it reminded Yakov why he left the area in the first place. The days were long, working conditions were anything but ideal, unless one had a fondness for 4:30 AM alarms clocks. Outside conditions ranged for sopping wet to searing heat, fields that seemed as though the major crop was rocks, weeds, living pests of every kind, size and description, all basically mindless eating and biting machines, manure loading and unloading, other than that, a life of ease and relaxation. But from time to time, there were periods of rest and relaxation and this was one of those times, with Yakov, his brother and Griggory, seated atop a mound of rocks recently harvested from the adjacent field, that Stepan could stand the pain of curiosity no longer.

"All right Yakov, what's all the mystery about the other reason for your visit?"

"Not really a mystery, Stepan. It's just that it will take some time to explain it all. But," and turning to both Griggory and Stepan, "if you're ready and have about a half hour, I'll try explain what it's all about."

The timing was good for all of them. The field work was about done for the day and it looked as though they were in for a little rain fairly soon anyway. The temperature had dropped a bit, a slight wind freshened and it was comfortable, at least for the time being. Yakov began the tale.

"A few years ago, we learned that a Dr. Miroslav Oborski in Moscow had received funding from the Barkov brothers for an expedition to the Tunguska Valley. Remember the day of the explosion Stepan," he continued, looking directly at his brother who remembered quite well indeed, shaking his head in the decided affirmative. "You probably don't know who the Barkovs are but to say they are crooks would be a world class understatement. I will explain about them later. Anyway, we contacted Dr. Oborski ... " Yakov continued recapping the events. "... and so the exact location of the object is, at this point in time, a matter of conjecture. How Kazamin has been able to keep his financiers at bay all this time in another mystery," concluded Yakov.

There was a long period of total silence, broken only by the sound of the freshening wind slapping the leaves of a couple of poplar trees nearby and flocks of blackbirds and the small herd of sheep heading for shelter from the rain they sensed was on its way. Neither Griggory nor Stepan looked at Yakov, only at each other, saying nothing but communicating volumes.

"I can see why this place would be, well, handy for you if you plan to hunt for the object but there are a couple of things that I... we aren't sure about. I have met Joakim a few times but Griggory here knew him far better than most. I don't know if you know it or not but Joakim's house burned down a few years ago and nobody seems to know where he is but I don't think he died in the fire. Strangely, no one in that community says much about him – or says anything, for that matter." Griggory showed agreement with his father's comments. "So, I don't know where he is. And another thing Yakov, and please don't take this personally, but what does all this have to do with us?"

"First of all, no offence taken. I will tell you the reason why in a minute. Second, Joakim is alive and well, by the way, he's married now, no children yet, as far as I know. I can't reveal where he is located but he and his wife Oksana are quite safe. I knew about the fire, probably before you, but it's not the house that we are interested in; it's the barn and I know it burned as well. The object, by the way, was in neither building. It was buried beside the barn, the side next to the house, according to Joakim. Now here's where you come in, or Griggory more specifically. Ivan and I want to go to Joakim's old home and try and retrieve the object but we need a guide and we are asking if you would release Griggory for a few days to be our guide. I won't say that this trip is entirely without an element of risk, but hey, life in Russia is a risk these days anywhere."

"About the only surprise, Yakov, is that Joakim is married and we're happy for him. I had it pretty much figured out where you were going with this tale sometime ago. Tell me something Yakov, why, after so many years, is your Foundation so interested in this thing that Joakim had?"

"Good question Stepan. The Foundation really hasn't been all that interested in it at all until now, that is. But since it's not known what it is or what it does, our concern is that whether or not there will be another war, whatever this thing is could be a technological windfall for Russia. We are also concerned about why the Barkovs are so interested in getting their hands on it, although we have reason to believe, for them, it would just be a commodity, something to sell for profit. So basically, we want to keep it from getting into their hands until we can figure out what should be done with it."

"But why haven't the Barkovs gone after it themselves," asked Griggory.

"I'm not sure Griggory," responded Yakov, "Only one of the brothers is of concern now, Kazamin Barkov. His younger brother Slava, tried to pull a fast one on Kazamin, dealt with the wrong people and was rewarded with a one-way ticket to a labor camp, not that Kazamin would lose any sleep over it. I suspect Kazamin either doesn't know where to start looking or, more than likely, he thinks Dr. Oborski has it but he hasn't had any better luck than we have in locating him. A few years ago, there was some suggestion that he may be alive and living near Kazan or, later, somewhere in Finland. It's a bit of a dilemma for Kazamin. According to our information, he may have been extremely well paid by some very nasty people to dispose of the good Doctor."

"Does the Barkov brother know you're here," asked Stepan.

"I don't know, but I hope not. We did our best to cover our tracks when we left Sevastopol, but I can't say for certain that we were successful, hence the element of risk that I mentioned. Kazamin, I'm sure, is fully aware of the family connection, however, and I know that's not very comforting."

"So Yakov, what if the Barkov brother is in this area?" asked Stepan. "What do you think he would do? Is this venture going to put anyone's life at risk: Griggory, you, Ivan?"

"You know the Barkovs are pond slime, without doubt," answered Yakov. "And if we were going after a stash of money or gold, I would say the risk would be great. But we are going after an unknown and this area, as remote as it is, is still populated. I don't think Kazamin would risk leaving the landscape littered with bodies. Yes, there's risk, no doubt, but not the deadly variety. Still, I don't want you to think this is risk-free, it isn't. So it's up to you and Griggory."

"I'm still not sure what this is all about but I will discuss it with Griggory and Polina," said Stepan's, leaning back and pondering the darkening sky. "For now, let's get things put away before the storm hits. Griggory, would you tend to the sheep and chickens? I saw a number of foxes prowling around the edge of the field this afternoon."

With that, Griggory climbed down from his perch and started toward the out buildings next to the house.

"So, Yakov, when do you want us to leave on this grand tour?" asked Stepan as they bedded down the horses and cattle after the evening meal. This was the only chance the two had to talk privately.

Yakov turned to look at him with a grin that was a mix of puzzlement and knowing.

"What about Griggory" asked Yakov.

"Yakov, you sly dog. You know as well as I do that there is a chance of danger and it's me you want on this venture more so than Griggory. And I can appreciate that. You knew darn well that you couldn't turn him down but that I would be the only one who could do it so that he didn't feel hurt. You have forgotten that we had the same father and he was a master at this sort of thing! And, yes I know the route to Joakim's place, perhaps not as well as Griggory, but well enough to get us there."

Smiling ear to ear, "Can't fool the son of a master. Yes, you're right. I do believe there could be some trouble. There's a lot at stake as you realize. I don't think any of the Barkov gang are in this area, at least not yet, but it's always good to be prepared and I sure wouldn't want Griggory, or any of us, for that matter, to get hurt," said Yakov, jumping down from his rocky perch."

"Stepan, on another matter, would you mind if Ivan took Griggory with him into town to pick up supplies and I have a few things I would like Ivan to attend to at the same time? And as well, perhaps Yuri and Katrina would like to go along for the ride."

"No. Of course not, and the children would love it. First time in an automobile for both of them," replied Stepan. "And I think this will be Griggory's first ride in an automobile as well. It should be something of an adventure for all of them."

Having received the approval he wanted, Yakov sought out Ivan and they spoke quietly for a few moments, spiced with a number of hand gestures and pointing. Ivan returned to the house.

"So," continued Yakov, "they will go tomorrow morning. You will inform Griggory and the children, will you?"

Stepan actually felt a mix of excitement about Gregory's pending adventure and a slight hint of jealousy that he too was not going. But, as small as the farm was, it wouldn't run itself.

VANAVARA

Even as the first rays of the newborn day filtered through the few clouds that still hung around, and the tall evergreens along the road displayed the real meaning of forest green, it was clear that it was going to be a warm day with no hint of rain. Unfortunately, another kind of rain came: the news from Ivan that the automobile would simply not make it out of the farm yard to the road, let alone along the road into town. It was still very muddy and would take a day of warm weather to make it travelable. Griggory was disappointed and both Stepan and Polina felt his sense of disappointment although Griggory said nothing and, outwardly, took it in stride. But for the smaller children, it was a very deep disappointment for they had talked about nothing else during the evening meal and stayed awake hours beyond their usual bedtime.

"Tell you what," said Ivan, kneeling down to speak with them, taking their hands in his and even though the touch was gentle, the children could feel that these were hands that knew more about aggression than kindness. He ever so gently wiped the tears from their innocent, heartrending eyes. "Griggory and I have to go into town today and we will be taking the horse and wagon. How about a nice horse and wagon trip?"

With deeply furrowed brows, pursed lips and frowns that spelled even more disappointment, they responded, almost in unison.

"No! The horse makes a stink!"

This caught Ivan completely off guard and he looked up to Polina first and received something of an embarrassed smile, then to Stepan who mouthed what the children were taking about.

"Oh… oooohhhh. The horse makes a… well, we can't have that, can we?" said Ivan. "How about this then; as soon as the road dries up, how would you like it if I took you both for a nice drive, just the three of us… oh perhaps we should invite Griggory as well. Would that be okay?"

Polina joined the little group and put her hands on the children's shoulders.

"But you have to promise Ivan that you will do your studies before you go. Agreed?" she asked.

The disappointment faded faster than a bolt of greased lightning. Jumping up and down and yelling 'yes… yes… yes,' they both threw their arms around Ivan's neck, squeezing as tight as they could. Ivan felt emotions he had forgotten he even had. Polina finally released Ivan from their grip and guided them toward the table and the waiting books but not before Yuri turned around and asked, "can we sit in the front?"

"Of course you can. I would be honoured" replied Ivan.

The trip into town was anything but comfortable. It wasn't so much the ruts, although they were present in prolific measure, but the endless battle to keep clear of the mud flying from the wheels and the horses hooves.

"You know, Griggory, the children were right" said Ivan.

"What do you mean? Right about what?' asked Griggory.

"That horse does make a smell!"

Ivan left Griggory and the mud encrusted wagon near the centre of the small town with a list of supplies to buy and with funds more than sufficient to pay for them. Ivan walked the short distance to the west edge of the town to attend to other business matters. Griggory was amazed by the service he received when the retailer discovered that he would receive real money at the time of the sale and not a promise of payment down the road, if ever.

When Ivan returned, two men were with Griggory.

"Friends of yours Griggory?" asked Ivan.

The shorter of the two, dressed in a leather jacket that had clearly been around the block more than once, square jawed, enough scars to pass for a surgical class manikin, turned to Ivan and took an aggressive karate stance. Without a micro-second of hesitation, Ivan brought up his left foot and caught the wannabe martial arts opponent solidly in the groin. A swift uppercut with one of Ivan's anvil sized fists and it was all over in little more than a few seconds. The runner-up slammed into a wagon parked next to theirs, slid down to the side boards and onto the street, splayed unconscious, face up, sitting in the mud.

The other unwanted visitor was taller, dressed in a long black overcoat, equally pock-marked facial features with a scar that ran from his left ear all the way to his chin, short cropped black hair and a mouth full of teeth that ranged from non-existent to yellow with more than a hint of black. Releasing Griggory whom he had pinned to the side board of their wagon, he turned to Ivan while, at the same time, going for a pistol in a shoulder holster. Ivan grabbed his left hand that now had a solid grip on the pistol and got hold of one finger on the other hand, bending it as far back as he could without breaking it. The assailants knees started to buckle and Ivan kept up the pressure while easing the assailants gun hand slowly down, the assailants fingers forcibly wrapped around the trigger but no longer under his control.

Slowly, with a smile of satisfaction from Ivan and a growing look of horror on the face of the assailant, not entirely certain what the outcome would be but entirely certain that it was out of his control and probably not in his favour, Ivan brought the gun hand to a sudden stop, the barrel of the pistol pointing directly at the assailants right leather boot clad foot, and his head shaking as if to say *no! Don't do it... please!* For Ivan's part, his head was shaking in the affirmative... then the blast came, the nine mm bullet tore a smoldering hole in the right boot. Ivan released the horror stricken assailant as he collapsed onto the mud street next to his slightly luckier partner, releasing the hand gun to Ivan. Semi conscious with not even so much as a whimper, he just stared at the hole, now covered with oozing blood. In a few moments, the shock effect would wear off and there would be more than a slight whimper. Ivan reached down, grabbed the two assailants by the coat collars and dragged them to the sidewalk, propping them up against a building.

Although uninjured by the events, Griggory was in as much a state of shock as the would-be assailants and it took several tries for Ivan to get him sufficiently mobilized to get onto the wagon and start the journey home. For the best part of half an hour, Griggory sat motionless, staring straight ahead, barely holding onto the reigns, saying absolutely nothing.

"That went well, don't you think Griggory? Were you able to get all the supplies?" asked Ivan, clearly unshaken by the events.

The pause was far more than protracted. Griggory continued to stare at the road ahead, not outwardly conscious of the jarring ride or smelly horse, mouth open but saying nothing. Finally, after a few kilometres of rut avoidance gymnastics, Griggory asked, "was it necessary to shoot him?"

"I didn't shoot him. He shot himself. All I did was provide direction. Would you rather that he shot you, me or someone on the street?" replied Ivan. "What did those two labor camp grads want anyway?"

"They wanted to know what the supplies were all about and who they were for. I didn't tell them anything, then you arrived."

"Did they ask your name," said Ivan.

"No. They seemed more interested in the supplies" replied Griggory.

"Curious, they didn't ask your name but they probably knew who you are anyway. Umm," pondered Ivan. "This isn't good. I should have frisked them but I doubt they were carrying any identification anyway. Probably just a couple of local thugs but hired by who is the question."

When Yakov was informed about the excitement in town, it was decided between Yakov and Stepan, that they should leave to retrieve the object as soon as possible and that Stepan and his family should begin packing to leave the farm soon as well. It would be a virtual certainty that they would be observed and although they could split up, taking different routes, it was decided that such a move may prompt whoever may be observing them, to intercept them at the house; not a good idea! So, as insurance, Ivan was to follow about three or four hours behind them and camp next to a clearing about a three hour ride from the farmhouse. The clearing, according to Griggory, was something of an intercept point for a number of trails in the region.

NEAR
VANAVARA

SATURDAY, JUNE 12, 1926

The morning was a repeat of the day before and, for Ivan, a promise made is a debt unpaid, especially when that promise is made to young children.

"Are we ready," asked Ivan.

Stupid question, he realized for before he could look around, Yuri and Katrina were well on their way to the automobile.

"Sorry guys, but this is more important," said Ivan speaking to Yakov and Stepan who were ready for their trail adventure.

"That's no problem, Ivan," said Yakov. "You can ride to the intercept point when you return. That should work out alright."

With the plan firmly in place, Ivan and Griggory strode slowly to the automobile and the super excited front seat passengers. And away they went, bouncing around, up and down, sideways but ever forward to constant squeals of joyful fun from Ivan's front seat charges.

About an hour later, Polina was relieved to see the automobile turn into their farm and come to its usual steam puffing stop. Bounding out of the front seat, they flew toward Polina's waiting arms, both telling of the adventure at the same time.

With a finger to her lips, Polina leaned down and whispered, "isn't there something you're forgetting?"

Yes there was and they quickly realized what it was. Running back to Ivan, who was now down on one knee, they leaped into his arms, wrapping theirs around his neck and said, "thank you, Uncle Ivan."

Ivan wasn't sure what to think. *Uncle Ivan,* he murmured to himself. And he felt as though a great weight had been removed from his back. He had just escaped from a darkness from which he had long felt there would be no escape. *To love and be loved in return,* he was thinking, *must surely be the greatest of all gifts.* In that instant, the human Gibraltar became little more than a hundred kilograms of soft putty. This was new territory for Ivan and he liked the neighbourhood. And so with a renewed spirit and recharged enthusiasm, he packed his provisions, saddled a horse and hit the trail as planned.

With Griggory's directions mapped out, the group left on horseback. It was not a particularly pleasant journey. As the day wore on, the temperature had taken a turn for the worse and a sporadic misty rain characterized the two days they were on the trail, pelted constantly by waterfalls from sodden trees. The trail that would have been almost unrecognized as such without Griggory's map and instructions, wound its way around and over low hills, through dark green forest cover that rarely gave witness to light or human traffic. Wet and cold, they arrived at a hill overlooking what was left of Joakim's property late in the afternoon of the second day.

"Not much left," observed Stepan. "I can barely make out where the house and barn used to be. It looks as though whoever set it, didn't want to leave much behind."

To their relief, the weather showed signs of slight improvement as set up their camp on the east side of the hill, about a kilometre from the site so as not to cause any undue alarm for the local residents.

WEST OF
VANAVARA

SUNDAY, JUNE 13, 1926

The following morning, under partially overcast skies and with a cool wind blowing from the northwest, they rode down to the site. There was nothing left standing with the exception of the old ceramic stove leaning at a crazy angle. Everything else was burned beyond recognition. The site was littered with charred pieces of timber, shards of glass and remnants of metal hinges and other metal objects. Nothing at all remained of the old fence (not that there ever was much to start with) and many of the older trees adjacent to the property showed clear signs of burn damage. The fire had caused total destruction and, from its obvious intensity, seemed a deliberate act of arson.

Still, as dead as it first appeared, life was present everywhere. New forest growth was all over the site, mostly black spruce and maple. Although the ceramic stove was the only solid clue that this may have been someone's residence, it was quickly being embraced by a spindly maple sapling, now almost twice as high as the stove itself with other smaller saplings nearby. It was clear that the site would be entirely reclaimed in a very few years and probably lost to memory.

It took a little time for Yakov to get his bearings as far as the location of the buried object was concerned since the shed itself was completely gone leaving virtually nothing behind save bits and pieces of charcoal that had once been the structure itself. However, after about an hour of cruising the site, the location of the target wall was estimated. "Stepan, the object was apparently buried somewhere along this line. You start at that end," said Yakov pointing to a location where they assumed the barn had stood, "and I will start at the other end." They both began the process of digging; not an easy task when the soil, left undisturbed for almost a decade, was now populated with thousands of roots, but not as difficult as they originally thought it might be.

"What do you two think you're doing in there," screamed a voice from behind them.

Standing about thirty meters from what used to be the front of the shed and well outside the property limits was an old lady and a younger gentleman, clearly upset by the goings on.

"This place is cursed. He's been buried once. Leave him be. Get out and stay out unless you want to end up in Hell with Joakim and Satan," she continued.

The gentleman said nothing but simply nodded in agreement.

"Do you think that disturbing his remains will save him now," she asked.

"Would it be acceptable if his remains *were* buried… After all, we knew Joakim'" continued Yakov with a bit of an exaggeration; well okay then, a lie.

"I don't care what you do with them so long as they stay on this unholyest of unholy ground. But I tell you, leave when you're done and leave this area. We don't need to be cursed as well."

And with that parting remark, they gave a wave of disaffection and walked quickly away from the site.

"As Ivan would say, that went well, don't you think Stepan," said Yakov with a smirk before turning to the task at hand which was not to bury Joakim who was very much alive, so far as they knew.

"Yes Yakov. You handled that like a master. Strange though, it was almost as if she thought Joakim was already buried there. Now the locals will think that we have added something to the gravesite for Joakim. I wonder if he will ever come and visit himself someday?" Laughing quietly, they continued the dig.

About an hour later, Stepan called to Yakov.

"I think I've found it."

Stepan picked up a leather bound item from the dirt at the bottom of the trench and held it up. Unwrapping the leather pouch, there it was; a chunk of lead pipe just as Joakim had described.

"That looks like it," replied Yakov with obvious glee. "The only thing is Stepan, that we cannot open the pipe to make sure. According to Joakim, if you mess with whatever is inside, those lights appear and that would be all we would need right now."

"I understand," said Stepan. "But I think we're pretty safe in assuming that this is what we believe it to be. We didn't find any other pieces of lead pipe, or anything else for that matter although the soil wasn't as compact as I thought it would be." After removing the partially rotted leather wrapping and leaving it behind in the trench, they packed the pipe in one of the saddlebags and prepared to leave 'this unholyest of unholy ground' when Stepan said, "I think we had better fill in the hole to make it look like a grave."

Yakov agreed and they shoveled the dirt back into the hole, leaving a bit of a mound but no grave marker, then mounted their horses and left the site.

The trip back to the meeting point was somewhat of a replay of the trip to Joakim's place, cold, wet and no creature-comforts! Yakov and Stepan had little trouble finding Ivan's campsite, the hollow in which the campsite was located was completely engulfed in ground fog as the cooler air flowed down the hillside to the waiting valley below, releasing its cargo of water as condensation. Through the eddying mist, the fire burned brightly, throwing eerie yellowish-orange shadows in every direction. Yakov reined his horse to a halt as did Stepan a moment later.

"Do you see that," asked Yakov.

"Yes, Ivan's campfire. Why?"

"Either that isn't *his* campfire or he's trying to send us a message. He wasn't supposed to build a fire until we returned in case anyone was following us. Something's not right."

"So whose fire is it then if it's not Ivan's," replied Stepan.

From the darkness to their left, announced by the unmistakable click of a pistol hammer being cocked into firing position.

"Get off those horses. Now!"

Two men emerged from the black trees next to the trail, both armed with hand guns and both pointed at the two brothers in a manner that clearly meant business. The shorter of the two had a bandaged nose and jaw while the other had one boot missing, and in its place, a bandage that ran almost to his knee.

"They must be the two that Griggory and Ivan met in town," said Yakov.

The two hijackers grabbed the horse reigns and, after a quick frisk to make sure Stepan and Yakov were unarmed, retrieved their own horses from the woods, mounted them and prodded the two brothers to lead their horses, descending along the trail toward the campfire.

Entering the camp, they spotted Ivan sitting on a log next to the roaring fire and standing guard behind him, a poker faced man, average height, about thirty something, wearing a brown leather flight jacket and cradling a rather mean looking rifle with a scope and a demeanor that said he not only knew how to use it but would welcome any excuse to do so.

"Sorry Yakov. They were here when I arrived."

"It's all right Ivan. Not to worry. So, how about introducing us to the welcoming committee? "

"Oh really? Well he should worry 'cause I'm gonna blow his #$%#@ head off before we leave," said one-foot, waving the cocked pistol directly at Ivan, much to the pleasure of broken-jaw, executing a toothless smile as best he could.

"We'll do no such thing," came another voice from the trees behind the lean-to. Out stepped a tall man, well dressed, broad shoulders, mean black eyes, short black hair with the look of someone truly in-charge. One foot and broken-jaw immediately stepped back, and with a withering look from the speaker, holstered their firearms. "Well, look who we have here," motioning to Yakov. "Treschev's favourite lackey."

"Oh great," whispered Yakov to Stepan, that did little other than intensify his concern.

"Gentlemen," said the speaker, waving his hands around and finally pointing to Yakov and Ivan. "It's like a re-union. Yakov, Ivan. By the way, where are your manners, Yakov? Introduce me to this other gentleman," pointing directly at Stepan.

"Stepan, this is Kazamin Barkov," and, pointing to Stepan, "this is my brother, Stepan," looking skyward and gesturing nonchalantly toward Kazamin with an open hand.

"How wonderful: older and younger brother, together, here, in the woods and in the middle of… well, nowhere. How very nice to meet you Stepan. Too bad your brother ended up as a gofer for Treschev. He has so many useful talents going to waste. By the way Stepan, did Yakov tell you I have a brother as well? At least I think I do," turning toward the others who were unsure of whether to smile or to continue to look bored. "Slava is on a somewhat of an extended State-paid vacation at present, actually not that far from here, thanks to your brother. Well, no. That's not quite true. Thanks really should go to the good Doctor and Anton, I suppose, for accomplishing a somewhat distasteful task, at least in part. And speaking of Miroslav, I don't suppose you would know where he is, would you Stepan." There was a long pause during which Yakov and Kazamin engaged in a staring contest that ended in a draw. "Silly question," continued Kazamin.

"And Anton," inquired Yakov without blinking in this contest of who-blinks-first. "I don't suppose you know where Anton is?"

"Anton? Of course. Anton has… retired shall we say. Serious injuries you understand."

"Retired?" continued Yakov. "Nobody retires from your organization, Barkov."

"Really? You did," concluded Kazamin with a grin that was well received by the others of his group, even the silent guard with the leather flight jacket came dangerously close to an incipient grin.

Stepan had a look of both shock and disbelief.

"What's he talking about Yakov? Retired from the organization?"

"It's a long story Stepan. I'll tell you later. This is not a good time," knowing full well that 'later' wasn't good enough and he had just stepped into a swamp full of alligators.

"Look, let's get on with this and get back to civilization," muttered one-foot, retrieving his pistol and clearly prepared to use it. "I've had enough of this love-in. I'll take care of the three of them right now, Mr. Barkov."

"Put that gun away, you brainless monkey," responded Barkov. "Nobody is going to shoot anybody. That would be all we would need, to have Treschev and his self-righteous bunch of do-gooder fanatics hunt us down like a pack of rabid wolves." Kazamin, with a forced grin, turned toward Yakov. "Good help is so hard to find these days, don't you think Yakov?"

With that, the two wannabe executioners reluctantly did as they were ordered, much to the relief of Stepan.

"We came for one thing and we will leave when we get it. So, gentlemen, enough of the chit-chat. Where is it?"

Yakov thought about continuing the game by playing dumb, but, upon reflection and noting the rising level of irritation amongst his captures, particularly Kazamin, wisely decided to cooperate – to live and fight another day.

"It's in my saddle bags, Barkov."

Gesturing to one-foot and broken jaw, they searched the saddle bags and, in less than a minute, held up the piece of lead pipe.

"There's nothing here other than a few cans of beans and a piece of pipe. That's all they have."

"Oh, it's not just a piece of pipe, is it Yakov," Barkov said, snapping his fingers and gesturing to one-foot to bring it to him immediately.

Turing it over and over, and trying to un-do one of the caps that would not turn, Barkov was both pleased and clearly confused. Giving the piece of pipe a shake, he noted that 'something' was inside.

"All that fuss and expense for… this! Well, I don't know what's inside and quite honestly, I don't care. But there are some people who do care and that's all that matters to me. How are you going to explain this to your glorious leader, Yakov?" concluded Kazamin with a smile that reeked of pent up maliciousness. Turning to one-foot and broken jaw, "cut their horses loose, get our horses and let's get out of this horrid place. I have a long way to go if this miserable weather decides to cooperate."

Business concluded, the four left the site but not before unhitching Yakov's, Stepan's and Ivan's horses and sending them on their way with sound slaps to their rumps.

"I don't know where they came from but they had to have been behind me when I left the farm. Had you and Stepan arrived earlier while it was still light, they would have had that rifle trained on you and I didn't doubt for a moment that the one in the flight jacket would use it if he suspected anything wrong," explained Ivan.

"It's alright Ivan," replied Yakov. "We're all okay and that's all that matters, for now. Let's see if we can round up any of the horses and get something to eat and bed down for the night. We'll head back to the farm in the morning."

Stepan said not a word and was clearly drowning Yakov in silence.

Little to nothing was said as Yakov prepared a gourmet feast of beans and black rye bread that Ivan had brought with him. It was Yakov who finally broke the ice.

"Well, it looks like we are back to square one… again."

For the longest time, neither Yakov nor Ivan said a word, staring at the ground as if expecting some startling revelation to pop out at them.

"We *have* to get it back," announced Yakov.

Ivan threw a furrowed brow glance at Stepan at the same time as Stepan did the same to Ivan.

"I don't know how," Yakov continued, "but we can't let Barkov sell that thing, whatever 'that thing' is. You know, none of this seems logical or reasonable. All this time and effort chasing after something and we don't know what the something is. But I suppose logic and reason doesn't necessarily explain everything."

"Yakov," said Ivan, "I'm certain they came here by aircraft since Kazamin was so concerned about the weather and one of those guys is probably the pilot. The silent one with the rifle would be my guess."

"I think you're right Ivan. We are at least a half day from the farm," noted Yakov, "and they could be gone by the time we get back. And even if we were at the aerodrome now, how would we get it back? They will probably keep a pretty sharp eye on it. I think asking for it back is sort of out of the question!"

For several minutes, absolutely nothing was said as all three just stared at the ground. Yakov lifted his head and surveyed the sky above, nodding his head up and down.

"Look at the sky," said Yakov finally. "It's been raining and right now it doesn't look like it's going to clear up for a while. If we're lucky, they may be grounded for a day or so, long enough for us to put a plan together, wouldn't you say?" asked Yakov.

"He's very good at making plans, Ivan," said Stepan and to his surprise, it drew some quite chuckles from both Ivan and Yakov.

"I think he's pretty good at carrying them out as well... from time to time," concluded Ivan, moving slightly back to avoid a friendly punch on the shoulder from Yakov.

"Let's sleep on it," said Yakov. "Who knows? As the saying goes, *'it ain't over till the fat lady sings.'*"

WEST OF
VANAVARA

MONDAY, JUNE 14, 1926

A miserable night blended with an equally miserable sunrise. Sleep was minimal at best. The on and off drizzle lasted all night, and the protection of the lean-to was more physiological than real and breakfast was not on the agenda. Wet, cold and all sense of humor washed away, they packed up and headed out on shanks mare for the 5 hour plus trek back to the farm. As pointed out by Stepan, *"once you get soaking wet, you can't get wetter"* and so, as they slogged their way along the trail, the on-going drizzle became little more than natures unkind gesture.

"You know," observed Ivan, "as Yakov mentioned yesterday, it's not likely that Barkov and his pilot will be able to take off." That observation, while possibly true, did little to restore their spirits or prompt lively discussion.

NEAR VANAVARA

TUESDAY, JUNE 15, 1926

It was very early morning when two of the saddled horses ambled into the barnyard. Polina was the first to see them and yelled to Griggory to come quickly. He identified them as the ones Ivan and Stepan were riding.

"Something must have happened, mother. I'll take the horses with me and go to Ivan's campsite. I know where it is. I will be back as soon as I can. Don't worry. They may have gotten loose during the night; who knows."

The sun had been awake for an hour and a fine mist was in the air, showers pelted them from even the slightest touch to the overhanging branches and tall, saturated grasses and ferns assuring that the walk along the trail was less than pleasant for all three of them but even more so for Stepan and Yakov, one wrestling with how he was going to quell the others fears about the past and the other seeing his future in an entirely different light, filled with uncertainty.

It was Yakov that finally broke the log-jam, much to Ivan's relief.

"Stepan, when I arrived in Moscow after leaving the farm, I was broke, hungry and totally lost and more than a little scared," began Yakov. "I seriously thought about returning home but, I didn't. I had no money anyway. It was useless to beg on the street. Nobody had any money and nobody was going to give me food, so… I stole it from local merchants. I slept in alleyways, park benches when one was available or anyplace that I could. But one day, I apparently stole from the wrong store and the merchant gave chase and almost caught me before a car pulled up, two men grabbed me and threw me into the back seat and we drove off. They had seen me pull off the theft and apparently I was the 'type' they were looking for."

"You can guess that they were part of the Barkov organization," continued Yakov. "Anyway, to make a long story short, I kind of adopted the Barkovs. At least I had food to eat and a place to sleep and even some money from time to time. But after a few months, they got me involved in things that were a lot worse than just stealing food. They would go into businesses and extort money in exchange for protection from rivals and if the merchant didn't pay, fires would occur or break-ins would occur – really nasty stuff. And yes, I was involved in some of it. I told you when we arrived that I had done things that I wasn't too proud of, so there you go! Stepan, have you ever heard of the Mafioso?'

"No, can't say that I have. Why?"

"Stepan, you don't get out much do you," responded Yakov, a statement that drew a large grin from Ivan and a deer-in-the-headlight look from Stepan. "Well Stepan, the Mafioso is a criminal organization with origins in Sicily. They are involved in every illegal activity you can think of: drugs, prostitution, human trafficking, you name it. Because they have infiltrated just about every sector of the private and public sectors where they are located, they are extremely influential and incredibly dangerous. Actually, there is a joke about the Mafia that sort of says it all. Sometime ago, the economy was so bad in Italy that the Mafia had to lay off five judges."

Ivan and Yakov were the only ones to muster something closely akin to a smile while Stepan wasn't sure if had just heard a joke or a short history lesson.

"Anyway," continued Yakov, "one night we met with a business owner who had not paid his, how did they put it, his… 'premiums' for a number of months. Anyway, they beat the crap out of him, handed me a gun and ordered me to put a bullet in his head. I was scared out of my mind but I wasn't about to be part of a murder, so I took the gun, pointed it toward the poor slob in the chair then turned and pointed it at the legs of one of Barkov's men and pulled the trigger. Nothing happened; just a click. There were no bullets in the gun. I knew then that this was a test and I had just failed. I threw the gun at the one I had intended to shoot and bolted for the door. Incredibly, it was still unlocked so I got out of there and found a place to hide. I hid out for a week or so. I had some money so food wasn't a problem but I knew I couldn't check into a hotel. Some of them were under Barkov's control but I didn't know for sure which ones. But the money ran out and I thought I would try my hand at begging but I soon found that I either wasn't too good at it or there was no money anyway. But then I remembered something the Barkovs had said, *follow the money*. So I did; to a fancy hotel that I was fairly sure was not part of the Barkov's and started to beg for money and that's when Ivan came out of the hotel and, as the saying goes, the rest is history."

Stepan looked at Ivan.

"All true my friend. Every word of it. Well, I'm not sure about the five judges thing," assured Ivan.

Stepan said nothing for what seemed to both Ivan and Yakov to be hours. Finally, hugs were not something that any of them were used to but, after all, they were, to use Kazamin's words, in the middle of the woods and in the middle of nowhere.

"Welcome home, brother. Welcome home," assured Stepan.

It didn't take too long for Griggory to find them, safe and sound but pretty much worn out from running after a horse that was decidedly uncooperative. They rounded up Yakov's horse which wasn't far away and headed for home.

It took a while, a long while for the three of them to get over what had transpired but, by late evening, they came to the inevitable conclusion.

"We have to get the object back, if for no other reason than to assure that the efforts by all those people has not gone in vain," articulated Stepan to the agreement of the other three.

"I think I may know where they are headed," said Ivan. "We believe they arrived here by airplane as well and they plan to leave as soon as the weather improves. Remember what Kazamin said about the weather? The airdrome is on the other side of the town so there is a pretty good chance that they are camped there."

"Who's their pilot? He may still be in town. If we can, shall we say, detain him. That will detain Kazamin as well; buy some time for us." asked Yakov.

"Won't work Yakov," replied Ivan. "I'm certain the one with the rifle is also the pilot."

"What about the two we met in town Ivan," asked Griggory. "they could be a problem if we are going to get whatever it is back."

"I doubt that those two clowns are flying out. I'm certain they're locals. So, I don't think they will be a problem," responded Ivan.

It was clear that planning had to be done and done well to pull this off successfully. It would involve all four of them and possibly even Polina. It was also clear that their targets would take off as soon as the weather cleared, and, if they did, all would be lost.

After arriving back at the farm, work began with no time to spare and no time to fully explain to Polina what had happened and what was about to happen but she understood… for now.

After getting what they needed from Stepan's small machine shed, a lead pipe similar to the one they retrieved at Joakim's burned out homestead, filling it with a couple of pieces of waste iron, and leaving the two youngest with Polina, they saddled up and headed for the aerodrome on the east side of the town, next to the Tetere River.

Leaving the horses with Griggory (for the time being), Ivan, Yakov and Stepan walked then crawled in the sopping wet grass to within a hundred metres of a tent, navigating by a healthy fire roaring near the front of the tent, about twenty metres off the port wing of a parked aircraft. About fifty metres off the starboard wing was an old, ram shackled hanger. Ivan made his way toward the hanger and positioned himself out of site of the campfire but such that he had a clear view of the aircraft and the tent.

Two men were seated on folding chairs between the fire pit and the tent, busily engaged in conversation. After observing the two for some time with a set of binoculars, it was determined that neither of them had the object in hand and concluded that it must still be somewhere in the tent.

While Stepan and Yakov eased their way across the wet grass to the rear of the tent. Griggory, right on cue, dressed in the worst, worn and raggedy and appropriately dirtied clothes he could find at the farm, mounted his horse and took a long, circuitous route around the perimeter of the field so as not to be highlighted by the flame in the fire pit and positioned himself so that he could approach the tent from the front next to the tail of the aircraft.

His heart pounded heavily and his breathing became irregular. He tried his best to get control of himself. Everything depended on it. Finally, ready for his performance, he gave the horse a gentle kick and they started a slow trot toward the campsite. On target, Griggory and his steed passed Ivan, his hand gun drawn, laying prone on the grass at the corner if the hanger. Griggory emerged into the light of the campfire, much to the surprise of Kazamin and his pilot. Griggory reigned the horse to a halt and pretended to study the plane from tail to nose, giving little or no apparent attention to the two seated by the tent.

"… and you know that this thing, whatever it is, is going to make me a lot of money," said Kazamin to the less than attentive pilot. "What I did, my idiot brother failed to do and now he's paying the price for his treachery," concluded Kazamin, the slurred words clearly showing the effects of a long evening of drinking as he gave coup de gras to a near empty bottle of vodka.

Just then, they both noticed Griggory ride in from the shadows and stop near the tail of the parked aircraft.

"Hey, you," called the pilot. "Get away from there." Griggory just waved and continued to 'inspect' the craft as if not having heard the command and not even glancing toward the voice.

"What's the matter with you? Are you deaf? I said get away from that plane – now."

As if completely unaware of the insistent commands (and having more than a little trouble maintaining a look of composure), Griggory continued his visual tour. The pilot got up from his seat, handed the rifle to Kazamin and started toward the plane while Kazamin rose shakily from his chair but stayed in place.

Yakov and Stepan were in position at the rear of the tent when Griggory rode up. Stepan, with the fake lead pipe in hand, started to lift the back wall of the tent for Yakov to make his entry but stopped, pointing to their left. Yakov turned to look at whatever Stepan was pointing out. It took a second or two for him to realize that he had just been duped by his brother, turning around again, just in time to catch a glimpse of the soles of Stepan's boots disappearing into the tent. Snapping up the tent wall, he saw Stepan turn around, and with a wide grin, gave him a salute and a wink that said "got ya!" A feeling of impending disaster filled Yakov's head. This was not part of the grand plan but he could do nothing about it.

The tent was small and Stepan found himself to be remarkably calm, glancing out the half open front flap as the pilot handed the rifle to Kazamin. Looking past Kazamin and the pilot and under the aircraft fuselage, Stepan could just barely make out the outline of Ivan, crouched next to the old hanger, ready to defend Griggory if needed.

The object was not on the cots or under them, or in either of the suitcases. Stepan, clearly frustrated, realized that it either had to be in the aircraft (which he figured was unlikely) or being carried by the pilot or Kazamin.

"When I say stay away, I mean stay away. If I see you here again," yelled the pilot, "I'll break both your arms. Is that clear?"

Griggory, his role having been played, slowly rode away from the site and disappeared into the darkness, circled around and returned to his starting location.

"While you're up Pavel, get me another bottle from the tent," demanded Kazamin, plopping himself back into the chair.

The pilot, although not happy with being ordered about but realizing that he had little choice in the matter, passed behind his chair, and strode across the three or four meters to the tent.

Yakov was horrified and peeking around the edge of the tent, caught Ivan's eye who just threw up his arms, not realizing that Stepan was still in the tent.

Stepan heard the demand from Kazamin, started moving toward the back of the tent for an escape but very quickly realized that he didn't have time. He dove under the cot to his left and cuddled up against the case of vodka. The pilot entered the tent, throwing up the flap with enough energy to send it half way to the river. He looked around and but was unable to spot what he had been sent to fetch.

"Where is it?" he yelled.

His voice caused Stepan to freeze, break out into a cold sweat and his entire body temperature to drop although his heart rate was off the scale! Expecting the pilot's hand to come at him any second, he braced himself for the inevitable and his brain raced for believable explanations, all to no avail.

"Next to my cot Pavel and don't be all night," replied Kazamin.

The pilot grumbled something not clearly understood by Stepan but he was quite certain that they were not words of kindness or endearment.

Stepan, seemingly without thinking, quickly but silently eased the half case of liquor toward the edge of the tent wall next to the cot. The cot spring above him sank within centimetres of his chest as the Pilot kneeled on the cot, and with his left hand, felt along the edge until he connected with the case. Grabbing two of the bottles, he got off the cot and left the tent. It was then that Stepan realized that he couldn't remember breathing during this whole episode.

For a few moments, he simply laid under the cot, not moving a muscle, breathing more or less normally. He was only to be startled again when the back of the tent flipped open and Yakov head filled the hole. At first he didn't see his brother in the semi-darkness, but when he did, a cyclone of relief swept over both of them. He signaled for Stepan to get out and Stepan didn't need much more encouragement.

The plan having been executed, all four gathered at a spot about 200 meters or so from the campsite, well out of sight of the campers.

"Did you get it," asked Yakov of Stepan.

Stepan shook his head in the negative. Yakov was plainly discouraged, rubbing his chin trying to plot their next move.

"It simply is not in the tent Yakov," stated Stepan, placing the fake object into the saddlebag on his horse.

"I know Stepan. I know. I just wish I knew where it is, that's all."

Griggory spoke up and said he had noticed Kazamin reach into the right pocket of his coat several times but withdrew nothing.

Ivan and Yakov looked at each other.

"You and I both know where it is," said Ivan.

"Yes, I know."

They all knew. It had to be in the long coat worn by Kazamin.

"We could wait around until Kazamin either passes out or goes to bed and make another try," replied Yakov.

"We would still have to contend with his pilot and he's not drinking. He would probably go to bed at the same time as Kazamin but if he hears or suspects anything, we could be dead meat... literally, especially if Kazamin's coat ends up inside the tent," responded Ivan.

There was a very long pause; a micro-eternity during which no one said anything. There was just serious thought of actions and consequences. Yakov wandered away from the others who made no attempt to follow. They understood completely. Leaning on a cedar rail fence, head down, Yakov reviewed what had happened and weighed alternatives. After about 5 minutes, head up, he returned to the group.

"Okay. That's it for tonight," said Yakov. "The risk is just too great to chance another mission. I don't know what we've lost, if anything but I do know we gave it our very best and that's all anyone can ask. To pursue retrieval now would not be in anyone's best interest, so let's pack it in and head home."

"As a sort of remembrance of this adventure," asked Griggory, "may I keep the fake lead pipe... perhaps as a souvenir?"

There was no objection raised by either Yakov or Stepan. Stepan reached into his saddlebag, retrieved the object and handed it to Griggory.

Dejected yet somewhat relieved that, after all those years, it was finally all over, they mounted their horses and headed toward the town. Even though it was still several hours before sunrise, there were a few lamp lights visible in the town but none what so ever beyond its limits. As they rode down the main street, Yakov announced that he and Ivan would be staying back.

"I have a number of telegram messages to send and we must wait for a response, so you and Griggory head back to the farm. We'll catch up with you later, probably this afternoon."

Only a non-verbal response was required and, with that, Griggory and Stepan rode off in the direction of the farm.

Griggory and Stepan rode side by side both thinking pretty much the same thing, but saying nothing.

This whole effort, the people it involved and the time it absorbed has been irrational by any standard of explanation. Yet, here we are, totally enmeshed in this seesaw of irrationality, with no perceivable means of escape other than to simply give up.

The very thought of that only deepened the irrationality of it all.

NEAR VANAVARA

WEDNESDAY, JUNE 16, 1926

Ivan and Yakov returned to the farm late in the afternoon, announcing that they saw the aircraft over the town just as they were leaving, heading southwest, probably bound for Krasnoyrsk. They had received replies from the telegrams that they shared with the others.

"Our pilot will be bringing the plane to Vanavara the day after tomorrow", announced Yakov. "We must be ready to leave the following day. As well, I will read the telegram from Mr. Treschev."

> YOU HAVE NOTHING TO BE ASHAMED OF. STOP
> PLEASE PASS ON MY MOST SINCERE THANKS TO THE
> OTHERS FOR THEIR HELP AND ASSISTANCE. STOP
> PLEASE PROCEED WITH THE MOVE AS QUICKLY AS
> POSSIBLE. STOP
> I LOOK FORWARD TO YOUR RETURN. STOP.

"By 'the move'", asked Polina, "I assume he means our move to Krasnoyarsk?"

"Yes", responded Yakov, "and Griggory will be returning with us to Sevastopol as we discussed."

"I have no problem with our move, but you know I will miss Griggory so very much. But please Yakov, don't misunderstand. I approve the plan but it's very painful for us."

With that, Stepan put his arm around Polina that he knew would not be all that comforting. They both realized this day would come and come it did.

"Of course Ivan will stay with you until you reach Krasnoyarsk. You will take the automobile to Tulun where you will board the train for Krasnoyarsk. We have a fine place to stay in Tulun while you wait for the train. And don't worry about Griggory. I will make sure that he visits your new home several times a year. Would that be all right?"

The weather was unusually favourable and the crops were performing well but the toil in the fields was almost without end, requiring every member of a farm household, from seniors to toddlers. It was warm. No, it was hot, and both Polina and Stepan, unloading field stone at the edge of the field, were near exhaustion. They could see Griggory and his two siblings some distance away, weeding the plot of vegetables and they had to assume that Yakov and Ivan were packing the automobile in preparation for the journey. They all realized that the work they were doing was now redundant – that they would not be here to see the harvest. They were, in point of fact, working for someone else, but it kept them occupied and freed them from over-planning the move.

"Do you know something Polina?" asked Stepan, not really expecting an answer.

"Well, Stepan, I know that if you keep on talking, I will be left to unload the rest of these rocks!" she said, half joking (but only half).

"I was thinking about our conversations with Yakov and do you know if it wasn't for him, I wouldn't realize how unhappy we are!"

They both broke out in a very loud laugh, falling into the wagon box, starring skyward, realizing what the answer had to be. It was the beginning of the end and the end of a beginning.

There had been a lot of discussion during the past few days and the sense of urgency did not escape their attention. In the final analysis, it was decided that the move, as difficult as it would surely be, would be good for all concerned, and plans were immediately finalized.

"Father, may I take the pipe thing with me, just as a keepsake of our adventure?" asked Griggory.

"Fine with me," responded Stepan. "Is it okay with you Yakov?"

"Sure, take it. It's no good to us or to anyone for that matter."

With that, Griggory stuffed the pipe into his rucksack.

2,000 METRES AGL (ABOVE GROUND LEVEL)
BETWEEN VANAVARA AND
KRASNOYARSK

FRIDAY, JUNE 18, 1926

The parting at the Vanavara aerodrome was both exciting and painful. Certainly, Griggory was excited and scared as never before at the
prospect of flying and tearful, not knowing when he would see his
parents, brother and sister again. Yakov was clearly emotional about
leaving his brother and extended family but was comforted by the
fact that Ivan would stay behind to guide and assist in the move. Ivan,
to the surprise of all except Polina, was unable to hide the full extent
of his emotions but, on the other hand, was clearly looking forward
to helping with the move and spending more time with his adopted
family. Polina was the most tearful of all for the same reasons as her
eldest son. But leave they must and they leave they did.

The weather was overcast but the pilot made the trip to Vanavara
without incident and was confident that the return trip would be
just as uneventful. The pilot, Alexi Lenchenko, was clearly a man
who loved flying. An ex-air force type with more than 5,000 hours
of flying time under his belt, he had a slight build, graying hair and
an overgrown Chevron moustache. He exuding confidence with the
disposition of total control and calmness that only comes from experiencing just about everything in flight that there is to experience.

With Alexi and Yakov in the front seat and Griggory behind, the
take-off was accomplished easily, if not a bit jarring for the passengers

as the plane rushed toward the trees at the end of the runway, picked up speed, it's rubber tires bouncing along the rough grass surface. But, eventually they were airborne with room to spare, climbed to about two hundred meters before turning southwest (the steep turn proved to be a white-knuckle event for Griggory for whom it seemed his first flight would end as a big smoking hole in the ground) and, continued to climb to the cloud base, at about two thousand meters.

It wasn't at all what Griggory had imagined. Instead of a smooth, seat-at-the-kitchen-table feel, it was bumpy in a series of unending, unpredictable jarring motions that sent the craft five to ten meteres up or down. It was noisy. Every firing of the five cylinder engine could be heard in the cockpit. It was cool to cold. It was exciting and Griggory never ceased to gaze in wonder as they crossed the river and the only sense of speed were the wisps of cloud that came at the craft at better than 50 meters per second, then disappeared only to be replaced by another, and another.

Everything below was a hundred shades of green, yellow or blue and the sky ahead was grey and it was almost impossible at times to see where land and sky actually met at the horizon.

It was about 90 minutes into the flight. Alexi saw it first. Just a black speck in the sky ahead of them and slightly below their altitude.

"That's another plane," Alexis yelled, pointing to the 11 o'clock position. "Very unusual in this area. Seems to be heading for Vanavara."

By now, they could all see it. Only now, it was no longer a speck on the horizon. It took on the unmistakable shape of an airplane, a bit similar to theirs; a high wing mono-plane, but distinctly different. Within a few minutes, it whizzed past them about two hundred meteres below their craft and a half kilometre off their port wing.

Griggory, totally fascinated by the sight of yet another plane as seen from a plane, followed it and was about to return his gaze forward when he noticed something odd.

"Hey, look at this. That airplane is turning now."

Sliding over to the starboard side to see if he could catch a glimpse of it. Yakov looked at the pilot.

"Griggory," said Alexi. "Keep an eye on that plane and let me know when you see it again and tell me where it is; exactly. Okay?"

"I lost it again. Oh, just a second," replied Griggory, sliding back to the port side window. "Yeah, there it is. He's behind us on this side."

"Above us or at our altitude," asked Alexi.

"Same altitude as us, I'd say," responded Griggory.

By now, Yakov had turned in his seat and also spotted the other craft. For Alexi, it was business as usual with no sign of concern, unlike the passenger seated next to him.

"Griggory, I want you to be prepared to hang on tight. Grab anything you can because I'm not sure what's going on and I may have to make some rapid and steep turns but I need you to keep me informed of where that other plane is."

Griggory looked around and there wasn't much to grab as he mentally prepared himself for the totally unexpected.

"The plane's gaining on us. He's still on this side and... there's something fla... "

Before he could finish the sentence, their craft shook as if hit by some unseen force, and Griggory was propelled to the right side of the seat as a bullet pierced the fuselage next to him and smashed into the lead pipe. In quick succession, another shot tore into the window next to Griggory and embedded itself in the aircraft roof over Yakov's head. Before Yakov and Griggory could comprehend what was happening, the pilot pushed the throttle to the firewall and slammed the aircraft into a vicious, near vertical turn to the left that sucked

Yakov and Griggory solidly into their seats. Yakov trying desperately to grab a hand-hold next to the windscreen and Griggory laying almost flat on the seat, grabbing the seat in front of him as best he could. Their aircraft passed over the other plane with only a few scant meters to spare.

The pilot maintained the super tight turn and screamed at Yakov and Griggory.

"Watch for that other plane. I need to know where he is every second."

Griggory saw the other plane first.

"He's on our right. He's turning as well; turning left. I can see the top of his wings."

"Keep watching. Tell me where he is in relation to us… quickly!" yelled the pilot.

"He's gaining on us but he seems to be getting farther off to the side," replied Yakov.

"Okay, that's good news. He can out run us and he sure can out gun us but I don't think he can out turn us. Let me know when he's abreast of the starboard wing; the right one."

A few seconds past as both Yakov and Griggory kept their gaze glued to the other craft in spite of the turbulence, noise and added discomfort of a lot more outside air and the high pitched whistle of it ripping through the holes in the fuselage.

"Okay, okay. He's just off our right wing tip," yelled both Griggory and Yakov.

"Hang on," was the only phrase from the pilot as he rammed the yoke to the right and the plane immediately responded with a brutal, 2G turn to the right that again glued the passengers into whatever position they had been in.

To both Griggory and Yakov, it seemed the other plane rocketed sideways toward them before disappearing under their aircraft at which point, the pilot sent the plane into a steep climb that left them too numb to experience fear. Then they leveled out, totally engulfed in dark grey cloud and the temperature dropped even more.

Throttling back, and changing the fuel selector valve to feed from the port side tank, the pilot turned to Yakov and then Griggory.

"Is everybody alright?" Alexis asked. "If it's any consolation, I don't think the pilot of the other aircraft is military. He missed too many opportunities."

After a few moments, white as ghosts, they both nodded that they were fine but were at a loss to put together what had just happened.

"Are you two not well loved or something? Been messing around with somebody's girlfriend? What's going on?" inquired the pilot.

"I'm not sure," responded Yakov, "but I think the one doing the shooting was Kazamin's pilot. That was probably Kazamin in the back seat but I didn't get a look at who was flying their plane. Did you Griggory?"

Griggory just shook his head in a negative response, still recuperating from the event.

"Well here's our situation," said Alexi. "I don't know if you noticed or not, but we have a small hole in the port wing. That wispy stuff coming out is fuel. The starboard tank is near full but we don't have enough to make it to Krasnoyarsk. I don't think the other aircraft will risk hunting for us inside these clouds for fear of finding us; a nasty collision and a couple of flaming wrecks to show for it. We can't drop out of the cloud base yet but the problem is that the clouds seem to be breaking up, so very shortly it's going to be a bit of a problem staying hidden."

"Can we land somewhere?" asked Griggory.

"Well, yes and no, my friend," answered Alexi. "We're going to land somewhere, that's a certainty with any flight, including this one. There's an aerodrome at Bratsk to our east or we could return to Vanavara… maybe. Either way, we would probably end up as sitting ducks for the other aircraft which I'm sure hasn't given up the chase and are probably mauling over the same alternatives. For what it's worth, I think our best bet would be to fly west. The clearing is taking place south of us so we may have enough cloud cover to make it to… somewhere but there are no reachable aerodromes in that direction. So gentlemen, what's your pleasure,?" concluded Alexi. "Oh, by the way, did anyone think to pack a lunch? I'm starved. Missed breakfast this morning."

Neither Yakov or Griggory said a word. There didn't seem to be an adequate response.

All three spent the next few moments trying to figure a way out of this dilemma. Finally, Yakov broke the ice.

"Here's how I see it. We're still alive and uninjured but the plane isn't. The good news is that the shooter doesn't know how much damage was done. He also doesn't know what our plan is."

"Neither do we." interjected Alexi, a statement that brought some small form of comic relief to all of them.

"Roughly, where do you think we are right now," Yakov asked the pilot.

Consulting the map on his lap.

"Probably close to Boguchany, a town on the Angar River. Flows west into the Yenisey."

"So, if we turn west, that should take us to the Yenisey? Right?," asked Yakov.

"It will but then what? Where do we land? There's no aerodrome in that area."

"True. However, the shooter doesn't know how much damage he did, only that there was damage. After all he did hit the plane with three shots. He may think we will continue on to Krasnoyarsk or fly east to Bratsk. Does that make sense?"

"And when we get to the river?"

"We land!"

Alexi leaned over his seat to study the look on Griggory's face. A kind of deer-in-the-headlamp look that told him what he was thinking, *I'm just along for the ride at this point. Just get us on good old solid terra firma, preferably alive, if that's okay.*

With the strategy receiving universal approval, the pilot eased the craft onto a heading that he calculated should take them about parallel to the Angar River. Cloud cover was getting thinner and several course changes were required to provide them with hiding spaces. As they hopped from one cloud mass to another, all eyes scanned the sky for any sign of the other craft, and, to their enormous relief, none was found.

After about an hour, with the port side tank having gone dry sometime before, the throttle was eased back and the plane began a shallow, cautious descent. At about 1,500 meters, they broke out of the clouds, but only slightly. All on board scoured the skies around but could see no sign of the other craft, even after several turns left and right were executed. Still, for insurance purposes, they kept close to the cloud base, ducking in and out from time to time.

The Angar River was nowhere in sight but the heading was correct, insisted Alexi. So, that's the heading he maintained in complete certainty that they had not crossed the Yenisey River.

"We couldn't have flown that far. There's a bit of a tail wind, but not that much. Keep looking… the river should be on our right… somewhere."

Much to their relief, about a half hour later, in light rain showers and a descending ceiling, the Angar River appeared off to their right, near the town of Kulokeyovo identified by the pilot.

"The Yenisey is only about thirty or forty kilometres ahead of us so we had better start looking for a place to set down," said the Alexi. "The area looks pretty rugged so let me know if you see anything that looks reasonably level and at least three hundred meters long, preferably straight."

Neither Yakov nor Griggory had the slightest idea what three hundred meters looked like at this altitude but, with little choice in the matter, any reasonable guess would do.

As they passed south of Kulokeyovo, Alexi spotted what looked like a potential spot about five kilometres ahead and slightly to the right of their current course. Pointing it out to the others, they all agreed that it was the best so far (any port in a storm, crossed their minds!). Alexi reminded them that once a site is selected, that's it; no changes allowed! There was no response from the others: just tightening of seat belts, bracing of feet and… more praying.

"Great," replied Alexi. "Please fasten your seat belts, put your trays in the upright position, extinguish all smoking materials and remain in your seats until the plane has come to a full and complete stop at the terminal. The crew of Crash Air thank you for choosing us as your carrier and we look forward to serving you again in the future."

That was too much for both Griggory and Yakov and they sat back, relaxed and had a much deserved and long awaited laugh.

Banking to the right, the plane lost more altitude and Alexi continued to bleed off excess speed as the 'runway' came up on the starboard side. As he was about to make his turn onto final, the engine began coughing. Fuel was almost exhausted so Alexi reduced power, leaned the mixture as much as possible and continued his turn onto final. About a half kilometre from the edge of the field they had selected, the coughing increased and stopped and so did the engine. The planes rate of descent increased and it was clear that they would not make it to the threshold. To make matters worse, the field was bisected by a depression to their right that would intersect their landing run about two hundred metres or so from the threshold, a detail that escaped notice from the previous altitude and the observation angle.

The wind was causing the plane to drift to the right of the desired glide path and Alexi skillfully set the plane at a crab angle, normally an easy maneuver but not so flying dead stick. Yet, he remained totally calm as the nose seemed destined to make a large hole about fifty meters short of the landing point. At the last second, with both Griggory and Yakov planted as deep into their seats as possible, sweating like Olympic athletes and stone-like appearances, expecting this to be their final moments on earth, Alexi straightened out the craft, dipped the right wing to compensate for the right to left drift, eased the yoke back enough to have the nose clear the edge by less than a meter.

The loss of airspeed was too much and the craft stalled. It barely missed the fence but slammed into the ground with a metallic thud that sent all of them even deeper into their seats, then bounced about four or five meters into the air, followed by another, although less severe contact with the ground. Alexi held the yoke firmly back as far as it would go. Although he tried to nurse the craft into a left turn to avoid the rapidly approaching depression, the rudder and tail wheel refused to cooperate and over compensated, causing a sliding left turn to accelerate. The starboard wing began to rise. The pilot did what he could to arrest the turn and was partially successful just as the plane hit the depression on the starboard forward quarter, nosing over, the propeller digging into the grass and dirt and sending it in showers over the aircraft. The plane finally come to a sudden and jarring stop, with the tail pointed high in the air.

All three stayed completely still, simply staring through the windscreen at the propeller that was now just a mass of toothpick fodder, the dirt, and the grass, as the tail ever so slowly, began its fall to earth. All three braced themselves for the inevitable smash of the tail wheel, or what was left of it, as it rammed itself into the soft, moist earth to the awful sound of tortured metal. Then all was still. Just the unmistakable sound of heavy breathing, rain falling on the craft and birds in the distant trees.

Turning to both Yakov and Griggory, both of whom appeared to be in a mild state of shock, eyes as big as plates, sweating up a storm and clearly well into white-knuckling anything they could grab.

"Is everybody alright," inquired Alexi.

Looking around the planes interior, Yakov was still holding the hand brace as if he were a bronco rider and Griggory looked as though he was completely comatose with eyes fully open.

"Don't you just hate it when this happens?," said Alexi, with a grin and a look of total comfort and peace with the world.

Exiting the aircraft, both Yakov and Griggory found that their legs had turned to rubber and they could do nothing as they both collapsed, kneeling in the mud that surrounded what was left of the aircraft. Finally summoning enough strength to get shakily to a standing position, while Alexi carefully inspected his beloved aircraft, they each hoped that washroom facilities were not too far away. It was then that Griggory noticed the gaping five centimeter hole in the side of his rucksack and realized his life had been spared by a simple yet fortuitous request.

Although the walk from the crippled plane to Kulakovo in the rain was anything but pleasant, they enjoyed every contact their feet made with the earth, solid terra firma and none complained. They were still alive and, with the exception of a few bruises, uninjured. Griggory was totally involved in instant replays of this, the greatest adventure he had ever known.

What a tale to tell my parents, he was thinking.

For Yakov, it was a grand adventure but not his first. His thoughts were on why the event had happened and that's when it hit him like a blow from a sledge hammer.

"Kazamin doesn't have the real one and he apparently thinks we do. What Stepan and I got from Joakim's place wasn't the real one. It wasn't the real one. Don't you see," he screamed in obvious delight. Dancing round and round the other two, waving his hands in the air. "Only question is though, who has it and where is it?"

There were no answers.

300 KILOMETRES NE OF KRASNOYARSK

FRIDAY, JUNE 18, 1926

"That was them! They just passed over us! Get this thing turned around – we've got to get that object back. Don't you two understand anything?" screamed Kazamin, waving his TT-33 handgun around.

"Calm down," said Pavel, leaning over the seat from the right front. "The pilots' turning the plane. It will only turn so fast."

"Get this contraption turned around or I'll blow his head clean off his shoulders," replied Kazamin, continuing his irrational rant, ramming the pistol up against the pilot's right ear.

"Yeah, that would be a good idea, Kazamin," responded Pavel. "Right now we need all the eyes we can get if we have any hope of finding Yakov's plane. Now, please, put that toy away before a stray bullet hits one of those tanks up there," pointing to the overhead fuel cells in the wing roots. "BOOM, and they pick us up with spot remover!"

"Ahg," grumbled Kazamin in complete disgust, sliding the gun into his shoulder holster. "If we don't find that plane, you two will have a lot more than a stray bullet to worry about.

After about a half hour of circles and more circles, and not the slightest sign of the other aircraft.

"For what it's worth, Kazamin," began Pavel, "I think they have gone into the clouds to get away and I doubt they will be coming out, well, at least until they have to land or crash."

By this time, the pilot, who was somewhat more concerned about whether he would ever see another sunrise or even a sunset, was soaked in sweat and shaking like a stop sign in a hurricane.

"Well, what are you waiting for? Get us up there and flush them out!" yelled Kazamin, except this time, it was not punctuated with a handgun.

The pilot gave Pavel a look of absolute horror.

"That's not a good idea Kazamin," said Pavel turning his gaze to Kazamin. "We're on a hunting trip I agree, but that other plane isn't a flock of ducks. If we hit that plane, we're both goners. I have no idea where they are in those clouds or even if they are. It's extremely risky."

"Look you weak kneed wimps," responded Kazamin. "I didn't get to where I am by not taking chances."

"True," replied Pavel, trying his best to calm the situation, "but you didn't get to where you think you are by being stupid either!"

That put an end to the argument that didn't entirely go over all that well with Kazamin who seriously thought of terminating Pavel's employment on the spot! Pavel Nishnokeyov had been in Kazamin's employ as a both a pilot and bodyguard for several years. In his mid forties, ex-military, he had a full head of close cropped salt and pepper hair, clean shaven, clear blue eyes, lean and muscular and he was slightly shorter than the average Russian male his age.

"The weather doesn't look that great. Looks like a storm front coming at us," spoke the pilot, a shaky finger pointing to the grey to dark blue clouds "And besides that, we are getting low on fuel. About another hour and a half at most I would say."

Pavel surveyed the sky in all directions then leaned over the seat.

"I doubt that Yakov returned to Vanavara. The weather wouldn't allow that and I think I may have caused some damage to their aircraft, perhaps even punctured one of the fuel tanks," he reasoned. "So, if I we're in their shoes, I would head for Bratsk. After the dogfight, they may not have had enough fuel to make it to Krasnoyarsk."

Kazamin said nothing, simply stared at Pavel and looked around at the ever worsening weather conditions.

"All right. Bratsk," he agreed, not taking the loss well (something to which he was not accustomed), clearly dejected and madder than a wet hen.

The city of Bratsk came up off the starboard side and, by this time, they were down to less than three hundred metres AGL, a combination of deteriorating weather and the elevation of Bratsk. Spotting the aerodrome off the port wing, the pilot continued his downwind leg toward the Angara River, noting that both fuel gauges were on the "E" (that he knew didn't stand for "enough"), turned steeply onto a very short final and continued his approach as the plane was thrown from right to left, up and down, constantly buffeted by a gusty wind blowing from the NW. With less than a text book landing, that amounted to a one then a two point touchdown, followed by another two pointer and, for the grand finale, a pelvis splitting, very solid, semi-controlled full stall, three pointer and a collective sigh of relief. At least it was survivable!

The aircraft no more than came to a stop in front of a long, metal covered and well rusted building with a sagging roof line, when the pilot opened his door and literally fell to the tarmac, got up and raced toward the side door of the building, crashing though it in his panic to get away from the aircraft and it's passengers. Pavel grabbed for the rifle to his right, but realized he was too late. And that's when he noticed the other aircraft.

"Kazamin," he said, pointing through the misty rain to a large bi-plane parked next to the far end on the building. "Yes. What about it?" replied Kazamin.

"It's a military craft. A Polikarpov I think. It can fly circles around this crate which means the military are here somewhere."

"I know where," said Kazamin, pointing to a group heading toward their craft: two armed soldiers, another uniformed, somewhat hefty individual with a well worn captains hat, all followed by the wayward pilot.

"No sign of Yakov's aircraft. They couldn't have landed here, refueled and left before we arrived. So where is that sleaze-bag?" asked Kazamin, for which there was but a shoulder shrug from Pavel but nothing verbal.

The apparent leader of the troupe, Nikita Vanzin, approached Kazamin and Pavel as they exited from the aircraft and introduced himself as the Aerodrome Manager. "Your papers gentleman," demanded the Aerodrome Manager in his most officious tone, overflowing with self importance. The pilot told the Manager that he was forced to fly them to Bratsk and that Kazamin and Pavel were both armed. All the while, standing under a wing of the aircraft, Kazamin and Pavel were staring down the business ends of two large bore rifles in the possession of two young, very nervous soldiers. Vanzin motioned to one of the soldiers. He went to the aircraft, retrieved Pavel's rifle and relieved Kazamin of his 'toy'. Kazamin and Pavel were abruptly marched to the steel clad building without a word of being said.

Locked in a small, windowless holding cell in what appeared to be the airfield "office" building, Kazamin and Pavel did little more than wander around the room, as though inspecting every square centimetre in the vain hope of identifying a way out. It didn't take very long to discover that there was none. Damp concrete walls and floor, a high wood ceiling and a steel door surrounded them. It was highly unlikely that the décor of the room would qualify it to be listed in Russia's 'Places to Stay' brochure, unless the traveller had a particular fondness for two cots sans blankets, one very wobbly wooden table hand carved with every obscenity known to mankind, one equally wobbly wooden chair and a yellowish 15w light bulb hanging from a cord from the ceiling that cast sporadic remnants of light, but only if the cord remained completely motionless.

Steel is frequently a good transmitter of sound and it wasn't difficult for the prisoners to eavesdrop on the vodka boosted discussions in the adjacent room. While the pilot may not have been a world class foul weather flyer, he most certainly excelled as a story teller. Luxuriously embellished to maximize literary impact, had it all been true, his bold abduction, flight bravado and subsequent "hair-raising escape" would have caused Attila the Hun to have a coronary arrest! "I'm not sure that pilot was on the same aircraft as us," mused Pavel, stepping away from the door following the pilot's gut wrenching tale. The observation had outward no effect on Kazamin's persona.

There was no sleep to be had, even if it were remotely possible. They needed a plan. Extradition to Krasnoyarsk was out of the question and spelled a one-way ticket to a labor camp at best and the end of the Barkov dynasty. *'Anywhere was better than here'* formed the basis of their plan.

Bratsk, early the following morning

"Are you ready? The watch should be changing in about ten minutes or so." said Kazamin.

"I'm ready. Let's do it!" replied Pavel. "I've had all I can take of this place," as they both moved close to the steel door.

"You know, if it wasn't for your blatant arrogance and stupidity, we would be in Moscow now enjoying a nice meal and good Russian vodka."

With that, Pavel threw himself against the door that shook every inch of its steel shell.

"You want to shove, you miserable excuse for a human. How about this?"

It was Kazamin's turn this time; not quite as resounding but followed by a very convincing yell of pain.

"Can't take it, eh. Maybe this is more to your liking since you enjoy pain so much."

And another door smash with an appropriate pain filled groan. Now it was time for a superlative climax: the compulsory chair demolishing ritual complete with a deluge of profanities and a string of less than complimentary ancestral descriptions, body smashes with a chair leg and yelps of intense pain; oldest ruse in the book, but it worked, if for no other reason than curiosity.

They heard the key going into the lock and one of the soldiers cautiously opened the door. Seeing Kazamin on the floor, face down, his attention was distracted for only a second but that was long enough for Pavel to grab the rifle barrel and slung the terrified soldier all the way across the room where he slumped semi-conscious to the floor. Pavel, now in possession of the rifle, jumped into the office area. The horror-struck pilot and Vanzin were seated at a table, both completely immobile and in a patent state of shock. Kazamin relieved the semi-conscious soldier of his side arm and joined Pavel in the office. Pavel herded the pilot into the holding cell, slammed the door shut and locked it.

With the soldier and the pilot safely secured in the luxurious Bratsk Aerodrome guest suite and dawn but a half hour away, Kazamin and Pavel retrieved their own weapons from the office and with Vanzin, seated themselves comfortably at the table. They heard the other soldier returning from his watch. Pavel stood behind to door, and as it opened, a look of complete puzzlement flashed across the soldiers face. Pavel raised his pistol, drew back the hammer and pressed the barrel of the gun against the soldiers neck.

"Good morning Private'" said Pavel. "I trust all is well on the eastern front." Kazamin promptly disarmed the dismayed soldier and pushed him toward the door to the guest suite, Kazamin unlocked the door and shoved the soldier inside. After making sure the door was secure, he tossed the key to the corner of the office.

"Now, let's take a walk outside, shall we Comrade Vanzin?" said Kazamin. "Where's the fuel tender?"

The Manager pointed to a steel tank mounted on a rubber tired cart.

"We're going to push it to our aircraft and you're going to fill the tanks. Right?" said Kazamin.

He nodded 'yes' and all three maneuvered the cart to the plane. Once completed, Kazamin told the Manager to push the cart over to the military plane.

"But it doesn't need fuel. I filled it yesterday and it hasn't flown since then," protested Vanzin.

"Push the cart you moron if you want to see tomorrow," yelled Kazamin pointing his pistol directly at his forehead.

"Pavel," ordered Kazamin. "You take Comrade Vanzin back to join his friends and I will take care of things here then get back to the plane as quickly as you can."

As the duo walked quickly toward the office door, Kazamin pumped fuel on the ground and over as much of the aircraft as he could, leaving the flowing hose laying on the ground. Pavel made quick work of securing the prisoners and was on his way toward the plane and was the first to notice it. Pointing toward the road that led to the airfield, both now could see faint lights flickering through the trees that surrounded the area. It wasn't long before they could hear the sound of gasoline engines and there was more than one.

"More soldiers coming Kazamin," yelled Pavel.

"Get in and let's get out of here right now," yelled Kazamin.

Both piled into the cockpit and Pavel started the engine. The sun was just barely clearing the horizon dead ahead of them as their craft started to taxi toward the closest end of the runway. The trucks, full of replacement soldiers, had just cleared the gate and were pulling up to the office door as Pavel swung the plane around, ready for the take-off run. A soldier ran into the office and, a few seconds later emerged, ran to the lead truck and spoke to those in the front seat. In less than 10 seconds, following a string of loud orders and pointing, about five or six soldiers were on the run toward Kazamin and Pavel's plane. Kazamin, seated on the right, opened the window, raised a rifle and took several shots in the direction of the military plane. But other shots were heard as well. The crouched soldiers were firing on Kazamin's aircraft, and hits were being scored all over the fuselage with one piercing the right side of the windscreen.

The firing came to an abrupt halt as the military aircraft burst into flames. The aircraft, at first, seemed to suddenly bloat, followed by a thunderous explosion that saw the tail of the aircraft hurled 50 meters into the air and the forward section disappeared in a horrific fireball that crashed into the end of the building. The heat and force of the explosion peeled back the metal roof and siding as if they were made of paper. A loud 'whomph' sound echoed from the tank on the fuel tender and in less than a second, it also erupted into a fireball that sent white hot shrapnel sized pieces of metal and flaming chunks of wood in every direction, instantly igniting anything they touched.

Pavel lifted their aircraft skyward and they climbed steadily toward the west. Kazamin was more than just relieved, he was downright joyous at their well planned and executed escape.

"You know, once we get to Moscow, we'll be safe. They can't touch us there."

"If we get to Moscow." answered Pavel.

"What do you mean 'if'? We're on our way and the weather looks…

oh no." It was then that Kazamin noticed the expanding red smear on Pavel's right shoulder. "How bad is it," he inquired, gazing at the rapidly expanding blood stain on Pavel's shirt sleeve.

"Well, it's never good when you're shot. See if you can patch it up and I'll try and get us to Kolpashevo."

Kazamin was anything but comfortable playing the role of a doctor but, if he was to get to Moscow, he knew he had to do what he could. He cleaned the wound as best he could and made a bandage from his own shirt sleeves and kept pressure on the wound during the flight. It slowed the bleeding but it was obviously not enough. He needed professional medical attention and soon.

Pavel was a close friend and had been for several years. But survival was uppermost in Kazamin's mind. While they may have enough fuel to make it to the intended destination, it was highly unlikely that Pavel could remain conscious that long and a crash was virtually inevitable.

They could fly to Krasnoyarsk but that would be going from the frying pan into the fire. Kazamin decided, without discussing his decision with Pavel, that the flight would continue on course until he decided that they must land if they are to live through this predicament.

While Kazamin was tending to Pavel's wound, un-noticed by him, they flew within sight of Yakov's crashed plane, now fully stripped and only the frame remained.

A short time later, Kazamin made the decision to land, prompted by a combination of Pavel's deteriorating condition and the sighting of a rail line heading south toward Achinsk, a line that would connect with the Trans Siberian Railway and Moscow.

There was no airfield and so Pavel selected a long narrow field that would serve as a runway. In spite of the pounding the aircraft took leaving Bratsk, the only apparent damage was Pavel's injury. On final,

Pavel was in and out of consciousness and the plane slewed back and forth and frequently pitched violently upward as Pavel fought to keep some semblance of control. They passed over the approach end too high and too fast for an early touchdown. Pavel side-slipped the aircraft in a desperate attempt to shed the excess altitude. It finally touched down on one wheel, nearly resulting in a ground loop before settling down on all three wheels but moving rapidly toward the left side of the field. Pavel lost consciousness and slumped over the control yoke. Kazamin, the experienced survivalist, reacted quickly enough to keep the nose of the plane from digging a trench in the ground, grabbed Pavel and pushed him back into his seat. Pavel's feet were still firmly planted on the rudder pedals and the plane swerved violently to the right. The left wing and landing gear rose slightly in the process. Kazamin reached over, turned the fuel selector valve to the 'Off' position and killed the engine. The plane slowed almost immediately to a stop.

Kazamin wasted no time in releasing his harness and opened his door. "Sorry my friend, but I have to leave you now," he said to the unconscious Pavel. "I'm in no shape to carry you. Unfortunately, you're excess baggage. Best of luck and hope to see you in Moscow." Kazamin wasn't sure if Pavel could hear him or not, nor cared, for that matter.

Kazamin quickly got out of the aircraft, kept the handguns for himself, made his way to the nearby road and headed directly for the railway line he spotted from the air, with no stops in between.

MOSCOW

FRIDAY, OCTOBER 15, 1926

To suggest that it was ostentatious would be almost an understatement especially considering the plight of most Russians. Large enough to comfortably house four average Russian families, Taras Laskin was dwarfed by his own surroundings that included a gigantic ashtray filled beyond capacity with cigarette and cigar buts. Not a slim man by any stretch of the imagination, weighing in at close to 130 kilos and counting, he hadn't seen his feet in almost a decade. Chin number 3 hid much of his shirt collar and the knot of his tie that disappeared under a black vest that was clearly under substantial stress to maintain its fastened state. But after all, he was a man of authority; Assistant to the Minister of the Interior and State Security, an imposing man with an imposing title. Although not mentioned in his resume, he was the epitome of total corruption!

"Comrade Novikoff to see you, Comrade Laskin."

It was the voice of his Secretary from the outer office, a prim and proper lady in her late forties sporting a hair bun tied so tight, it would be a good bet that her toes would curl every time she blinked! She was, to say the least, a true blue, died in the wool believer in the tenets of Stalinism or whatever dogma happened to be in vogue at the time that would assure her survival.

Maxim Novikoff, the complete antithesis of Comrade Laskin at least as far as outward appearance was concerned, opened the door separating the outer office, entered and quickly made his way to

Comrade Laskin's desk. Wearing a black well tailored suit, Novikoff was a high ranking official in the much dreaded OGPU. He was tall, built like a T-35 tank, square jawed, dark piercing eyes and the sense of humor of a wounded rhino, and corrupt!

Taras rose from his chair (with pronounced difficulty) and bade Maxim to have a seat in front of his desk, putting his forefinger to his lips and circumscribing a circle around the room at the same time, a message that *the walls have ears*. But it really didn't matter anyway. The radio on a small table next to one of the two huge windows in the one hundred sq. metre room was blasting out Military march music just shy of the threshold of pain.

"Welcome back to Moscow, my friend. And so you have good news I hope?" asked Taras clearly anticipating good news, but it was not to be!

"It was a fake," responded Maxim without so much of an iota of emotion.

However, Taras was not so calm. Obviously shaken by the bad news, he rose again from his chair (with less difficulty this time), strode over to one of the windows, one hand plowing through a mass of salt and pepper hair and the other supporting him against the window frame. Turning to Maxim, sweat rolling down his outsized forehead, hands out with the palms up.

"Where is he?"

"He bolted when he saw that it was another fake and I have no idea where he is. I chased him but lost him in the city. He could be anywhere."

"You lost him? You're OGPU! How could… " Tara's began. Then catching himself, he regained some composure and lowered his voice. Leaning over the side of the desk almost in Maxim's face, sweat dripping profusely onto the leather desk pad, he continued. "How could you lose him? One man. Alone! This, my friend, is a disaster for both of us. I can't believe it. One man in a room. How can this happen?"

Rising from his ornate office chair and carefully placing his overcoat over the back of the chair, his icy stare focused on Taras as he moved slowly to Taras's side, grabbed him by the back of his shirt collar, and solidly planted him in his chair (a testament to fine construction). Putting both his polar bear mitts on the table and leaning slightly in Taras's direction.

"Now you listen to me you bloated self righteous pig. You weren't there. He had an assistant… a partner as far as I know," bellowed Maxim.

Taras held up his hands, signaling Maxim to calm down.

"I'm the one that's taking the lion's share of risk in this venture," continued Maxim. "I pilfered the funds from the OGPU and so far I've been able to keep it under wraps. But I say this to you Tara's, If I go down that long dark corridor, so do you! Got the picture?"

"Listen Maxim," replied Taras, visibly shaken by Maxims' rage, "we are both taking enormous risks. My signature of approval is on the forged travel documents so there is no need to be threatening. It's just that I had hoped, that at long last, we could realize the reward and rid ourselves of Barkov. And as if I didn't have enough to be concerned about, there are those persistent reports of some kind of unexplained events going on around the oil fields in Megion."

Maxim went back to his chair, retrieved his cost, then turned to Tara's. "I'll see what I can do to find him." Somewhat to Taras's relief, Maxim left the office, slamming the door solidly behind him.

Tara's pressed a small white button under the desk, a door opened on the side opposite the outer office and a slim gentleman in his late thirties walked in and sat across from Taras.

"Did you hear the discussion?" asked Taras.

Lazar Koslow was Taras's assistant, a true lackey who was quite prepared to do anything asked of him, uninhibited by loyalty, morals or common sense. Shaking his head in the affirmative, he said nothing in order to preserve his self imposed secret agent persona. He relaxed in the chair, content and confident.

"I want you to follow him everywhere he goes. I want to know everything he does. Everything. Is that understood? I don't care what it is," instructed Taras. "I also want you to find Kazamin Barkov." Although Taras was doubtful that Lazar could find north if he was holding a compass, he felt certain that he could follow someone without being obvious about it."

Again the reply was a well practiced affirmative nod. Taras, with a wave of his right hand, told Lazar to leave and get on with the tasks at hand, then went back to the pile of papers, reports and forms that littered his desk.

MOSCOW

<u>**WEDNESDAY, FEBRUARY 9, 1927**</u>

In the summer months, Gorky Park was a most pleasant place to relax and do nothing. One was not even required to think in order to enjoy its pleasantness. The one hundred twenty hectare park surrounded a large lake used mostly for recreational rowing in the spring and summer months. But it was not summer yet the cold raw climate could not hide its beauty. It was just what Lazar needed - the solitude and coolness of the air to clear his muddled mind. Recently, his life had been anything but what he had expected.

Comrade Laskin was, it seemed, deep into crisis management and was never satisfied with any news that Lazar brought to him. Still, it provided him with a modest income, a degree of safety and, yes, even a bit of travel. To make things worse, he had not been able to spot his target for more than a week and a meeting with Comrade Laskin was coming up in a few days.

But, it was not to be. He knew, the second he spotted them, one at his 10 o'clock position and the other at his 2 o'clock position, that he was their target. Gripped by fear, sweating a river and filled with enormous apprehension, there was no place to run. The two gorillas, No.1 to his right and No. 2 left, and the partially frozen pond behind him, left no escape route.

"Comrade Koslow, you are to come with us immediately," said gorilla No. 1, grabbing Lazar's left arm and yanking him to his feet. With Lazar sandwiched in the middle, the trio walked swiftly toward a black Ford sedan parked at the curb on Krymskiy Val. Gorilla No.1 opened the back door and literally tossed Lazar into the sedan. He landed sprawled half on the floor and half on the back seat. Gorillas No.'s1 and 2 slid into the front seat, started the engine and pulled away from the curb into a mass of transition traffic: automobiles, trucks and horse drawn carts.

"Good afternoon Comrade. Good of you to accept my invitation."

"There didn't seem to be much choice," grunted Lazar, hauling himself to an upright position on the car bench seat and only then noticing who had spoken. He wasn't sure if he should be relieved or simply give up all hope. "Comrade Novikoff?" said Lazar fearfully.

"Well it's no surprise that you recognize me," answered Maxim. "After all Comrade, I seem to have been the subject of your close attention for a considerable period of time."

Lazar said nothing but glanced up at the rear view mirror to catch a wide grin from gorilla No. 2 displaying a mouth full of yellowish teeth with more than just a few gaps.

"Where to begin," said Maxim, opening one of two manila envelopes. He withdrew a number of sheets of paper and began reading. "Lazar Koslow born and raised in Tula. Lovely city, Tula. Isn't that right Boris?"

Boris, known to Lazar as Gorilla No. 1 replied, "Yes. Very lovely."

"He's faking it. He's never been there," replied Maxim to a round of quiet laughter from the front seat gorilla duo. "To continue. Not all that well educated though. Left school before completion . Most unfortunate," continued Maxim with a glance to Lazar. "Considers himself a master sleuth. What do you think of that Boris? We are in the presence of a master sleuth no less." Only a smile this time. "Enough of this nonsense," said Maxim, tossing the envelope and papers at Lazar. "Master sleuth? Hardly!"

Maxim's mood changed instantly from jovial to deathly serious, shaking Lazar to the core and accelerating his sweat production.

"You're in the wrong profession Comrade Lazar. You're no good at it and it could well get you killed. It says here you're twenty eight years old. Is that correct?" asked Maxim, to which Lazar simply shook his head in the affirmative. "Well, I have some other items that may interest you," he continued, opening the second manila envelope and withdrawing several large black and white photographs. "Here's a picture of you, enjoying food and drinks with General Dimity Goncharov at his home I assume. Nice photo, don't you think?"

"But… I never heard of General… whatever his name is," stammered Lazar.

"Well of course you know him; sorry, knew him" continued Maxim, putting on a look of complete puzzlement. "Are you not aware that he was executed 3 months ago for inciting antigovernment uprisings? How can you say you didn't know him? Is that not you seated next to him? Looks like you to me."

"Yes, that looks like me… but it can't be. I tell you, I never heard of him. I don't know where he lives… lived," replied Lazar in a near state of panic.

"Hummm. Interesting. Well then," placing the first photo under the pile and exposing the second one. "Here's a photo of you with Josef Popyrin also executed some time ago for involvement in an assassination plot. Oh! And what's in that briefcase your handing him? What is that anyway?"

"I don't know him I tell you. That's not me. I never heard of him," his voice shaky and gasping for every breath.

"Humph, yes. Quite fascinating. But it sure looks like you in the photo," continued Maxim. "Okay then. Now surely you recall this gentleman, actually from Tula, your home town. Nice photo of you with Col. Sergei Antakov in Gorky Park. Executed about a week ago;

theft and fraud. Hey! That's your hobby, isn't it?"

Another round of quiet laughter drifted from the front seat.

"No, no, no, no! I don't know any of those people," insisted Lazar. "Those photos are fakes. They're fakes!" By this time, Lazar was shaking like a leaf and in tears, with his head in his hands, sobbing like a baby.

"Tell me Lazar, would you like to see your twenty ninth birthday?" asked Maxim and received a quiet "yes" from Lazar. "Good. It may be possible but not if you continue to work with low life scum such as Taras Laskin, especially in surveillance. You aren't even aware of the most basic of techniques, do you understand?" Maxim's voice was becoming more aggressive and animated with every word. "You know that you're living a very dangerous existence, do you not Comrade?"

Lazar, unsure of what was coming his way next, simply looked at Maxim and said nothing.

"But I'm not without compassion, my friend," said Maxim, staring out the car window at the passing panorama of everyday life in Moscow.

"Yes. Filled to the brim with the milk of human kindness, as it were", he continued, returning his attention to Lazar. "I think it was Shakespeare who coined that phrase, was it not Comrades?," directing the question to the gorilla section to which the two simply looked briefly at each other and shrugged their shoulders at the same time.

Lazar was still shaking and sobbing, staring at the floor of the automobile, totally oblivious to everything around him, drowning in an ocean of hopelessness and fully believing that he was headed for a date with a firing squad, a fate for which he was entirely unprepared.

Maxim was the picture of total contentment, staring out the window again. "Tell me Comrade, have you ever wondered how long it will be before we no longer see horses in Moscow? That would be most unfortunate, don't you think? Gives some added character to the city. And they smell no worse that the automobile."

"Sit up Comrade. Get yourself under control! You're embarrassing us!" demanded Maxim. "Nothing is going to happen to you today if you do as I say; exactly as I say; no argument! Do you understand?"

Lazar sat up in the seat, head back and eyes closed. "Yes, yes. What do you want me to do?"

"Just so we understand each other Comrade, you're of course right. The photos are fakes, somewhat doctored, as they say," said Maxim, staring coldly at Lazar, now little more than a mental basket case. "But do you know something, my friend? It was photos such as these that spelled the end for those unfortunate gentlemen. The justice system doesn't care. It goes by what is presented to it, real or fake, it's all the same thing these days. And those I showed you are only three. There are numerous others I have or can have, along with supporting documents. So now that we understand each other, let's get down to business, shall we?"

There was the slightest of nods from Lazar who had just received an unexpected education and a wake-up call to the realization that there was no escaping the fact that his survival depended solely on the whims and mood of the man seated next to him. Lazar Kozlow was in charge of absolutely nothing! He was the proverbial puppet on a string!

"First," began Maxim, "you will retrieve a number of documents from Comrade Laskin's office. I will tell which ones later and tell you how to do it. Second, you will continue to tail me as though this meeting never took place. From time to time, I will have Boris or Leonid (whom Lazar assumed to be gorilla No. 2) give you the information that you are to feed Comrade Laskin. This will keep up until either Laskin or I end it and you better pray that Laskin's doesn't end the relationship before my requirements are satisfied," warned Maxim. "Thirdly, as soon as this is over, you will leave Moscow for good. I don't care where you go or how you go, but if you ever return to Moscow, I guarantee you will be on a one-way trip to a labor camp in Siberia before week's end. Is that clear?"

With that, Maxim beckoned the driver to pull over to the curb, reached over, opened the door and literally pushed Lazar out before pulling back into traffic and speeding off. Lazar had an urgent nature call.

Orders and instructions received, the word 'nervous' didn't even begin to describe Lazar, pretending to work for one boss while actually working for another; master sleuth turned double agent. He was what he once thought he wanted to be, a spy, and, as Maxim put it, he was no good at this and he knew it but he only had two options: this or the numbing, deadly cold of Siberia winters!

TVERSKAYA OFFICE BUILDING, MOSCOW

MONDAY, APRIL 4, 1927

Laskin and the secretary had already arrived. Lazar received the usual 'get-out-of-my-face' response to his 'good morning', and continued into Taras's office. Taras had just removed his long coat and hung it on the coat rack next to the door. Lazar stood by the rack, his hand behind him, feeling for the pocket in which Taras put his keys.

'*Left pocket*,' Lazar was thinking, quietly removing the keys.

Lazar removed his coat and hung it next to Taras's.

"Well, don't just stand there like a department store mannequin! What do you have to report?" demanded Taras, hardly bothering to look up from his desk, lighting a cigarette with an assurance that only comes from years of relentless practice.

Lazar spelled out the rehearsed details of his surveillance.

"By the way, Barkov is back in Moscow. I spotted him the day before yesterday," concluded Lazar.

He hadn't, of course but that didn't matter even though it apparently was true that Kazamin had returned and was well protected in his downtown fortress, supported by a number of influential and untouchable government officials.

Taras just shook his head.

"What did you find in Megion and Surgut?"

"I spoke with the soldiers that reported seeing the lights. They think it's some kind of high speed aircraft but apparently there are more than one. Some said they saw three or so. Whatever they are, they don't seem interested in the wells in the area. I also spoke with a number of civilians in both places and none of them saw any lights and they didn't know what I was talking about."

"Trained soldiers high on vodka or filthy peasants high on dirt. Who to believe, eh? Get on with it then and keep me informed."

With a nonchalant wave of the hand and a puff of blue smoke, without looking up, abruptly invited Lazar to leave (to his relief and amazement, he had passed another test.)

Lazar, feeling more confident by the minute, walked by the stone-faced secretary and headed straight for the washroom, took a small bar of hand soap and pressed the proper key into it, leaving a very distinct impression. He then returned to Taras's office under the pretext of getting his coat from the rack but actually replacing Taras's keys.

"He's gone for the day," stone-face said as he was about to enter Taras's office.

Lazar broke out in a cold sweat and tried desperately to hide his panicked state.

"What? Where did he go?" he asked.

"How should I know. Got a phone call and off he went," she responded, returning to her work.

Lazar wasn't sure what he was going to do. Plan "A" was out the window and he had no Plan "B" but he knew he had to get those keys back in Taras's pocket before Taras had time to leave the building. He grabbed his coat from the inner office and rushed to the door without appear to be in a hurry.

The outer hall was crowded with people going in every direction but no immediate sign of Taras. Running down the hall was not a highly recommended practice since it seemed any excuse to arouse suspicion most always would. Lazar started thinking more logically even in his panic driven state of mind.

If Taras had his coat, he's not going to a meeting inside the building so he has to be headed for some other location in the city.

With that in mind, he hurried as best he could, down two flights of stairs, looking in all directions. He saw no sign of Taras in the front lobby. He leapt out the front door just in time to see a black sedan pull away with someone sitting in the rear seat that he identified as Taras.

'I'm a walking dead man. I'm dead,' he thought to himself, and began walking back up the street, then turning around, he stopped momentarily in front of the building, trying to think what to do.

He looked around in a faint hope of spotting one of the gorillas. No such luck, although he wasn't sure what to do or say had he seen one of them. That's when his heart skipped a beat and he couldn't believe his eyes. Out of the corner of his eye - there was Taras just coming out of the building. Lazar looked up the street and could see another black sedan trying to make its way around a horse drawn carriage that had no intention of yielding the right of way to the automobile.

He must have gone into one of the washrooms. I can't believe this! he thought.

The crowd of people on the street was just as thick as it was inside the building.

I don't care what Maxim says, he thought. *I am a master sleuth.*

With a renewed zest for life that comes from a near-death

experience, Lazar made his way through the crowd so that he was slightly behind and to the left of Taras, and delicately dropped the keys into his coat pocket without the slightest knowledge of Taras.

He returned to the building and headed straight for the nearest washroom in full realization that this activity was getting to be habitual.

While stealing a key to make a template was not a difficult task for a 'master sleuth' (discounting problems in replacing the errant key), he found that re-creating the key was another matter entirely, especially for one who had little idea of what he was doing. But, he eventually did it, or so he hoped.

Lazar had been around Taras's office long enough to recognize that both Taras and Stone-Face had fairly well established routines. The part of the routine that attracted Lazar's attention always occurred on Friday. Taras would leave the office around 4 PM and Stone-Face, around 4:30 PM. Lazar had his key, a key that opened both doors. He had the replacement files and he was familiar with the files he was to retrieve. He was pumped. After all, he had just come off a successful mission, albeit a shaky execution.

The building was old and the hallways were characterized by numerous huge stone pillars supporting the massive arched ceiling. Lazar stood behind one of the pillars, some distance from the outer office door but in a line of sight. Doing nothing while looking busy came natural to him, an art that he referred to as dynamic inactivity.

Almost on cue, Taras came out and waddled down the hallway, looking neither right or left, just looking his pragmatic, overbearing self! About forty five minutes later, out came Stone-Face, sporting an expression that would give the most fanatical poker player the willies.

Lazar walked cautiously to the office door and inserted the key in the ancient lock. With a little persuasion, the key worked and he was in the outer office and, happily noting that the second key worked perfectly, soon entered the sanctum sanctorum of the illustrious

Comrade Taras. He was amazed to find that the top right desk drawer was unlocked or, he surmised, the desk was so old that the lock had long since retired. He was alarmed and a rush of trepidation started to overwhelm him when he found that the records that he was to search for were not there nor were they in any other part of the desk and the room had no filing cabinets. Lazar stopped what he was doing and stepped away from the desk, took a deep breath and got his nerves back under some degree of control.

Returning to the task at hand, and recalling Maxim's instructions, he placed a bundle of records in the top right desk drawer, contained in a well used file folder so as not to attract undue attention.

Locking the door to Taras's office, he proceeded to the secretary's filing cabinet, a four drawer wooden piece of ancient furniture that was in surprisingly good shape. But all the drawers were locked and his key was clearly not going to fit the locks. After several tries, all unsuccessful, he went over to Stone-Faces desk to try and find the key, or, failing that, retrieve a letter opener.

His heart stopped and so did his breathing. Someone was inserting a key into the lock of the outer door. His confidence evaporated like a water drop on a hot griddle. He was trapped!

WESTERN ADMINISTRATIVE DISTRICT,
MOSCOW

THURSDAY, MAY 12, 1927

He just stood there, staring out of the second floor window, right hand on the right side of the window frame and his left on the other side. It had just started to rain and the crowds below thinned out markedly but it did nothing to relieve the congested traffic along the cobbled street.

His assistant, Vitaly Rusanov, a time-hardened, expressionless, blocky gentleman of about 50 years or so, entered the office and stood by the large, paper covered desk.

"Taras was here earlier. I told him you couldn't be disturbed. Maxim called for you as well as those two from the Ministry," said Vitaly.

Without warning, Kazamin rammed his right fist into the window frame, shaking it from top to bottom but the old panes withstood the onslaught.

"That bunch of blood-sucking leaches! If I knew where that bloody object was, I'd get it and they would have it! Do you have any idea what I've been through these last years?"

He picked up a bunch of papers from the desk and tossed them all over the office.

"Dragged my carcass all over Siberia in the cold and rain, saddle sores that will probably stay with me for the rest of my life, thrown into a rat infested jail, two friends gone, and I lost track of how much this mess has cost so far."

He leaned over the back of his desk and pointed toward the south and Sevastopol.

"Everything would have been fine except for those meddling fools of Treschev and that bunch of crack pots."

"Kazamin," said Vitaly, "I warned you about burning the candle at both ends, didn't I? And you know as well as I that Slava screwed it up right from the start. And I also warned you about him. did I not? So even if you had it, who would you release it to?" questioned Vitaly.

Although he felt he had just ventured onto very thin ice, Vitaly banked on his long-standing relationship with Kazamin to avoid physical retaliation.

"I know. I know. I don't need to be reminded. I don't know who would get it. But right now, I don't have it so it doesn't matter anyway. I should have listened. All right, you heard me say it, but I didn't see how am I going to handle this?"

"There's only one way my friend. You have to get that object thing back, or whatever it is, and right now, none of us know where it is. You know that Yakov doesn't have it. There hasn't been a peep from Treschev's group and if they had it, it would have surfaced somewhere by now, don't you think?"

"I've had a lot of time to think about this. Slava certainly didn't have the real one and I think that Yakov believed he had it when we stopped them on that trail with Ivan. We searched their saddlebags and there was only one pipe and nothing else that could have been the object. I guess shooting at their plane was a bit of a waste. Oh well! But here's the strange part, and it's been driving me crazy for weeks. If Yakov believed that they had retrieved the real one, and it wasn't, then the real one must be with the group that Slava left behind. Slava, my idiot brother, had the real one in his grasp. Can you believe it?" slamming his fists onto the desk then throwing his arms up in complete disgust. "In other words Vitaly, that bunch that were with Slava may still have it! And get this - Treschev's group probably doesn't know any more about where it is than we do!"

"You're probably right Kazamin," said Vitaly, "but what do you make of Yakov's visits to Kazan over the past few years? Do you think that may have something to do with this Tunguska object thing? You know he did a lot of inquiring when he was there but we couldn't find out much; nobody would speak to us."

"Yes, I'm aware of those visits but if it does have something to do with the object, I don't think it was to retrieve it but what that bunch are up to well… I have no idea but I think we should find out." said Kazamin. Moving next to Vitaly, putting an arm around his shoulder, "Just to be sure, I want you to find out who all was on that grand venture and where they are now… except for Slava and Anton of course." Giving rise to a round of impassive laughter from both of them.

TVERSKAYA OFFICE BUILDING, MOSCOW

OCTOBER 26, 1927

The windowless outer office was Spartan by any definition: one filing cabinet, one desk and one chair (with the social graces of an amoeba, Ms. Stone-Face had little need for more than one chair).

Through the frosted glass in the office door, Lazar could see that it was Ms. Stone-Face inserting the key into the lock and, much to his temporary relief, the action was not going smoothly. He knew that a game of hide and seek in this office wouldn't last more than five seconds. The only safe refuge was the inner office and although that door was less than 5 meters away, for Lazar, it might as well have been in Zimbabwe!

The desk; that was the only choice, and he dove for it, huddling up in the cramped space just as the outer door opened. He couldn't see her but he could hear her.

'Clop, clop, clop.'

She made her way gingerly toward her desk. Lazar was sure anyone in the next building could hear his heartbeat. No one could hear him breathing because he wasn't breathing and it took almost a full minute before he realized that he wasn't breathing. He was starting to turn blue before realizing that he had better draw a breath or pass out! This wasn't the way spying was supposed to be, at least not how he convinced himself it was supposed to be. This was deadly stuff and he wished he was anywhere but where he was at present.

Lazar was ready to bolt from under the desk, out the front and try and make it to the door before she recognized who it was, knowing full well that would be a futile move. And even if he made it out, Stone-Face would raise an alarm and he would be up to his armpits in security staff before he got ten metres down the hallway.

Did she lock the door when she came in? Was she looking at her desk or somewhere else in the room? Can I crawl part of the way un-noticed?

The office was toasty warm to say the least, but Lazar was freezing, covered in cold sweat and shivering like a puppy in a February blizzard. He could see her shoes, not a meter away. To his horror, she left her position in front of the desk. He could hear her walking around the side of the desk, and the shoes appeared again behind the desk. She grabbed her desk chair and rolled it to the right side of the desk.

I'm dead, he thought. *She knows I'm here!*

But after moving things around on her desk, she proceeded to the filing cabinet. She used her keys to open several drawers and, followed by the sound of rustling papers, she came back to the front of the desk.

Lazar could sense that she removed something from her purse. She mumbled something he didn't catch, then the sound of the desk lamp being turned on. After a few moments he could hear a strange noise.

'Click, scrape, scrape, rustle, click, scrape, scrape, rustle.'

It took a few seconds for Lazar to figure out what she was doing.

She's taking photos of papers on her desk, winding the film and shooting other papers. Stone-Face is a spy! He wasn't sweating anymore and the temperature of the room was much warmer and Lazar actually smiled, shaking his head. *Well, isn't this something. Taras has a spy for a secretary.*

All of a sudden, the party ended. The outer door rattled. To Lazar's left, the camera dangling on a chord, not a half meter from his head, and appeared to be hanging from Stone-Faces right hand. The outer door opened. A security guard stuck his head through the opening.

"I'm fine," said Stone-Face, with no sign of panic or any emotion. "Just cleaning up my desk."

"Yes, I see that," answered the guard. "But you signed out down stairs. Perhaps you should have… cleaned up before leaving."

"You're quite right. Of course. But I forgot to re-file these papers," she continued, "and I didn't want to leave them sitting around for the weekend."

Grabbing the papers, she turned off the desk lamp and walked slowly toward the filing cabinet. The guard didn't budge; just waited for her to put the papers away (Lazar noted the drawer). She grabbed her purse (stealthily putting the camera in it without the notice of the guard), and left the office, closing the door behind her.

'She didn't lock the cabinet drawers,' thought Lazar, now breathing almost normally. 'Great! My job is over and I'm out of here.'

He put the last bundle of papers into the cabinet drawer. Getting by the security staff, for Lazar the *Master Sleuth*, would be the proverbial piece-of-cake, given what he had just experienced.

The following morning, he and Maxim met. There was a less than cordial exchange. He handed the papers to Maxim (but no mention of Ms. Super Spy's activities) and received a stern warning to leave Moscow before being unceremoniously turfed from the sedan. Lazar started his trek, selecting to travel northeast, the shortest direction to the city limits.

SATURDAY, APRIL 18, 1928

The office was not large: perhaps twenty five sq. metres, two average sized windows that looked out on a building with lots and lots of average sized windows. For furniture, it had an average sized desk and several average sized chairs, including three small sofas. But it was comfortable and completely unlittered with paper, books and magazines. Maxim pressed a button on a black box sitting on the desk.

"Leonid, Boris, come in here," demanded Maxim.

The door to another office opened in stepped gorillas No.1 and No. 2; well dressed as two gorillas can be but unable to disguise their profession; enforcers for clients that required additional encouragement! They both strolled over to Maxim's desk, one at the front right and the other at the front left, hands in their pockets.

Maxim handed Boris a piece of official looking document and said, "Read this."

It took a few moments for Boris to get through the six line paragraph, while Leonid did the heavy looking on. Once finished, a mordant smile broke out as he looked at Maxim and handed the document to Leonid.

"Don't you just love it when a good plan comes together Comrades? Taras Laskin was arrested last evening on charges of treason and fraud and I hear that his secretary will be arrested later today. Calls for a drink, wouldn't you say. That clears up the mess on the playing field a bit," continued Maxim, "But we still have that snake Kazamin to deal with. He's made promises that have yet to be kept and I've covered for him far too long? I want my money back, I want that object and then I want Kazamin's head, with or without the platter. What say we cut him some slack for a bit and see what he does and where he goes. I still want him tailed but don't make any moves to arrest him. As long as he's holed up in his fortress, he won't be able to go after the object, if he knows where it is. The games afoot, as Sherlock Holmes would say, or maybe it was Shakespeare."

The gorillas simply looked at each other and shrugged. They couldn't recall meeting either one.

SEVASTOPOL

TUESDAY, APRIL 3, 1928

The room on the fourth floor (the top floor actually) was fairly large and furnished with taste and dominated by a large, oval, solid and somewhat ornate table. The ebony mahogany table, inlaid with several exotic woods, each surrounded by a copper thread and matching chairs with needle point seat covers, was clearly a satisfying mix of masculine and feminine influences, as was the entire room décor, for that matter. Tall, wide windows occupied most of one wall, overlooking the extensive harbour facilities and just beyond, the Black Sea and the gateway to the Aegean.

"Griggory," began Viktor Treschev, seated at one end of the table and speaking in an uncharacteristically stern manner, "you've been a total embarrassment to all of us."

Griggory looked at Yakov, who was seemingly without emotion and then to his fiancé, Elsa Sergeyovna, who was almost in tears.

Treschev said nothing; just kept the stern expression and his eyes fixed solidly on Griggory who was now in a near state of shock. But a crack in the rock appeared – then widened – and both Treschev and Yakov, who could hold the act no longer, broke out in laughter loud enough to be heard in Istanbul.

"Griggory, it is true, you know," began Viktor Treschev. "You managed to embarrass all of us." Getting up from his chair, Treschev went and stood behind Griggory and put his arms around he and

Elsa. "Griggory, you have graduated top of the class; honors no less and have been accepted as a graduate student at the State Technical University in Leningrad. A bit of a rocky start but you found your way. The problem my boy, is this - none of the rest of us ever got beyond eighth grade. You're a first for us, Griggory, and we are so very proud and pleased."

Griggory, now relaxed, was a bit uneasy with the stream of accolades.

"And Elsa," continued Treschev, "we have all fallen in love with you. What a magnificent couple. Don't you think Yakov?"

"Indeed I do sir. Indeed I do," responded Yakov.

The door to the conference room opened and a uniformed gentleman entered, carrying a tray with several glasses: two bottles of Stolichnaya Elit vodka and a bottle of Prascoveya red wine.

"I took the liberty of ordering drinks to celebrate the occasion"' said Treschev. "Vodka for Griggory; you can't be a true Russian Griggory, without at least some appreciation of vodka and, Elsa, can I offer you a glass of one of the finest red wines in the region?"

All agreed and the ice was broken.

"Well Mr. Treschev, uncle Yakov," said Griggory, "we are truly thankful for all that you have done for us, and true to your word, I have had several opportunities to visit my family. And to have paid for my education. How can I ever repay you?"

"Griggory, we didn't pay anything for your education; we invested. Education is never a cost; it's an investment. We invested in you, we invested in your future and the future of this stumbling country. And I assure you, we have invested wisely. Who knows, perhaps someday we will be fortunate enough to have leadership that actually leads! You know," continued Treschev with a impish smile, "I could be sent to one of those rest homes in Siberia for that statement!"

SURGUT

WEDNESDAY, JUNE 18, 1930

He felt uneasy; very uneasy, more than he had ever been in his life, but it had to be done. To wait much longer would be to risk everything up to this point in time: all the work, the people, all would be for naught. It was a long way but he was certain of the information he had acquired and of the information given to him by the very one who had it all along. Miroslav didn't think he was being watched but there had been several inquiries and that made him nervous and fearful and it surely affected those around him and who believed in him. It wasn't a matter of if; it was a matter of when he would release ownership, of the object and it was going to be his when. So, it was necessary to take the next step, albeit a dangerous step and one so long in coming. Fear had been an ever present companion for more than a decade, but now there were higher orders of concern. Soon, he would be boarding the train for the fourteen hundred kilometre journey back to Kazan.

SEVASTOPOL

WEDNESDAY, AUGUST 20, 1930

Yakov had been back from Kazan for more than a week and his desk was still a mountain of "IN" with virtually nothing in the "OUT." Viktor Treschev knocked at his door.

"Come in Viktor," said Yakov.

Treschev took a seat to the left side of Yakov's desk, staring with obvious amusement at the work yet to be done.

"I read your report and I agree with your analysis, Yakov," began Viktor. "I think you're right. Europe is headed for war and it's a virtual certainty that Russia will be involved."

"I hate to say it Viktor," said Yakov, "but that harbour out there will become prime real estate for an aggressor and I doubt that we will remain in business if it happens."

"Not if, Yakov, when," stated Viktor, to which Yakov held his hands open in agreement.

"So you believe we should move the operation as soon as possible to Kazan. Is that correct? And why Kazan?"

"While western Russia has felt the impacts of war before, as has Kazan, it's impact that far east, while significant, has been far less than other centres. Kazan won't provide us access to the Black Sea but staying here won't either... eventually. We can ship some on the Volga but that would be about it. If nothing else, it would provide us some degree of continuity. If we stay here in Sevastopol, it's debatable whether or not we could even survive," concluded Yakov.

Viktor Treschev rose from his chair, walked slowly to the window, placed his hands on its ornately carved frame, and stared at the outside world that had every chance of imploding in on him in the not too distant future. With arms crossed and one hand rubbing his chin, he sat down.

"Okay then. We move the operation. It's going to take some time to relocate; a lot of things and a small army of people. Get whatever staff you need Yakov, lay out the strategy and get back to me as soon as you can," said Treschev, getting up to leave.

"Oh, I almost forgot Viktor," said Yakov. "While I was in Kazan, a gentleman introduced himself, well, kind of."

"What do you mean, 'kind of? Who was he?" inquired Treschev.

"That's just it. He said he didn't want to tell me his name right then but said you would know of him and that it was important that he meet you as soon as possible. It was important, he said," answered Yakov. "He said to say this to you and that you would know; '*Moscow 1925, Yermac Janeskanov.*' That was all he said. Does that mean anything to you?" said Yakov.

Treschev scratched his head, eyes looking upward.

"No. Doesn't ring a bell at all. Very odd, very odd indeed."

Viktor left the office, clearly puzzled, closed the door quietly and made his way back to his own office.

Moments later, Treschev burst into Yakov's office, slamming the door open, rattling everything in the room and scaring the wits out of Yakov and half the people within earshot.

"I know who it is, or was, rather. I know who you were talking to! What an absolutely incredible stroke of luck. Can you believe it Yakov? Wow. You know who it was? Do you know what this means? Well, of course you do. Wow. What a way to start the week"

With a spring in his walk and a smile as wide as the Grand Canyon, Treschev closed the door as noisily as he had opened it and danced toward his office, swinging one of the passing secretaries as he went. Yakov just sat there, uncertain of what he had just witnessed but reasonably sure it was a good thing!

KAZAN

TUESDAY, NOVEMBER 4, 1930

"Are you sure that's him," asked Yakov, pointing to a tall gentleman on the floor below them. The building was alive with activity. It was a large building; not as large as the one in Sevastopol, but large enough. Old as it was, it was determined to be structurally sound. Location was important and the location was perfect with access to both the Volga River and the streets of Kazan. Still, it had been under renovations for a long period of time and soon that task would be complete and the next stage of the strategic plan could be implemented.

"I'm certain," answered Ivan. "He's been here several times but hasn't spoken to anyone that I know of. He just pretends to be one of the crew."

"All right then, let's get the show on the road," replied Yakov. "Is our friend still parked on the street?"

Ivan wandered over to one of the windows that looked out over the busy street paralleling the river.

"Yes he is. But look at this Yakov." He gestured for Yakov to join him at the window.

"Well, well, well. It seems that Kazamin is tailing our friend downstairs but he's being tailed himself. Any idea who it is Ivan?"

"No idea."

With that, they both came away from the window and Ivan proceeded downstairs to join the visitor who, with a clipboard in hand, was pretending to check items off a list as they were being unloaded from a truck.

"Good morning sir. Fine day wouldn't you say?" said Ivan, standing next to him. "There is no need for the charade. We are completely aware of who you are and we are ready to assist you. By the way, my name is Ivan Kozinsky, Yakov's assistant, and I believe you had already met Yakov on an earlier visit."

The gentleman kept his composure and barely gave Ivan more than a glance.

"Unfortunately, we are being watched so just keep doing what you're doing, if you don't mind. Yakov looks forward to meeting with you but not here. There is a taxi parked out front in which I'm certain you will feel quite comfortable," Ivan continued.

With no sign of uneasiness, the two of them strode toward the street and the waiting taxi.

"Good morning Doctor," said the driver as Ivan and his charge seated themselves in the taxi.

The gentleman, mouth wide open and in a mild state of shock, looked at the driver, who had turned around in his seat, then at Ivan who was all smiles.

"Yermac? Yermac Janeskanov? This can't be so. Is it really you?"

"In the flesh, Doctor Oborski. In the flesh. You remembered my name as well. And how have you been sir? It's been what, five years?"

"Well, I don't meet that many Cossacks. Yes, I remember your name. Wonderful to see you. Absolutely wonderful."

With relaxation in the air, Ivan informed Miroslav of the plan; a bit of a circuitous route but necessary to preserve Miroslav's identity and location.

"Is Barkov following us," inquired Ivan.

"Yes," replied Yermac.

"Good. Don't let him lose us."

Yakov watched the parade pass along the street. Yermac and his passengers, Barkov then the third vehicle. Yakov was unable to determine who was in the third automobile as all three disappeared from sight.

Yermac pulled to the curb in front of a small warehouse and Ivan and Miroslav exited the vehicle and entered the building. Barkov also pulled to the curb about a half block back but did not get out. He just kept watching as Ivan and Miroslav enter the building.

Once inside, Ivan went over and spoke with a group of workers but Miroslav walked behind a number large crates, emerging at the other side in a few seconds. Motioning to Miroslav that his business was concluded, the two walked back to the street and re-entered the taxi.

"Everything went smoothly," asked Ivan.

"Yes. Just as planned."

"Yermac, it's time to get out of the parade. You can lose our tail now please," said Ivan.

A thumbs up from Yermac and it only took a few moments for Barkov to be alone with his own tail, known or unknown to him. Near a theatre in the downtown core, the taxi pulled over and a gentleman got out, walked into the theatre and Ivan and Yermac drove off.

"I hope Miroslav will be alright," said Yermac.

"He should be alright," replied Ivan.

"The switch went well. All he has to do is take a taxi to the restaurant, a short walk and everything should be okay. Still, I would really like to know who's tailing Barkov."

There was a quiet, almost imperceptible knock at the door separating the two hotel suites. Yakov opened the door to allow Dr. Oborski entry into his room.

"You had no problems, Doctor?" asked Yakov.

"No. None at all. I did just as you suggested and took a taxi to the restaurant down the street from this hotel, went in, waited for a crowd to fill the establishment, slipped out the back entrance and walked to the back of the hotel and here I am."

"Barkov may still figure out where you went. He certainly realizes that it is critical that you and I meet. It's probably only a matter of time before he realizes you're in the room next door."

"It really doesn't matter Yakov. I won't be staying any longer than it will take to conclude our business, tonight I hope."

"But are you not coming back to Sevastopol with us? Mr. Treschev will be most disappointed. He's certainly looking forward to meeting you."

"I appreciate all you and the Foundation have done for me over the years, and perhaps we shall meet again someday. But for now, at my age, I think it best that I stay with my friends in the east. They need me, if for no other reason than moral support during these difficult times. To that end, I will be leaving tomorrow morning. So, shall we get down to business, as it were" concluded Miroslav.

Handing Yakov a file folder, thick to capacity with notes and drawings and a short length of lead pipe. Miroslav certified it to be the real one.

"As you may have guessed," began Miroslav, "I left the group at Mutoray after our rescue and went back to Joakim's home, or what was left of it at that time. I was concerned that Slava or Kazamin would figure out where the object was and did not want to risk it getting into their hands. Joakim told me where the object was buried so it didn't take long to find it. I knew about the relationship between Joakim and his neighbours and that took a bit of time to explain my presence. I have had it ever since. My notes will explain the tests I carried out and what was concluded from them."

SEVASTOPOL

MONDAY, MARCH 30, 1931

He had been away for several months and, as usual, the "IN" box was piled high. But this time, there was a difference. It was business as usual but the building was considerably less crowded as the various phases of the strategic plan were implemented. Sitting on Yakov's desk was a short length of well worn lead pipe, sealed at both ends.

"There it is," he said, as Viktor Treschev entered his office. "That's what all the fuss was about. I'm not sure if I am to be amazed or not. Outwardly, It's just a piece of grey pipe. Lead, you say?"

"Yep. A piece of lead pipe. But it's been a while since so much interest has been generated by something as innocent as a piece of lead pipe," explained Yakov. "Miroslav said not to open it. Apparently not that it's dangerous but, according to him, it releases some form of energy that we don't yet understand; nothing dangerous so far as he was able to learn, but it just attracts a lot of attention. What do you think we should do with it?"

"Good question, Yakov. Wish I had a good answer. Let's look at this objectively. Fact one: this… thing isn't Dr. Oborski's. Fact of the matter is, we don't know who it belongs to. And it sure isn't Barkov's' either, or ours for that matter. Fact two: we have only a rudimentary idea what's inside the pipe, other than descriptions from those who have seen it and Dr. Oborski's notes, so we're far from certain of its purpose although he did determine a number of very interesting properties and possibly a technology that we have yet to discover.

Fact three: a number of very nasty people want it and feel it has great monetary value, a commodity of some kind, possibly military applications, I don't know. Fact four: Russia is not the place for it, at least for the time being or at least until we find out just what it is. Agreed?"

Yakov, rubbing his chin and staring at Viktor.

"So Viktor, you're suggesting that we have to get it out of Russia until the future becomes more settled and keep it out of the hands of people like Barkov? Is that correct?"

"Yes." replied Treschev.

"I agree Viktor, but where do we send it and how?" asked Yakov.

"I've been thinking about that, a lot. I think we should send it to Canada."

There was a long pause. Yakov just stared at Viktor but didn't question his rationale. He knew better.

"So... how do we do that? I don't think we can put it in the mail and send it addressed to *Canada*", Yakov said with a bit of a sarcastic smile.

"Not exactly, my acerbic friend. Very cute, by the way," said Treschev. "No, we can't send it to any government office. We know too little of their philosophy. But let's suppose we could find an ordinary Canadian that would, shall we say, retain it for us until we can find its owner or decide what to do with it."

"You know Viktor, you old fox, I have a feeling that I'm coming into a motion picture at the half way point. You've got this all planned out. Am I right?"

"Something like that. I assume Griggory is rested from his trip to Sevastopol. It was unfortunate that he had to leave his new bride behind but I'm certain that, very soon, they will be re-united. Kazan is a pleasant place anyhow so I'm sure she will be fine."

SEVASTOPOL

WEDNESDAY, APRIL 26, 1933

It was warm in Sevastopol, a welcome relief from the cool to cold weather in Moscow and it was dry. The pleasantness belied the heating up that was taking place in western Europe, a situation that Viktor felt would soon spill over into Russia. There had been numerous trips back and forth between Sevastopol and Kazan and both Viktor and Yakov were getting weary from the task of relocation. But, the move to Kazan was almost complete and it was now just a matter of tidying up loose ends, not the least of which was the somewhat troublesome piece of lead pipe.

Barkov or one of his lackeys, were constant companions of Yakov, Ivan and Viktor, no matter where they went. It didn't bother any of them all that much. Their lack of familiarity with the region, especially the city itself, coupled with their total incompetence, made them easy to lose, although, they wondered, it must have been frustrating for whoever was tailing Barkov. Only once did Barkov's' surveillance auto try to follow Yakov. Although somewhat more persistent, the tail was soon lost. But the message was sent to both; they had been spotted.

Viktor and Yakov met for lunch in a quiet bistro not far from the harbour, the Ukrainsky Shinokey, a favourite of Treschev. While both recognized that discussing business in a public setting was perhaps, not highly recommended, the owner provided them with a private area, secure from prying ears. Besides, it was good to get away from time to time, especially from the ever present noise. It would be unlikely that the surveillance 'teams' would be able to track them down until it was too late.

"I think I have it figured out," began Viktor. "There's a ship in port right now." He pointed in the general direction of its berth. "It's been here for a couple of weeks; Canadian Merchant Marine Service; '*The Lisieu*'. It sails for Halifax on the east coast of Canada next month sometime. I understand that there are a number of mechanical problems that need attention. Anyway, I've done a bit of digging and there's a crew member, a Norman MacLeod, who will be leaving the Service after the return voyage. Apparently his father is quite ill and he's leaving the Merchant Marine Service to take care of him. Just the kind of person we need, wouldn't you say Yakov?"

Yakov was totally amazed.

"You did bit of… *digging* and you found all this out since we returned from Kazan?"

"Yes, pretty much. We are in the information business, are we not?"

Without any attempt to hide an amused laugh, Yakov said "Okay. So now what? And if we do pull this off, how do we ever find this Norman MacLeod person in Canada when the time comes? And how do we… persuade him that we are not total lunatics and to take a piece of lead pipe to Canada and not open it? And how do we do all this without raising the suspicion of Barkov or the authorities?"

"Questions, questions, questions. Don't get your knickers in a twist Yakov, as the British say. We'll figure it out. However, there is one… hmmm… minor problem we will have to address; MacLeod doesn't speak a word of Russian and you, me and Ivan are anything but fluent in English."

"That's quite a *minor* problem!" said Yakov.

"Yes… and no. That's why I had Griggory come to Sevastopol. He's completely fluent in English. It won't put him in any danger so there's nothing to be concerned about in that sense but I haven't discussed it with him. I leave that to you. How is your пέрвое?"

MARIA NIKIFORNOVA CAFE, SEVASTOPOL

TUESDAY, MAY 3, 1933

The old coffee house, situated near the corner of Sevastopol Street and H19, was ideal. It's large, although less than pristine windows that probably hadn't seen a squeegee since the Bolshevik Revolution, offered a straight line view of the harbour guard house on the opposite side of the wide thoroughfare.

The café was showing its age. Built around the turn of the century and renamed several times since, it's low, wooden beamed ceiling assured that every puff of cigarette smoke was safely archived within the structure. Although the walls were almost completely covered with photos, mostly of military figures and engagements dating back to the Siege of Sevastopol, they drew little attention from patrons representing seafarers from every corner of the globe. To date, the café had successfully eluded a listing as a 'Must See' tourist destination in the Crimea. It was perfect!

It had been determined that MacLeod frequented the café when not on watch and that, on this day, he would probably go to the café around lunch time. On a pre-arranged hand signal from the Guard, MacLeod would be identified. Griggory, seated facing the window, saw the signal first, poking Yakov to look for himself.

He strode away from the Guardhouse, walked up the street, passing a number of decaying, mostly abandoned shops, taking no notice whatsoever of a dark figure standing in the shadows of one of the doorways. Then crossed the street in a game of dodge-ball with the mix of traffic. He was average height, stocky build (although slightly heavy), black hair under a hat with the ships name embroidered on the front, but not in uniform. He came straight to the café, entered, looked around and spotted Griggory and Yakov who stood out from the crowd like two ostriches in a chicken coop.

Griggory got up, went over to him, asked if he was Norman MacLeod (and he said he was but expressed no apparent surprise by the query). Griggory introduced himself and invited him to join Yakov at the table. After introducing Yakov as his uncle (Yakov did his best to respond in English), Griggory went about the somewhat lengthy explanation for the meeting. He basically stated that the Foundation wanted to express its gratitude to the Canadian Merchant Marine Service for honoring their port and the Canadian people for their support in assisting the Ukrainians in Canada to become an established society and that a gift to a crew member of the Canadian vessel seemed appropriate.

As flimsy as the rationale was, MacLeod expressed no concern with it and gratefully accepted the gift of a small ornately hand carved jewellery box. Both Yakov and Griggory were more than pleased with how smoothly the meeting went although Griggory was clearly less comfortable with the proceedings. Still, he saw no reason for the discomfort and wrote it off to unfamiliarity with Canadian traditions.

After a short discussion, during which MacLeod confirmed that he was leaving the Service to tend to his father on the farm in New Brunswick, MacLeod thanked both Griggory and Yakov for the gift. He indicated that it would be highly treasured; shook hands with the two Russians and left the café with the box tucked under one arm. He crossed the street and started walking toward the guardhouse.

"Uncle Yakov, I think you had better come and see this," said Griggory.

To their unbelieving eyes, MacLeod didn't go back to the guard house, but stood near the curb across the street. A black sedan pulled up and MacLeod handed the box to the driver who handed him an envelope, then drove off, into street traffic. MacLeod walked quickly toward the guard house. Before Griggory could even begin to comprehend what was happening, Yakov flew from his chair, sending it into a half gainer that barely missed taking out a window. Faster than a cheetah going after a noon time snack, bolted out the door and into the street full of automobiles, small trucks and horse drawn carts to the yells of those bowled over by this unstoppable hulk.

Unnoticed by MacLeod who had just entered the guard house, Yakov went straight for the auto, still trying to get into traffic. Yakov was too late to stop the driver but not too late to identify him; Kazamin Barkov. It was only then that the magnitude of his mistake struck home. He had just been a participant in handing Barkov the very thing he and others had been trying so desperately to keep from him and there was nothing he could do about it!

Macleod emerged from the guard house, saw what was going on, and high tailed it like a scalded cat in the opposite direction, down Sevastopol Street. Yakov saw nothing to be gained from chasing him down. The irrevocable damage was done.

To the stunned amazement of both Yakov and Griggory, who were now standing next to the curb in front of the café, the black sedan came back toward the café. Slowing to a near stop, drivers window down, box in hand, Kazamin blew a kiss then sped off in a cloud of blue-black smoke, up the hill and out of sight, his bellowing laughter almost drowned out by the whine of the transmission and misfiring of the tired, old engine.

FOUNDATION HEADQUARTERS, SEVASTOPOL

WEDNESDAY, MAY 4, 1933

At this point in his life, especially after the fiasco of yesterday, Yakov wasn't sure whether he was comfortably crazy or sane with uncertainties and doubts. Yet, only sane people admit they are crazy! The events of the day before played like re-runs. He couldn't be sure if he was starting down the denial path or just being selective about the realities he was prepared to accept.

After a long hour of reflection, he recalled what Griggory had said to him several months back when the move to Kazan was getting more than he felt he could handle. He remembered that it was a quote from Anton Chekhov.

"My business is to be talented, that is, to be capable of selecting the important moments from the trivial ones."

There was knock at the door to his office.

"Come in", said Yakov.

The man was average height, wearing a wide brimmed hat that hid his dark, steely eyes. He was dressed in a long coat that came almost to the floor and he slowly made his way to a chair in front of Yakov's desk, removing his hat.

Yakov looked up at his visitor. For a second he wasn't sure but soon realized that they had met before.

"I recognize you. You're the one that wanted to kill me, my brother and Ivan that night at the campsite. So what is it now? Didn't steal enough? I hate to tell you but you're too late this time! Your boss has it now and that's the truth."

"I know that. I saw it all yesterday. Only thing is though, I no longer am in his employ. He doesn't know I'm in Sevastopol or that I'm even alive, for that matter."

He had Yakov's attention but Yakov wasn't sure why because none of this was making any sense.

"Just what are you talking about?" demanded Yakov, now standing with both hands firmly planted on the desk top and a look of pure anger in his eyes and on his rapidly reddening face. None of which seemed to have any influence on the demeanor of his visitor. "You were the one who threatened us with a rifle, took the object, or at least we thought it was the object, shot our plane down, and now you come here! Are you totally insane or just incredibly malicious?"

Yakov returned to his chair, leaned back and folded his arms across his chest, still shaking from the encounter.

The visitor said nothing for what seemed to Yakov to be an eternity, maintaining a completely emotionless, poker-faced expression, all the while looking into Yakov's furious eyes and without a single blink.

"My name is Pavel Nishnokeyov," he began in a voice that dripped with self assurance and calm. "You're correct in that I was in the employ of Kazamin Barkov for a period of time, as his personal pilot and bodyguard. Unfortunately for me, Comrade Barkov has… umm… shall we say, a limited sense of loyalty. He sees it as a one way street. But, I'm sure this is not news to you."

It wasn't!

"So, you come here with the idea of what. Switching loyalties? Thanks but no thanks Nishnokeyov," responded Yakov with an equally assured comportment.

"No, of course not. I saw what took place yesterday and I'm here to get that object back."

Yakov leaned over his desk and simply gazed at Pavel with a look that said, *are you nuts?*

"Let me get this straight. First you try and kill us, twice that is. Then, you stand by and do nothing while Kazamin gets away with the box and now you want to be declared a Saint! A knight in shining armor! One of us is crazy, my friend, and I'll give you a hint - it 'ain't me!" concluded Yakov with a shake of his head.

Pavel remained stone cold emotionless.

"Kazamin deserted me. Left me for dead after I had been shot and we landed just ask I passed out. I don't have any love for the man. No more than you do. I won't rest until he pays."

Yakov tapped his fingers on the desk and retained his stare at Pavel.

"What do you want of us? We can get the box back ourselves. What makes you think we need you?"

"And just how do you plan to do that? Do you know he leaves for Moscow tomorrow morning? So what are you going to do? An armed assault on his hotel room? Perhaps a kidnapping on the way to the train station? That's very much in style these days anyway and I doubt it would raise too many eyebrows. Or perhaps a nice neat assassination and a robbery? Same thing; communal blindness! But these tactics aren't your style, are they? That only leaves going up to him and asking him to turn it over," Pavel said, ending his comments in distinct mockery.

Another long pause, Yakov rubbing his chin and forefinger up and down over his mouth.

"So then I take it you have a plan or else you wouldn't be here."

"I just told you, I will go up to him and ask that he turn the box over to me. It's that simple, comrade."

"Yeah, I'm sure and I'm also sure there's more to it than that and, frankly, I don't want to know. And if we decide to, shall we say, engage your services, what do you want? You don't strike me as an experienced volunteer."

That drew something that closely resembled a smile from Pavel.

"Simple. I want my freedom. You know that I'm a wanted man. Apparently the Russian military were not very happy about the plane we blew up and I guess a building or so got demolished along the way," said Pavel. "I escaped from the hospital. I have friends that took me in until the wound healed, but agents are still searching for me. I want the search to stop and the charges dropped and your organization can do that. Do that for me and I guarantee, I will get the object for you before Kazamin's train gets to Simferopol."

BETWEEN SEVASTOPOL AND SIMFEROPOL

FRIDAY, MAY 5, 1933

Blazing along the tracks at a mind numbing sixty kilometres per hour, the cars swayed back and forth in an unceasing rhythm of sound and motion that required some degree of seamanship to successfully navigate from one car to the next.

He knocked at the compartment door. The train had left the station more or less on time (mostly less) and was about half way between Sevastopol and Bakhchisaray.

"What is it," demanded the voice from inside.

"Tickets, Comrade. I need to inspect your papers and punch your ticket," was the response.

After some shuffling around, the door slid open in an anger driven slam. Kazamin was instantly paralyzed by the speaker but more so by the feel of the cold steel barrel of a TT-33 pistol rammed tightly against his forehead. Kazamin's ticket fluttered silently to the floor.

"You! I thought you were… " Kazamin didn't get to finish.

"Yes Comrade; back from the dead. And they said no one ever comes back! Keep those hands where I can see them unless you want to become a notice in tomorrow's newspaper."

He pushed Kazamin back into the small compartment and, with his free hand, slid the door closed and latched it.

"Now Comrade, here's what you're going to do," taking two pair of handcuffs from the pocket of his long coat and with the gun still pressed tightly to Kazamin's forehead, shoved him down onto the floor next to the bed. "Before we talk about old times, let's get comfortable. I don't want you to be distracted by violent thoughts so grab the leg of the bed with both hands... NOW."

Kazamin did so. Pavel cuffed his wrists with the chain wrapped around the leg of the bed and then proceeded to cuff his ankles. Bending over Kazamin, Pavel removed the pistol from Kazamin's shoulder holster, a small gun from his right boot and a nasty knife with a keen serrated edge from the other boot.

"You know Comrade, you're a real creature of habit." Spotting the ornate box on a small table next to the bed, Pavel added, "So this is what all the fuss is about."

"Listen Pavel, I have the connections. You and I can make a lot of money with that box," pleaded Kazamin.

"Gee, you think so? Now you listen to me you pompous moron. If there are people other than you looking for this thing, then anyone who has it in their possession can profit from it. So why would I need the likes of you?"

"Perhaps, but I'm not wanted by the entire Red Army and you are. Therein, my friend, lies the difference."

"Perhaps Kazamin I neglected to mention a couple of things. First of all, I am not your friend and secondly, I am no longer a wanted man, thanks to a deal I cooked up while vacationing in Sevastopol. Thirdly, although your name wasn't mentioned in that trouble we got into, I can soon rectify that. Fourthly, I don't know if you're aware of it, but there have been a couple of heavy weights tailing you since you left Moscow. Why do you think that they are watching your every move? You've become careless Comrade, very careless and it's costing you."

Pavel sat down on the only chair in the close quarters of the compartment, flipped the box over and with Kazamin's knife, pried open the bottom panel of the box, removing the chunk of lead pipe.

"This is really what it's all about Comrade, isn't it?"

"Pavel, listen to me," said Kazamin. "It's not too late. I know now I was wrong to leave you after we landed. I was wrong, but I thought you were dead, and that's the truth. So put the pipe back, let me loose and we can talk a deal that will be great for both of us. What do you say, old friend?"

Pavel put the bottom of the box in place, slid the knife into his right boot and the small gun into his left boot and the TT-33 into his shoulder holster. He walked over to

Kazamin who was sweating profusely and looked on in dread that bordered on panic, fully believing that with the knife or the gun, he would be dead within a few seconds. Pavel reached into Kazamin's valise, withdrew a pair of socks and rammed them into Kazamin's mouth, all of which heightened Kazamin's terror. But, nothing happened, much to Kazamin's relief.

"I'm not going to kill you Comrade. I should and it wouldn't bother me much to do it, but that's not the purpose of this visit. I have what I came after. Partnership? You have to be kidding! I've been Satan's partner so never again."

With that, and the box in tow, Pavel got up, unlatched the door, stepped outside and closed the door on a relieved but very angry Kazamin. Pavel started down the passage between the compartments and the windows of the car. Noticing that he was being approached by a man easily twice his size, he did a 180 only to see a clone coming from the opposite direction. Pavel was well armed but had to choose his time, but he was too late. Both goons were also armed and with guns drawn, pinned Pavel between them. With a gun pressed tight to his ribs, one of the goons frisked Pavel and removed the holstered TT-33.

"The box please Comrade," he said.

Pavel didn't resist and handed it to him.

"Thank you for doing our job for us." He turned to the other goon and said, "I told you all we had to do was wait."

Both turned and walked away. With an enormous sigh of relief he was certain they could hear, Pavel went in the other direction, laughing and complimenting himself on his shrewdness.

Seated next to the window, Pavel watched with obvious glee at the passing panorama, more than just pleased, not only with the events of the day but with his stellar performance.

Everything went exactly as planned and Pavel, my boy, you're a free man and a rich one at that, thinking to himself.

The train pulled into Simferopol behind schedule, of course. But Pavel didn't care. He looked out the window but there was no sign of Yakov.

Good, he thought. *Perhaps they are late as well. It's only a short stop then on to Moscow.*

After about thirty minutes, Pavel knew that the train would be leaving shortly.

"Papers and tickets please," came the voice behind him.

Without thinking, Pavel handed the items back and to his right.

"Going to Moscow Comrade," asked the voice.

"Yes. How soon does the train leave," Pavel asked.

"Well Comrade, the train leaves in about five minutes, but you won't be on it!"

Pavel looked back. At first he didn't recognize him but after a few seconds the fog lifted and his face sunk like a lead balloon, taking with it all his dreams of fame and fortune.

"It's you. Where did you come from," he asked.

"Right here. I got on the train in Sevastopol", said Ivan. "You see Pavel, that whole story about bad guy turned good guy was just too much for us to swallow. You've been too long with Kazamin and his slimy crew. But still, we also realized that we could use you to get the object back. And by the way, if it's any consolation, you performed brilliantly. Now before you get any fancy ideas, I want you to remove the gun from your holster with two fingers and hand it to me. By the way, I have one pointed directly at your guts."

"I don't have it any more. Two baboons took it off me after I left Kazamin's compartment."

Ivan checked to make sure.

"Now I know that Kazamin always carried a gun in one of his boots and I suspect that as his bodyguard, you taught him that trick. So dig it out, two fingers, slowly."

Pavel did as he was told. Ivan caught sight of a handle protruding from the top of Pavel's right boot and demanded that be removed in the same manner.

After stashing the arsenal in his own coat, Ivan stood up and told Pavel to do the same and walk to the door at the back of the car. On the station platform, joined by Yakov and Griggory, the final indignity came for Pavel. Ivan reached into the right pocket of Pavel's coat and retrieved the lead pipe and handed it to Griggory just as the train pulled away on its journey to Moscow.

Pavel watched its departure with trepidation.

"You could have at least let me board the train and continue the trip," said Pavel. "But then again, I suppose I'm still a wanted man."

"No you're not, Pavel," answered Yakov. "Unlike your intent, we kept our part of the bargain. The kidnapping of the pilot and his plane and the destruction of the military plane and building never took place. And as far as re-boarding the train, think about that for a moment. Kazamin is not a very happy man right now and, very soon, the two heavy weights are going to be even less happy. The train may not be a good place for you."

Pavel thought on the comment for a moment.

"I don't have that object nor do the others but I'm alive and plan to stay that way. You know, this whole thing has been about money. Anytime an organization or a government gets involved in just about anything, it's always about money. You three may think you're doing this out of some noble aspiration, but I guarantee you, at the end of the day, it will be about money."

Pavel gave a true military salute, turned and walked in the direction of town.

FOUNDATION HEADQUARTERS, SEVASTOPOL

TUESDAY, MAY 16, 1933

"Come on in gentlemen," said Viktor Treschev, pointing to the chairs on his right and left at the board room table. He picked up the lead pipe with both hands and rolled it around and around. "Well, we have it back again and you three made it back safe and sound, so it's a good day, wouldn't you say?"

"It is Viktor," replied Yakov, "but we were doing some analyses on the way back to Sevastopol and you realize as well as we that our performance to date in all of this has been less than spectacular. In fact, had it not been for Ivan's foresight here," pointing to Ivan who was seated across the table from him next to Griggory, "we wouldn't have that object even now. It was Ivan who cautioned that we were dealing with a crook."

Treschev gently placed the pipe on the table and looked over the glasses low on his nose.

"You're absolutely right Yakov and I assure you, all of you, that I'm also part of the lack luster group. In my position and having had to deal with Barkov and others like him over the years, I should have made sure you were better prepared. That said, where do we go from here?"

"Should we send the object to Canada," asked Griggory. "Barkov obviously knows about MacLeod and will be expecting that the item will be delivered to him somehow or other."

"Well, the alternative is to keep the object," responded Yakov. "But the problem I see with that is that Barkov may not realize that it hasn't left Russia. And even if we put the word out that it has left Russia, he may see that as a decoy or a ploy and go after MacLeod anyway," concluded Yakov.

"How would he be able to go after MacLeod? He's being watched by, what's his name in Moscow; the boss of those two monkeys I saw on the train," asked Ivan.

"Novikoff. Maxim Novikoff," responded Treschev.

"Right, Novikoff," said Ivan. "By the time the train arrives in Moscow, Novikoff and his cronies will be ready to nab him."

"There's nothing stupid about Barkov. If I were in his shoes, I would find some way to leave the train before it arrived in Moscow. It's true, Novikoff will leave no stone unturned to get to him and he probably will at some point but Barkov is still a player," said Yakov.

"The question is still open gentlemen – should we send the object to Canada with MacLeod if he agrees to accept our gift? I admit that I made a huge error in judgment by discussing this at our dinner in the restaurant. I should have known that Barkov's tentacles are everywhere. I may have put our Canadian friend in some danger so it's up to us to do everything we can to protect him," ended Treschev.

"I think we should go ahead with the original plan. One way or the other, Barkov will find a way of going at MacLeod whether he actually has the object or not. What we will have to do is keep extremely close tabs on Barkov in the meanwhile, extremely close," said Yakov.

"Do we all agree," asked Treschev.

All agreed.

"All right then. By the way, the guard at the docks was on Barkov's payroll. I have seen to it that he's decided to take early retirement and has been replaced with someone more friendlily to our cause. The guard apparently got a message to the real MacLeod that the ship's Captain wanted to see him at his hotel in the city and MacLeod left around 11 AM. The fake MacLeod was just an English speaking actor that Barkov hired for the day. I will get word to MacLeod and try and arrange a meeting at the Café. I know that Barkov's spies will undoubtedly see us but they probably would no matter where we met. I'm sure that MacLeod is being watched.

NORTH TAY, NEW BRUNSWICK, CANADA

FRIDAY, AUGUST 9, 1935

Norman loved the place. Left to him by his father who had passed away shortly after Norman's return from Merchant Marine Service, the farm and the farm house had seen better days. Built around 1865, it hadn't seen much by way of repairs or even modernization for a good many years. Yet, it was home; it felt comfortable and even smelled comfortable. Never married (he didn't think any self-respecting woman would take to his ram shackled farm and semi-recluse life style) Norman lived there alone with Sport, his old Collie dog (whose bark was far worse than his bite since he was at that stage of life when food had to be "gummed"), a few chickens, a rooster with an attitude, some milk cows, a few pigs and two horses. Life for Norman consisted of putting in a few crops (mostly oats, grain corn, a crop of hay and some potatoes and turnips), milking his cows and living in the old farmhouse, largely in the kitchen and adjacent bedroom. Norman's culinary skills, while not legendary, were at least adequate.

The place didn't have central heating. Just a big old wood stove in the kitchen with the traditional wood box next to it, and some ceiling vents to allow heat to the second floor. Not that he spent much time up there but at least he had room if and when guests came to visit which wasn't often but when they did come, the door was never locked (the lock was busted anyway and the key had long since gone missing). But the kitchen was the focal point of his life – the pantry, a couple of shotguns and an old Winchester 30.30, a cream separator, the table and the traditional cot that provided most of the 'comfortable' smell to the kitchen.

With the exception of a buried copper line that ran from the barnyard puncheon to the kitchen, the house had no plumbing or indoor "facilities" (use of the latter required a stroll of some two hundred meters, out behind the chicken house, and so bladder control was a must, especially during the long, cold winter months, something that Norman had mastered during the long watch hours at sea).

A few years ago, he brought electricity to the old house, not so much as a convenience for himself (although the electric radio was far better than the old battery operated one for listening to Foster Hewitt every Saturday night – "Hello Canada and hockey fans in the United Sates and Newfoundland"). Norman also enjoyed that fact that electricity now powered the motorized cream separator and he was able to replace the old ice-box with a small fridge.

Most of Norman's visitors were transient farm workers (who usually came in sometime during the night and plopped themselves down onto the cot for the night), as well as foxes and coyotes hoping for a free chicken dinner (Norman generally discouraged these guests with the help of the 12 gauge).

But to Norman, the farm was more than just a tired old house with a wood shed and an attic overhead, and a well house out next to the road to keep the milk cans cold (and provide a home to an interesting collection of amphibious lizards). It was punctuated with small fields and a bunch of nasty looking apple trees that hadn't been pruned since, well, in a long time… a very long time. It was home and that's where his heart was.

From the shed door or the dining room window, he could look out across the valley to the village of Northton where his mother was born, and east, down the road to the Williams farm (where he knew Clayton Williams, his best friend, was fighting a losing battle with TB and was having a lot of trouble coming to grips with the inevitable).

Then beyond that was Taitsville, about eight kilometres distant. Looking west, across the fields, one could see the Healey place which was perhaps one of the better farms in the area, and the Tay River, which was one of the best swimming holes that Norman cherished so in his younger days.

It wasn't with total surprise that Norman saw a car pull into the farmyard this afternoon in August while he was splitting wood and chucking it into the woodshed at the side of the house. Cars were getting to be more plentiful, even in Norman's neck of the woods. The car was new. A '35 Chevy Coupe he guessed; black and *shiny as all get out* he thought to himself.

The lone occupant, wearing a black suit and black shoes, made his way with considerable care past the chickens and the less-than-friendly rooster, to the woodshed extending his, right hand and with a toothy grin.

"I'm looking for Mr. Norman MacLeod sir. Might that be you?" said the suit.

Norman tended to be a quick judge of character but he wasn't sure about this guy.

It wouldn't cost nothin' t'be courteous, thought Norman. *If'n I don't owe you money, it would be me and if'n he does, Norman's gone to town and won't be back 'till winter!*

"How can I help you," replied Norman.

"Well Mr. MacLeod", said the suit, "you're a very difficult man to find. By the way, my name is Arnold Wilsey and, to come straight to the point, I represent a client who is very interested in paying you a considerable sum of money for your, eh… farm property."

Norman was stunned and looked it! No one had ever expressed even the slightest degree of interest in this place as far as he knew and that raised a red flag in his mind.

Why now? he thought.

"Perhaps we should retire to the house, Mr. MacLeod, so I can present the offer in detail," Wilsey suggested and off they walked, Norman lead the way in total silence while his brain spun like a top with a thousand "why's".

Sport raised his head as they entered the shed, opened both eyes, but decided it was too hot to get up and pretend to do the watch dog routine.

The kitchen table was both long and wide with legs that could take the weight of an elephant, a remnant of days gone by and large family gatherings. Mr. Wilsey was immediately struck by the cleanliness of the kitchen which was somewhat of a contrast from his trip through the barnyard.

"Plant yourself there Mr. Wilsey", said Norman, pointing to one of the chairs at the table, "while I wash up. Pour yourself a cup 'a coffee?"

Norman began scooping a pot of water from the tank connected to the old wood stove.

"No coffee for me, Mr. MacLeod," replied Wilsey, then continued. "I believe you can understand that I must first verify that you are the correct Norman MacLeod."

"The correct Norman MacLeod? How many can there be in this neck of the woods? Anyway, shoot," replied Norman.

"Well, your middle name is Stewart? Is that correct, Mr. MacLeod" asked Wilsey.

"Yep, same as my father; late father, that is," replied Norman.

"I understand you were in the Navy, is that correct? And that you served on the, now let me see… The Acadia, is that correct?" asked

Wilsey.

"Close", responded Norman, "but no cigar. I was in the Merchant Marines and the last ship I served on was the Lisieu, not The Acadia. But what's that got to do with anything?"

"In good time Mr. MacLeod. I must first make the proper verification… Ah yes. The Lisieu; quite so. My mistake" said Wilsey.

Red flags flew all over Norman's brain now. One thing was however certain, he was quickly gaining, not so much a dislike, but a feeling of distrust for Mr. Wilsey.

There's something fishy going on here, but what? he was thinking. *If this guy was able to dig up my history, it shouldn't have been all that difficult to find out which ship I served on or where I live unless he was just testing me.*

"Mr. MacLeod, I understand you visited Sevastopol, Russia from time to time while in the Merchant Marines. Is that also correct?" said Wilsey.

"Yeah, a couple of times. Why?" queried Norman.

"Oh, nothing in particular. Just an interesting place I imagine. Did you get to see much of Sevastopol?" asked Wilsey.

"Not much, the usual places: bars, restaurants, a hotel. That's pretty much it." responded Norman.

Norman was getting a very uncomfortable feeling about Wilsey by this time and hoped that this 3rd degree session would soon end or he would end it!

"Satisfied, Mr. Wilsey?" asked Norman.

"Yes, quite satisfied," replied Wilsey. "Now, about the offer. My client is prepared to offer you $15,000 cash for this property including land and buildings plus an additional $5,000 cash for everything in the house and buildings. But you must not remove anything and this offer will only be made this one time, Mr. MacLeod and you must inform me of your decision by Friday before 5 P.M. Is that clear, Mr. MacLeod?"

Normans felt as stunned by the offer as he looked.

Why would anyone in their right mind give me $20,000 for this place? There's no plumbing, minimal electricity, the veranda is close to falling off, the roof needs fixing and the windows leak air like a sieve. This makes no sense at all, he thought.

"Yeah. It's clear alright, Mr. Wilsey. $20,000? Is that what you are offering?" asked Norman.

"For the land, buildings and all contents, yes, $20,000. Generous offer, wouldn't you say Mr. MacLeod?" replied Wilsey.

"Well, perhaps it is. I don't know. But who is your client, anyway? And why this place? It's old and in need of a lot of repair and, as a farm, if you've done your homework, 'ya know it ain't that great as farms go these days," said Norman.

"I'm sorry Mr. MacLeod, I'm not at liberty to disclose the name of the interested client at this time", responded Wilsey.

"You know something, Mr. Wilsey, you may not be at liberty, as you say, to tell me very much of anything, but I'm at liberty to tell you this. You spent, I don't know how much time, lookin' for me. You drive up here, all this way, you ask me a few questions 'bout who I am and even fewer 'bout the farm but a whole bunch of questions about my time in the Merchant Marine Service then make this offer of some money. To be honest, the whole thing doesn't pass the smell test!" said Norman. "You know, I don't drive a very fancy car, just that old beat-up second hand Ford truck in the yard, and I don't even own a fancy suit and, yes, I was born at night; it just wasn't last night! Here's the problem; you and I know that this place, as a farm, ain't worth too much, 'specially when you look at some of the other farms in the North Tay area. Now unless your client thinks there's gold in the ground here 'bouts, I really don't understand why your client wants this place. So... why does he want this place? If you can answer that question for me, then maybe we can talk some more."

"Mr. MacLeod, perhaps my client can be, shall we say, a bit more flexible in his offer, but I can assure you that my client has only honorable intentions and... " Wilsey stammered.

"You ain't gonna answer the question, are you Wilsey", said Norman, cutting Wilsey off in mid sentence and without saying another word, Norman rose from his chair and made it clear that his next stop was to visit the shotgun. "Mr. Wilsey, I got no axe t'a grind with you and I'm certain that your client gave you some pretty strong marchin' orders, but unless you and that client of yours are ready to answer some pretty simple questions, your offer ain't worth a pound of fly dung, deadline or no deadline. Got the point?"

Wilsey quickly got the point. At almost the speed of a bullet, Wilsey grabbed his papers, stuffed them unceremoniously into his leather brief case and was out of the kitchen, tripped over Sport and out the shed door and into the Chevy. Seconds later, Norman got his wish; all he could see was a plume of dust and small stones as Wilsey's car ripped up the gravel, out of the short driveway, left down the gravel road and headed in the direction of Taitsville.

Norman watched from the shed door with mixed feelings as Wilsey's dust covered car disappeared over the hill.

Had I done the right thing or did I get too caught up in the session with Wilsey? Oh well, thought Norman, *What's done is done and I ain't about to go after him with my hat in my hand. Still, there was really something about the whole thing that just didn't set right.*

What disturbed Norman as much as anything else about Wilsey's was his mention of his trips to Russia.

Sevastopol? wondered Norman, *why Sevastopol? We were talking about my farm or I thought we were anyway besides, nothin' happened in Russia, 'cept I darn near cooked in the heat and went on a fool's errand for the Captain on the last trip. So what? There was them Russian guys at the cafe… a Yakov something or other and another guy… an Engineer or something… Greg was it? Something like that. Anyway they gave me a jewellery box.*

Glancing up at the shelf over the table.

Right! I need that thing real bad! First a bunch of crazy Russians and now, Wilsey. Should'a stayed at sea. I'll worry 'bout it later.

He then headed off through the barnyard and toward the distant fields to herd in his half dozen milk cows.

NORTH TAY

SATURDAY, AUGUST 10, 1935

Norman got up early on Saturdays to make sure he met the milk truck. It was no problem getting up on time. He hadn't slept much anyway, mauling over the pros and cons of his actions earlier in the week. Retrieving the cans from the well house next to the road, the milk truck arrived, emptied the cans, gave Norman his receipt and drove off to the next stop. Back in the kitchen, Norman thoroughly washed and rinsed the cans yet his mind was still pre-occupied with the events. Breakfast was pretty much routine: either a couple of fried eggs or a dish of porridge and milk. The fridge looked a little more bare than he thought it should be and he was getting low on bread and butter as well although he had just been to Tait's Store a few days ago.

Norman wasn't sure what to think and less sure what to do.

Maybe I should just forget about it and let it be. The offers probably dead anyway, he thought to himself.

Finally, he couldn't stand it any longer. He knew he had to tell someone and perhaps even get some advice. It was a short drive – out the driveway, left and down the hill, left again at the old one-room school house (where Norman regretted not paying more attention while he had the chance all those years ago), and on to Byron Healey's farm, a good friend and neighbour of Norman's. It was a large, rambling house that had had a couple of additions added over the years and in much better shape than Norman's place.

Doris was in the kitchen, cooking up a storm as usual and the smells made Norman's mouth water. There were rolls and bread cooling on the counter, a roast in the over and a salad large in the final stages of preparation.

"Hi Norm. Byron's in the machine shop – something to do with the new tractor," welcomed Doris, turning toward the window. "Oh wait; here he comes. Must've seen your truck pull'n in. Have a seat and I'll pour both of you a cup of tea. Just made it a little while ago."

Byron Healey was not what could be described as an imposing character, nor did he fit the stereotypical description of a farmer. Tall, lean, clean cut and even in his coveralls, neat.

"I'll tell you Norm, I just bought that tractor a month ago and already there's a problem. I called Len about it but he can't make it out here until Tuesday. Oh well, there's always tomorrow," Byron said as he washed up at the kitchen sink. "So, what's going on in your life these days, Norm?"

"Byron, did you ever think about selling this place and, well, I don't know… doing something else" asked Norman.

"Almost every day Norm," responded Byron.

"Don't pay any attention to that old buzzard, Norm. He would no more sell this place than, well…fly to the moon. He whines and complains a lot, all of us do, but, well, this is home," answered Doris.

"She's probably right Norm. Why do you ask?" said Byron.

"Well, to make a long story short, I had a visit the other day from a fella who wants to buy my place. Well, not him; he was representn' the actual buyer but I haven't the foggiest who the real buyer is or would be, If'n I sold the place. Thing is he offered $20,000. $15,000 for the land and buildings and another $5,000 for everything what's in the house. Cash! Wa'dya think of that?"

Both Doris and Byron stopped what they were doing instantly and just stared at each other for what seemed an eternity to Norman. Byron was the first to speak.

"$20,000 you say. That's a lot of money Norm. Especially... "

Doris's evil-eye glance stopped Byron in mid stream.

"It's okay Byron. I know what your think'n... and you're right for my place, that is a lot of money. But question is, what do I do if I sell. And the other thing is I don't know who the real buyer would be and, oh yeah, Wilsey, the guy who made the offer was real interested in my trips to Russia, to Sevastopol t'be exact. Why d'ya 'spose that would be?"

"I don't know, Norm" replied Byron.

"Did anything happen to you when you were there," asked Doris.

"Not really, Doris. On the last trip, I met these Russian guys; gave me a little kind of box thing; a jewellery box I guess."

"Is that the box on the shelf in your kitchen, Norm," inquired Doris. "It's absolutely beautiful Norm. Your wife will really appreciate it."

"My wife? Is there something you know that I don't Doris? I don't think I'd want to live with a woman that would live in my place," said Norm, jokingly (kind of). "Tell you what Doris, I'll trade you that box for a couple loaves of your super delicious bread."

"No need Norm. I was going to send a couple loaves with you anyway; got way more than we can use," said Doris, grabbing two loaves of bread from the table and handing them to Norm. "And Norm, as much as I appreciate the offer of the box, I want you to hold on to it. You never know what the future holds. You're a good man Norm and the right lady will come along sooner or later."

"Thanks Doris. Byron is a very lucky guy," said Norman "You

know, most of us picked up a lot of stuff over the years but that's the weirdest thing I got. But, ya know, a funny thing about the Russians that bothers me some. Before I left the café in Sevastopol one of them said something about he and I meeting again. What do 'ya think of that?"

"Got me, Norm," said Byron."I'm not sure what advice to give you."

"Well, I do," said Doris. "Don't sell. We would miss you around here. You and your parents have been a real part of this area for a lot of years. Besides, and I'm only joking Norm. I'd love to browse through all those gifts some day. How come you never mentioned those before? And I've never seen any of it at the house, except the box and I didn't know it came from your last trip."

"Doris, come up to the house anytime and do all the browsing you want. I ain't never put any of the stuff out 'cause there just no room for it. But you've got lots of room, so come on up and help yourself," said Norman.

"Norman, if you're serious, I'll be up tomorrow afternoon, if that's acceptable."

"Sure is", said Norman.

"Why not stay for supper," added Doris. "The boys will be back from their swim in the creek pretty soon and there's lots enough for everybody."

"Thanks anyway, Doris, but I've got to get the cows milked and bed down the horses and besides, I've got a roast in the oven as well and if'n I don't get back soon, it won't be nothin' but a black lump."

With that, Norman gulped down the last mouthful of the best tea he had tasted in months, got in the truck and drove back to the farmhouse.

The cows milked, horses bedded down, cream separated and the dishes done, Norman grabbed a flashlight and went to the attic. In most homes, the attic was in the upper part of the house. But in Norman's place, it was a large area directly over the woodshed reached by a set of stairs along the west wall. The room was filled with antique everything – spinning wheels, old hand pumps, trunks, suitcases, old clothes. It seemed that nothing had been thrown away for at least the last century. His duffle bag and several boxes were next to the stairs, covered with a decade of dust and it took the best part of a half hour to cart all the "stuff" down the stairs, through the woodshed, over Sport and into the kitchen.

It took several hours to go through it all, placing the items Norman thought Doris might have interest in on the kitchen table then back up to the attic with the unwanted "stuff". Then it was time for Hockey Night in Canada and Newfoundland.

NORTH TAY

SUNDAY, AUGUST 11, 1935

There was no church service, not until next Sunday when the circuit Clergyman would come in from town. Norman did the chores then prepared breakfast: the usual three fried eggs, a couple of slabs of back bacon that he bought last Monday at Tait's General Store and a cup of coffee so strong it took both hands on the spoon to stir it! Glancing out the window, he caught sight of the tail end of a car as it zipped down the road, toward the schoolhouse corner, but he thought nothing of it.

'Just some of the young folk out for an early morning ride,' he mused.

Doris and Byron arrived shortly before lunch and she was awestruck by all the things that Norman had set out on the table, at least a dozen dolls in various ethnic costumes, plates, silverware, picture book, carvings of every description and the hand carved wooden jewellery box.

"I was thinking about the offer you told us about yesterday, Norm" said Byron. "Like you, what disturbs me, is not knowing who the buyer is. It doesn't seem that they are all that interested in the farm, but if not, then what do they have in mind for this place?"

"That's what gets to me, Byron. Anyway, the answers goin' to be no. Better the devil I know than the one I don't, as dad used to say. See anything you like, Doris?" asked Norman.

"My heavens, Norm, there's so much. I had no idea. Are you sure you want me to have these things? I would certainly like to buy quite a number of them."

"Don't talk so silly, Doris. Take what you want. I will never have any use for them and you've got lots of places to display the stuff."

Doris selected a number of items, not including the jewellery box. She looked at it, her fingers going over the fine ornate carvings on its exterior, opened it to expose the soft, bright red felt that lined the inside in a semi-circle as if made to hold something round.

"It's truly beautiful Norm. It's odd too; I mean the shape of the inside. Most jewellery boxes are, well, square or rectangular. Are you sure it's supposed to be a jewellery box, Norm," asked Doris

"That's a good question Doris. Come to think of it, the guys that gave it to me didn't say it was a jewellery box. Just said it was an antique hand carved box. I guess I assumed that's what it's for. Other than that, I ain't got no idea what it is or what use it is or anything else."

"Do you know what kind of wood it's made from Norm? Seems a little heavy." continued Doris..

"Nope, no idea. I noticed its weight as well, just thought it might be made of some Russian wood that's heavier than the stuff we have here."

"Very odd. Well Norm, I would still like to pay you for these things," said Doris, pointing to a dozen or so items she lined up on the table.

"Doris, if you mention money to me one more time, I'll tell everybody you bake lousy bread. So, please take them. A gift from me to you. They collect dust here and of no value to me."

After a dinner of excellent roast beef, mashed potatoes and gravy, turnip, yellow string beans and peas, followed by apple pie and tea and, of course, the proverbial discussions of politics and hockey, Doris gathered up the gifts.

"Norman," said Doris. "I'd like to ask a favour."

"Anything Doris. What can I do for you" responded Norman.

"My sister is coming this weekend and I would really like to bring her here and show her that jewellery box. She would really enjoy that."

"Tell you what Doris," said Norman. "Why not take it with you and I'll drop by some day next week and pick it up. Would that be okay?"

"That would be wonderful Norm. Thank you so much." And with that, she and Byron thanked Norman and left.

The barn work done, Norman settled down in his favourite chair between the water heater on the stove and the cot. Like just about everything else in the house, it was old, worn, worn out actually, but incredibly comfortable. For some time, he stared at the shelf over the kitchen table where the mysterious box had been, wondering how such a thing could generate so much interest. The ancient clock on the same shelf ticked away in the near silent kitchen, a clock that actually kept reasonably accurate time, not that it mattered, except on Saturday night.

It began to rain and, as the evening wore on, it rained even harder until it was a genuine downpour. Out the window next to the table, Norman saw flashes of lightening, something he had dreaded since childhood. He recalled all those nights when his mother would drag he and his brothers out of bed, march them downstairs and into the kitchen to sit out a 'thunder and lightning storm' in case the house was hit and they had to get out in a hurry. Sport didn't like it either and this was one of the few times when he was allowed into the kitchen. He listened intently.

No thunder yet, he thought, *so it's a way off for now.*

A few moments later, there was a distant flash and Norman counted off the seconds.

'5, 6, 7, 8, 9,…'

Then he heard it.

Three kilometres or so, he thought to himself.

Another flash; more north this time.

'3, 4, 5, 6, 7,…'

Another low rumble of thunder.

"It's getting closer Sport" he said out loud this time.

The next flash came from another direction, sending fleeting blue shadows across the front of the machine shed.

Norman exploded from his chair and literally flew across the width of the kitchen to the window. Looking to his right and then left, saw nothing but empty barnyard. Completely unnoticed by him, Sport jumped up and sat, facing the kitchen door. Norman looked again and was totally puzzled. He was sure he saw a shadow of someone running down from the barnyard toward the house but there was no one there; everything was as it should be. Thinking back to the afternoon and the car that went tearing up the road.

That Wilsey fella. I bet that was him. He's been sneaking around the place and got caught in the rain. Good 'nough for him.

To satisfy his curiosity, Norman went to the window in the dining room that faced the road. Even in the growing intensity of lightning flashes, he saw nothing unusual: no car, no car lights, just darkness. Norman went back to his chair and continued the storm watch for most of the night.

NORTH TAY

<u>MONDAY, AUGUST 12, 1935</u>

Norman decided that it was time to make a few repairs to the roof over the main house. He was running out of pots! He had purchased shingles and nails from Tait's Store several weeks ago and left them in the shed. Going into the shed with Sport, who was a little reluctant to leave the comparative luxury of the kitchen, Norman noticed that the shed door was partially open but there was no water on the floor.

I'm sure I closed that door last night. I always do. Couldn't have closed it tight enough I guess. Looks like it got open this morning. No rain came in anyway, he wondered to himself.

After placing the old wooden ladder against the roof over the kitchen and hefting a bundle of shingles on his shoulder, he made a trip up the protesting ladder to the edge of the roof. It was a nice day. The rain had done more good than harm and there wouldn't be any field work to do that day.

A good day for roof'n, he thought, *if there was such a thing.*

At about 10 o'clock, Norman caught sight of a half ton truck coming up the road toward his place. He recognized it as Byron's truck. It pulled into the yard next to the ladder and Byron jumped out. Norman, with no encouragement, came down from the roof, removed his gloves and invited Byron "to set a spell" on two nail kegs next to the house.

"You know something Norm, going back to what you told us yesterday about some guy wanting to buy this place," said Byron. "Doris and I were talking last night during the storm and the more we think about it, there's more to this than meets the eye. You know something; he doesn't want the farm or the house. I'm willing to bet he wants something that's in the house, not the house itself."

"Yeah, I thought about that," (but Norman knew that he really hadn't at all but it would be embarrassing to admit it). "Problem is Byron, what would it be? Whatever it's supposed to be has to be worth a lot of money or he wouldn't be offering $20,000. Very strange, wouldn't you say?"

"True enough Norm. Anyway, stay alert and keep us informed. Strange stuff going on," said Byron as he got up to leave.

"I will Byron. There's a lot of strange things going on," said Norman, a comment that stopped Byron in his tracks.

"What do you mean, Norm? I mean other than the offer?" asked Byron.

"I guess I didn't mention it. The other night, I was sure I saw someone running across the barnyard in the rain but didn't see anybody from the window. And food has been disappearing. At first I thought it was just me but a whole loaf of Doris's bread disappeared and other stuff as well. Seems like every time I leave the house, something else disappears."

"Well, it wouldn't be that Wilsey guy. Sounds like he can afford food. What do you think is going on Norm?" asked Byron.

Norman just shook his head.

"Oh before I forget, Norm," said Byron, reaching into the truck, "here's the box you loaned Doris. She and her sister oohed and awed over it all morning. Doris sends her thanks."

Byron got into his truck and with a friendly wave, backed out of the yard and headed home.

NORTH TAY

Clayton Williams lived about three kilometers from Norman on the road to Taitsville. He had been a friend of Normans since childhood, his best friend actually. They had grown up together, played together, skipped school together to go swimming or fishing and even worked on one another's farms together and it was painful to see what TB was doing to Clayton and, according to the Doctor, there was no hope.

Each visit was more painful than the last; frequent coughing bouts that lasted longer and longer and drained just about every ounce of energy he had. And this evening was no different. It was taking a toll on his family as well who did the best they could to make him as comfortable as possible but they all knew, it was simply a matter of time. Marion, Clayton's wife of thirty years or so, looked tired yet was cheerful as she brought Clayton and Norman some tea and newly baked cookies. None of them took the slightest note of a black coupe going by the house, leaving a miasma of reddish brown dust in the air in its wake.

In spite of his condition, Clayton always mustered enough strength when Norman arrived to maul over old times, the music they played (both were pretty fair guitar players), they recalled better days and even the future crept in from time to time although both knew it was simply blue sky talk. While it was painful to make the visit, Norman found it equally painful to leave, fearing that this might be the last day to see his good friend alive. Norman knew it would be an even more lonely existence without these visits. Clayton had come to grips with the inevitable. It was Norman who had not.

As usual, the house was in darkness and Sport met him at the shed door. After the usual talk to The old collie with complimentary pats and rubs, Norman went into the kitchen, switching on the light. Immediately he sensed that something was not quite right.

Standing by the door next to the separator, he looked around the room. Everything was in place but not everything was where it should be. The wood box was full to the brim (although it had been nearly empty when he left or so he remembered), the cot blanket was flat and neat (too neat) and an old newspaper was laying on the floor next to the cot came from a rack of papers over the cot. The rack had not been touched in months.

He ventured into the kitchen, then into the pantry, taking the double barreled 12 gauge leaning next to a closet, broke it open and slipped in two shells. Snapping it shut, he cautiously went back into the kitchen again, then into the adjacent bedroom; found nothing unusual or anybody, back into the kitchen and eventually inspected the entire house, downstairs and up. Nothing other than a few things that may have been out of place but he wasn't 100 percent sure. He was certain of one thing; someone had been in the house while he was away and it probably wasn't a transient looking for a bed for the night or they would still be there. He had been visited by someone else.

It was a very uncomfortable night for Norman. He had no way of locking the front or back doors so he brought Sport in (thanked him for being a serious watchdog!) and braced both doors with two of the kitchen chairs. This was a move he realized could only be temporary at best.

SUNDAY, AUGUST 18, 1935

On the way back from church, Norman, with Sport in tow, stopped in to visit Clayton for a short time but he was sleeping and didn't want to disturb him. He got precious little sleep as it was.

Back at the house, Norman went to the chicken coop to get some eggs for his breakfast then, in the house, took the frying pan from the pantry and noticed that it was unusually clean; somewhat cleaner that he remembered when last using it.

It would be a long day for Norman. Although he had been invited out for supper by one of the neighbours, he declined the offer. Chores were a constant regardless of what day it was. Clayton weighed on his mind, heavily, and he spent most of the day in his favourite chair, strumming his old flat top guitar and remembering. Time flew and before long, the sun began to set. Still, he wasn't hungry, having eaten only breakfast, and so he sat, just staring at the cursed box on the shelf.

Something told him to get up and get it. He did and sat again in his favourite chair, starring at the ornate box. After a few moments, he recalled something that both Doris and her sister had mentioned. It was unusually heavy. He hefted it.

Yeah. A little heavy I guess, he thought to himself. *But how much are they supposed to weigh?*

Turning it over and over, he noticed that it seemed unbalanced; a little heavier on one side than the other.

Norman had always been a curious individual, always wanted to find out what made things tick as it were, an attribute that was highly appreciated while he worked in the engine rooms of the ships on which he served. Reaching into his pocket, he retrieved a rather mean looking pocket knife, another gift he had picked up in his twenty plus years at sea.

Turning the box over, he noted that the bottom plate was fastened to the walls of the box but not inset. It only took a slight pressure to release the corners. Prying the bottom plate up a few centimetres or so, he discovered a 15 -20 centimetre piece of lead pipe secured to one of the inside walls.

Putting the knife away, he unfastened the pipe and withdrew it from the box, replacing the bottom plate. Chucking the pipe onto the cot next to the chair, he got up and placed the box on the shelf above the kitchen table, next to the kerosene lantern, then returned to his chair, retrieving the pipe from the cot.

Norman looked at the pipe for several minutes, turning it over and over, end for end, noting the threaded caps on both ends. The curiosity factor kicked in again, big time. It felt to Norman that the pipe was not empty. There was definitely something inside.

He went to the workbench in the shed, placed the pipe into the vice attached to the bench, and with a pair of pliers, started to remove one of the caps. He stopped. He remembered a time in 1918 when he came across a pipe bomb that almost killed one of his buddies.

Norman stood by the bench for a long time, trying to decide what to do.

Was this thing worth dying for or losing an arm, he thought. Finally, he decided that it probably wasn't a bomb. *Why would someone he had never met send a bomb hidden in a box that would only explode if fused or opened?*

He went back to loosening one of the caps. It was on tighter than he thought and it took a lot of force to turn it, which was even more reason to believe that it wasn't a bomb.

Finally, the cap gave way and fell to the floor. Removing the pipe from the vice, Norman slid its contents into his left hand. He was surprised to find that it was about 10 or 12 centimetres long, silver and kind of metallic. It was actually quite soft, almost pliable and the surface felt gritty even though the object looked shiny.

Sport ran for the shed door to Normans left and, finding it closed, he dove for the other door that was also closed. In less than a second, the Collie jumped into the woodshed, ran to the back of one of the ranks of wood and hid. No amount of coaxing would dislodge him from his hiding place.

After a few moments, his curiosity satisfied, he put the object back into the pipe, picked the cap off the floor and loosely screwed into the open end of the pipe and tossed the pipe onto the bench before going back into the kitchen. Norman's hands began to itch a bit, he assumed from whatever was coating the object, so he washed them at the sink and that seemed to do the trick. It was getting late and tomorrow promised to be a busy day so Norman closed the kitchen door, placed the chair as a lock, turned out the light and went to his bedroom.

Norman's bedroom had two windows, one facing the granary and the upper end of the barn yard and the other facing the machine shed and chicken coop. He lay in bed but sleep didn't come. He wrestled with the purpose of the lead pipe.

What was so valuable that it had to be sealed inside a piece of lead pipe hidden in a jewellery box, he wondered.

It was a quiet evening. Not a breath of wind and a clear cloudless sky. At first he thought it was just fireflies but soon realized the lights were travelling far too fast, but then he wasn't sure what they were.

One went flying by the window to his left and it reminded him of the tracers he saw during the war. Norman instantly rolled off his bed and hit the floor as flat as he could but there was no sound of gunfire, no sound of bullets hitting the buildings outside, just the frightful, aerie silence and the awful parade of blue-white lights blazing by both widows, casting ghastly frenzied shadows dancing over every square metre of the room.

The fear that comes from being a shooters target is transitory once the source is located and survival mode kicks in, something Norman had experienced many times. But this was different and, for Norman, this was more than fear but not new. This was the terror he felt in his first battle experience. His heart beating wildly and covered in sweat, he stole a glance out the window next to his bed, a glance that was met with an unbroken string of lights moving faster than anything he had ever witnessed and they seemed to come from nowhere. Feeling totally defenseless, he crawled to the window at the foot of his bed. The same thing; they were there; they were everywhere and no source, no sound, just absolute, unearthly silence.

At this point, Norman didn't know what to do. He was frightened and he knew it but it hadn't paralyzed him. He decided to try and make it to the pantry and get his trusty rifle although he wasn't at all sure what he would do after that. They were very rapid moving targets and unless he opened a window to fire, he would have to go outside, not something he relished doing.

He finally made it to the pantry and took not only the 30:30 but the 12 gauge as well, grabbing enough ammo for both to stave off a Platoon for a week! Getting up to a kneeling position, he reached to open the pantry window and stopped dead in his tracks. The flash was so intense that it lit up the pantry and kitchen as though it was the middle of the day.

An explosion, he thought.

They collided with one another but the there was no sound; just the awful, cold dead silence that penetrated clean through to his spine then nothing. No lights. After a moment or two, the faint odor of burning wood but no sign of fire and no sign of smoke. Nothing. Then everything was in darkness under a clear, cloudless sky.

With his rifle in hand, Norman walked hunched over to the kitchen door which lead directly into the shed, removed the chair from the door knob and slowly opened the door just far enough to poke the barrel of the rifle into the shed area. There was nothing, just darkness, no sound although the smell of burned wood was slightly stronger. Poor old Sport was buried even deeper in his hiding place, clearly alive but completely immobilized by fear.

Norman ventured into the shed. The odor seemed to be coming from his left. He walked slowly to the shed door and cautiously opened it about half way, the creaking of dry hinges filling the night. Nothing: just a dark, quiet night and a sky full of twinkling stars, no mysterious lights, no movement, no sound, no fire. Closing the door and satisfied for now that any immediate danger had passed, he went back to the kitchen door, stopping long enough to call Sport but Sport wasn't about to move; not for Norman; not for anyone! Norman went back to bed to an uneasy and fitful sleep.

NORTH TAY

MONDAY, AUGUST 19, 1935

Norman awoke early. Actually, he had been awake long before he finally made the decision to get up. Going out to the shed, he noticed that Sport had decided to retreat from hiding and was, as usual, patiently waiting for breakfast. Norman realized that Sport's night was probably worse than his own, although he wasn't sure why. Sport knew about as much as Norman concerning the events of the previous night! Still, he felt a treat would be in order. Not the usual scraps but, this time, a real steak. So breakfast was steak and eggs (minus the eggs for Sport).

Clouds had rolled in overnight unnoticed by Norman whose mind was somewhat pre-occupied with other thoughts. It didn't matter though; it would be a day of weeding and the myriad of chores that plagued even a hobby farmer such as Norman.

I need one of them tractors like Byron, at least when you turn it off, it quits eating, he often thought.

Having washed and put the breakfast dishes away, Norman donned his coveralls, grabbed his straw hat and left the kitchen. Fetching a hoe, with Sport close behind, threw open the shed door that he so cautiously peeked out of last night.

It only took a fraction of a second for Norman to be thrown backward as if hit by a full body blow. He grabbed the side of the workbench on his left for support and keep from falling to the floor and hold his heart with the other, all the time, mouth wide open and eyes that spelled complete shock.

"Good morning Norman MacLeod. I'm sorry. I don't mean to alarm you."

But Norman *was* alarmed! Standing just outside the door was one who looked like a living nightmare (Sport wasn't the slightest perturbed and sat between the two, looking up at the stranger, clearly expecting at least a friendly ear-rub).

The man had scraggly hair that looked as though it was fashioned with a grain thrasher with bits and pieces of hay sticking out it. An unshaven face, reddish eyes with bags deep enough to hide small animals, a suit that looked as though he had slept in it for a month and body odor that would wilt the leaves on an artificial plant.

Partially recovered from the shock and breathing heavily, Norman started to speak.

"I… I know you. I've seen you before. You're… you're that… Russian guy." He searched his mind for the name and trying his best to regain some degree of composure.

"Yes. My name is Griggory… Griggory Semjonov. Pleasure to meet you again," offering his right hand.

Hesitantly, really without knowing what he was doing, now standing at the edge of the workbench but staring at the floor, Norman briefly shook his hand.

"May I come in sir," asked Griggory.

Norman stepped aside, still looking at the floor and gestures with his right hand for Griggory to come in.

"I assure you Norman MacLeod, it was not my… "

Norman held up a hand and cut off Griggory's speech in mid stream.

"Listen Greggory or whatever your name is. What are you doing here? You scared the living blazes out of me. What's going on anyway?" asked Norman. "And another thing, you look like something a cat would drag in out of a rain storm. What have you been doing? Living in… oh God, that's what you have been doing! You've been camped in my barn, haven't you? What for?"

"Yes. But if we can talk Norman MacLeod, I… "

Again, with a raised hand, Norman cut his delivery short.

"Will you quit calling me Norman MacLeod. It's embarrassing. Just Norm, Okay? Norm. Can you remember that?'

"Yes. Of course Norma… Norm."

Norman kept his stare fixed on the picture of desperation standing in front of him, unsure what to do next but certain that he was in no danger. His mind now back in normal mode, Norman quickly reasoned that if this excuse for a human was a threat to him, that threat would have been carried out long before now. Finally, he decided to offer him the same level of hospitality he would offer a migrant worker that frequented his farm.

"Great. Now what in blue blazes are you doing here? No wait… I can't stand the smell any longer. It's starting to rust my tools."

Griggory thought this might be a bit of Canadian humor but didn't express any emotion just in case he had misread the intent.

"I don't know why I'm doing this but get your carcass into the house. There's hot water on the side of the stove and get yourself cleaned up for God's sake. I'll be back in a bit to get you something to wear," continued Norman.

The way Norman had it figured is that if this guy had meant harm, he had lots of opportunity and if he was a thief, he didn't appear to be very good at it. So, giving him free reign of the house was not seen as any great risk. Besides, Norman wanted to check the barn that had been Griggory's quarters as of late.

There was little in the haymow except a small leather suitcase that contained some dirty clothing, an envelope which was filled with Canadian money and a large file of notes, written in Russian. Norman gathered up the items and walked back toward the house and the shed.

As he came by the machine shed, he glanced at the shed door and stopped dead in his tracks. Norman dropped the suitcase as if it had suddenly turned white hot. It was then that he noticed it, on the front of the shed door, near the top, not carved but burned neatly and precisely into the old wood boards.

461427665430

Norman starred at it for several minutes, remembering the smell of burning wood from the night before.

"What is this all about? Who… " No answers came. Still starring at the numbers, he bent down, picked up the suitcase and proceeded to the kitchen.

Griggory had washed up but was still in bad need of a shave and some clean clothes. Norman said nothing, just walked by Griggory, handing him the suitcase along the way and went into the bedroom, returning a short time later with clean clothes, and pointed to the bedroom. Griggory, took the clothes, went into the bedroom and returned a while later looking more human although Griggory was several sizes smaller than Norman.

Norman was in his favourite chair. Norman pointed to a chair at the end of the kitchen table. Griggory quietly sat down, not really knowing what to expect but sensing a degree of anger in Norman.

With both arms resting on the chair arms, Norman broke the silence.

"You know, for the past month, a lot of strange things have been happening around here, and to be honest with you, I'm sick of it. I want answers and I think you have the answers. Enough is enough. First, this guy in a fine new car rolls up and offers me a bag full of money for my place. Then food goes missing but I think I already have the answer to that one," said Norman, pointing to an emotionless Griggory. "Are you understanding any of this?"

"Yes. Yes. Go on," replied Griggory. "I'm quite fluent in English."

"Then someone searches my house while I was out. Was that you," asked Norman.

"No. It wasn't me but I think I know who it was," said Griggory.

"Then last night, I get the crap scared out of me, and scared my dog as well. And I thought my house was on fire. Then, just now, I see them numbers burned into my shed door. But you already know about that, don't you?" Norman was clearly getting more worked up as time went on. They both sat, looking at each other for almost a full minute. Norman, now calmed down, concluded , "What's going on?"

"Norm, you have every right to be angry, very angry, and I apologize for not contacting you sooner. But I wasn't sure what was going on myself until the other day. If you have about a half hour, I will explain everything and, if you wish, I will pay you for your kindness and leave. Would that be acceptable?"

"Look Greggory. I don't want your money. I just want to know what this is all about so I can get on with my life. Okay? And as anyone in the area will tell you, you're welcome to stay as long as you like so long as you help with the chores."

"Yes. That will be fine. And it's Griggory, not Greggory. All right?"

"Okay. So get on with it. What's this all about?"

For the next half hour, Griggory explained every detail of the events, going back to the Tunguska Valley and ending with the meeting at the café when the box was given to Norman.

"When it was discovered that Barkov had eluded Novikoff and left Russia, it was a foregone conclusion that he was headed here so I was dispatched to come here and make sure no harm came to you, and to try and determine what the object is and who does it belong to," said Griggory. "I'm the only one of the group that is fluent in English and, in case you're concerned Norm, I am here legally. I have all my papers."

Norman wasn't concerned. At the end, Norman was mentally drained, trying to keep all the events in order and comprehending the enormity of it all.

"But what about the lights? What do they have to do with this... thing, whatever it really is," asked Norman.

"I'm not sure. According to Dr. Oborski's notes, he thinks the light are an energy by-product; that the lights comes from very small particles, smaller than anything we have the technology to clearly see. He felt that the particles contain tiny bits of information that can be changed as needed. While each particle is capable of little or nothing, when grouped, the sum of their information or intelligence can accomplish many things. So, when they are active, they emit light. Dr. Oborski thinks that the object is coated with many thousands of these particles, perhaps millions and they may be self replicating but he wasn't sure. Interestingly though Norm, the particles can be washed off and are totally deactivated by as little as 5 cm of water and, as you know, the element lead eliminates their activity. Interesting, don't you think?' concluded Griggory.

"Interesting stuff, Greggory," replied Norman who didn't have the foggiest clue of what Griggory had just explained.

"Griggory," said Griggory

"Oh. Sorry. Griggory," replied Norman. "But tell me this Greggory, What do you make of those numbers burnt into my shed door?"

"Yes. Very interesting indeed," said Griggory. (who, at this point, decided to give up correcting Norman). "I've seen them once before and Dr. Oborski saw them once as well. But each time, they are different, not the same numbers at all. I have no idea what they mean, although I am sure they have meaning. The only reasonably sure thing is that they were burned by those lights. That seems unquestionable although no one has ever seen them being burned that I know of."

Norman and Griggory spent the day weeding and talking, mostly about where Griggory came from, his parents, his wife and his association with the Foundation and, by the end of the day, they had made peace although it seemed like a long haul to bonding.

"You know Greg, I do have a problem with you being here." said Norman

"Yes? And what would that be, Norm?" asked Griggory.

"How do I explain why you're here to my friends?" replied Norman, feeling more than a just a little apprehensive and unsure if Griggory's presence would cause him even more grief.

"Can you just say we met in Russia and I came to see Canada for myself, which isn't a lie, really. I looked forward to the trip but I cannot stay here very long. Even now, I miss Elsa greatly."

TUESDAY, AUGUST 20, 1935

Not much was said over breakfast by either Griggory or Norman.

"Norm," said Griggory, "when you leave the house, I would strongly advise that you take that piece of pipe with you. I saw it in the shed yesterday. Barkov may well be back. In fact, I'm certain of it. He's not one to give up easily."

"Be back," asked Norman. "You mean he's been here?"

"Yes. You told me that you know your house was searched. I saw Barkov and another man doing it. In fact, they made a real mess. After they left, I came in and put things away as much as I could before you came back. They were looking for the box but it apparently wasn't in the house."

"Well, at least that answers that question," said Norman "And as for the box; it's just a box now but Bar... what's his name?"

"Barkov," answered Griggroy.

"Yeah. Barkov. Well he ain't get'n the box either. That goes to a very good friend of mine."

Griggory smiled.

"You know Greg, them numbers on the shed door mean someth'n.

If someone told them their lights to carve up my door, they did it for a reason. I need to know who and what the reason is, wouldn't you say?" asked Norman.

Griggory marveled at Norman's exceptional logic. While he easily recognized that Norman had little appreciation of the advanced technology that was behind it all (nor did he, for that matter), he realized that Norman's down to earth approach exhibited a high level of intelligence and deserved an equally high level of respect.

"Norm, I have a suggestion to make. Neither of us know what those numbers mean. May I suggest that we go to the university in Fredericton and try and find someone who can unravel this mystery?' asked Griggory. "It's not that far away."

"Yeah. I know where it is. What do you think all them lab guys and college types can tell us that we don't already know?"

"Lab guys? College types? Is that what you think they are? You know, some of them may have picked up some knowledge along the way that could be useful. Perhaps they understand something we don't," responded Griggory.

"Ain't never met one yet," said Norman with obvious experience borne confidence.

"Oh yes you have," responded Griggory.

WEDNESDAY, AUGUST 21, 1935

The rain started late in the night, not a downpour, but rather a drizzle, the kind that generally lasts a whole day. Both Norman and Griggory rose early, had breakfast and set out to complete their chores before heading to Fredericton. As it turned out and to his immense surprise, Griggory knew as much about milking cows as Norman and so the job was over in half the usual time. By 10 o'clock, they were ready to leave.

Norman called Sport. The dog loved going for a ride in the truck and he quickly jumped up, into the box, over several sand bags and into a dog house that Norman had fixed to the floor of the box. Closing the tail gate, he and Griggory got into the cab and Norman started the engine. Griggory was surprised by the sound of the engine.

"How many horsepower Norm," asked Griggory.

"As much as I could ram under the hood. Ships engineer, remember," replied Norman.

"Aren't we forgetting something, Norm?' asked Griggory. "We have the numbers and the box."

"Nope. Just wanted to see if you remembered," replied Norman, having just pulled off an accidental, yet rewarding coup!

Norman just sat, hands on the steering wheel, the engine throbbing like a race horse at a starting gate but not moving.

"Well," said Griggory.

Norman said nothing; just slowly turned his head toward Griggory, raised both eyebrows and flashed a toothy smile, one finger pointing toward the shed.

"You're closer'n me," said Norman.

Griggory looked over at Norman, threw up his hands, got out of the truck, went into the shed and retrieved the pipe.

"Hi Doris," said Norman. "We can't stay. By the way, this is Greg. He's one of the guys I met in Russia last year. Come to visit Canada for a spell."

"Good morning Greg. Pleasure to meet you. You'll have to come back when you can stay longer; have supper with us," said Doris.

"That would be wonderful. We will do that," replied Griggory.

"Doris, I just wanted to drop off this jewellery box to you. It's yours. I have no use for it and I know how much you like this thing, my gift, actually, our gift to you."

Doris was beside herself and at a total loss for words. And so amid a stream of 'thank yous', Norman and Griggory left and headed for Fredericton, some fifty six kilometres away.

The distance from Normans farm to Taitsville was only about eight kilometers as the crow flies but about two hundred fifty meters as a dead crow drops. About a kilometre or so from Taitsville, the road was distinguished by a number of knolls and hollows. At just the right speed, the occupants of vehicles could experience Newton's Laws of Motion first hand, weightlessness followed by a slight g-force followed by weightlessness followed by a slight g-force and Norman was well acquainted with just the right speed.

The dirt road was full of water filled pot holes and small erosion gullies and while Norman successfully navigated around as many as he could without reducing speed, he managed to find as many as he missed but it didn't slow him down.

They had just cleared the top of a hill that dropped to a wooden bridge over a small stream when they both spotted it at the same time; the black Chev Coupe coming at them from the opposite direction. It didn't alarm Norman as much as Griggory and as it passed, Griggory recognized Kazamin in the passenger's seat and Wilsey, his eyes glued to the road and hands welded to the steering wheel.

When the Coupe disappeared over the hill after leaving the bridge, and without so much as a microsecond warning, Norman violently braked the truck as it left the exit end of the bridge, shifted to reverse, and the truck zoomed backward, just missing the bridge abutment on the left side. The truck came to a stop, tight against the concrete bridge abutment, about fifteen meters from the road. At this point, the top of the abutment was at least two meters or so above the top of the truck, hiding it from view from any vehicle on the road, and there they sat, motionless.

In less than a minute, the Coupe came back. Travelling fast, it hit a puddle at the exit end of the bridge, sending a cascade of muddy water and dirt into the air and onto the cab, engine bonnet and windshield of the truck and Norman smiled as the Coupe roared on and soon disappeared in the mist.

Putting the truck in gear, Norman eased the vehicle back onto the road but, instead of continuing on, he reversed direction, re-crossing the bridge, climbed the hill and drove off the road, into an old, largely grown up woods road, stopping when he came to a huge swampy area. Quickly backing up and out onto the road (no sign of the Coupe), continued back toward the farm but turned onto another dirt road and stopped after going about a thirty meters.

"What's going on Norm," asked Griggory.

Norman, with a pasty, devious ridden smile, beckoned Griggory to get out of the truck and join him in the short, crouched walk back to the main road.

In the Coupe, in spite of looking in every direction neither Kazamin or Wilsey saw any sign of Normans truck.

"Stop," screamed Kazamin. "We should have caught up to them by now. Turn around and go back and keep a watchful eye."

Wilsey did as he was told. A short time later, driving slower than before, they crossed the bridge and went up the hill.

"Stop you idiot!" Kazamin screamed again, "Did you not see their tracks? There! There."

He pointed to where the grass clearly showed recent vehicle wheel traffic.

"Follow them! Follow them!" he screamed.

"I really don't think this is a good idea, sir. That's an old…" protested Wilsey but Kazamin cut him short.

"I'm not paying you to think," Kazamin said removing his handgun from a shoulder holster and ramming it into Wilsey's side. "Now get this car onto that road – NOW!"

And he did.

Norman and Griggory, less than a couple hundred metres away, while not able to hear the 'conversation', saw Wilsey aim the car onto the woods road.

"Listen, " said Norman. "It should be any minute now."

Actually, it was less than a minute. The unmistakable sound of a whining transmission, and spinning wheels of a hopelessly stuck vehicle, followed by the smash of metal on metal and a string of anger ladened, unintelligible yells that seemed to be a curious mix of Russian and something that vaguely resembled English.

The remainder of the ride to Fredericton was relaxed with no sense of urgency. Norman stopped in front of Chapman's Clothing Store on York Street.

"Why are we stopping here," asked Griggory.

"Because I'm getting tired of you wearing out my duds. Spend a few bucks and get your own," replied Norman.

Actually, Griggory was quite happy to get a more Canadian look. Next stop was Lou Charters Esso.

"Good afternoon Lou," said Norman, getting out of the truck parked next to a gas pump. Norman filled the tank and asked Lou to check the oil.

"Down 'bout a quart," said Lou. "What weight does she take?"

"30 weight's is fine with me," responded Norman, fully realizing that Lou only had one weight of oil in his garage, 30 weight. It didn't matter what the client requested, it was going to be 30 weight anyway!

"Lou, is it okay if I leave the truck and Sport here? He's quite happy to just lay in the box and he's got lots of food. We've got some business up the hill and I don't want to take the truck." asked Norman.

"No problem. Sport and I go back a long way."

"Thanks Lou and if anyone asks about us… well just tell 'em we went up to the boot and shoe plant."

Lou nodded an "okay" but didn't ask why. He knew it was none of his business.

"We won't be all that long. Should be back in a couple of hours."

"Why leave the truck here? How are we going to get to the university," asked Griggory.

"Don't want to run into that Wilsey guy and his partner. It would be tougher to lose them in town." said Norman.

"So, how do we get to the university, walk? It's raining," asked Griggory.

Norman just looked at him and said one word.

"Taxi."

"Taxi's cost money Norm," replied Griggory.

"I don't care," answered Norman. "You're paying."

Griggory chose to have the taxi stop in front of the Forestry & Geology Building, apparently for no other reason than it looked newer than the others. After running up the steps to the entrance to escape a mist that, for the moment, turned into a downpour, they entered and Griggory went straight for the 'Directory Board.'

"How about this person, a Dr. H.M. Decourcey, Geologist?" asked Griggory after a lengthy period of studying the board.

"Fine with me – never heard tell of him, but then, I never heard tell of any of 'em," replied Norman.

Dr. Decourcey's office was on the second floor. On the way up, Norman, much to Griggory's amazement, asked Griggory to carry the conversation. Griggory knocked.

"Come in."

Norman and Griggory looked at each other; it was a female voice. Opening the door, they immediately spotted Dr. Decourcey getting up from her chair from behind a large, dark oak desk, neatly decorated with journals and papers of every description. The walls contained few photos; rural scenes for the most part but most of the area was occupied with soil and rock profile samples.

"Dr. Decourcey," asked Griggory.

"Yes," she replied with a most pleasant and warm smile.

Norman guessed her to be in her mid forties. She was average height, fashionably attired in a long pastel shade print dress, a little thinner than he preferred, but, for Norman, the bright blue eyes and short dark brown hair gave her the 'wow' factor.

"Good afternoon Doctor," said Griggory. Extending his hand to her, "My name is Dr. Griggory Semjonov and this is my good friend, Norman MacLeod."

After introductions, Dr. Decourcey invited them to be seated.

"How may I be of assistance, gentlemen," she asked.

"We are plagued with something of a mystery, Doctor," began Griggory, "and we wondered if you could help us resolve it."

Griggory briefly explained the mystery without getting into historic details or other issues currently in play.

"So, you see Dr. Decoursey, these number appeared on the outside shed door of Norman's home and we have no idea who or what carved them" (a slight deception but the truth would have probably ended the visit tout suite) "or the significance of the numbers. Do they mean anything to you?" he asked.

She looked at the numbers for several minutes, jotting down notes, rearrangements of the numbers and so on.

"Where did you say your farm is located Mr. MacLeod" she asked.

"North Tay, maam," replied Norman.

"Oh my goodness. Really? Isn't that interesting. I come from a bit north of the Tay, Northton actually. My parents still live there," she said.

"Yes. I know where it is. Go hunt'n around that area from time to time," Norman responded. Feeling a little more at ease he continued, "There is a lot of game in that area. Perhaps all the old apple orchards are the attraction."

"This is very intriguing you know. I have no idea what the numbers refer to," she said, leaning back in her chair with fingers clasped in front of her mouth, "However, I have a feeling that there is more to this mystery than you're telling me, a local farmer and an academic, from Russia I assume, not the mix that's that common, wouldn't you say? But that's alright; it's still a mystery and I expect, when you are ready, you will tell me the whole story, yes?"

"You're most astute, Doctor, and yes, in time, we will tell you the whole story, but I don't think you will believe it. However, just to put you at ease, neither of us have done anything illegal, this is not a game and those numbers are a true mystery," said Griggory.

"That's fine. I love a good mystery. Give me a few days to think about this. I will be going to my parents place for the weekend. Perhaps I could drop into the farm on Friday, that is, if I have learned anything. Would that be acceptable," she asked.

"That would be excellent Doctor," replied Griggory.

Griggory and Norman shook hands with Dr. Decourcey and they left the building after she arranged for a taxi to pick them up.

"Nice touch," said Norman, standing in the shelter of the buildings doorway as they waited for the taxi to arrive.

"What do you mean," asked Griggory.

"You know... calling yourself 'Doctor' as well. Kinda added some... I don't know. Made us not look so much like a couple of nut cases." answered Norman.

"Glad you liked it, Norm. However, it's also true."

"Get outta here," replied Norman. "You're not serious."

"Yes, I'm serious," said Griggory. "University of Leningrad, 1934."

"University of Leningrad," responded Norman. "Is that, well... you know, a real university?"

Griggory just smiled and pointed to the taxi coming up the hill to their left.

The drive back to North Tay was rife with silence, not the kind born of anger; the kind born of thoughts, the mystery of the numbers for Griggory and the mystery of Dr. Decourcey for Norman.

"You know she likes you Norman," said Griggory after about a half hour on the road. "And I saw the way you looked at her. I think you like... "

"Griggory... shut up!" said Norman without as much as a glance in Griggory's direction.

Griggory did, with a smile and said not another word, noting that this was the first time Norman pronounced his name correctly. The only sound on the return trip was the continuous splash of tires in the countless pot holes and the sporadic slap of the windshield wipers.

NORTH TAY

Friday was not a day like any other. It was a day of anticipation for both Norman and Griggory. Still, there was always an endless bucket list of work to be done and, rarely, not enough time to get it done. The seemingly endless job of roof repair was high on the days priority list.

It was about 4:30 in the afternoon when Griggory spotted a plume of dust coming from the road leading to Taitsville. He said nothing to Norman who was on the opposite side of the roof. Soon the plume disappeared as the vehicle slowed and turned onto the road leading up the hill toward the farm. It was not the vehicle they 'toyed' with a few days ago. This was a dark green pickup truck.

"Norman," called Griggory. "I think we have a visitor."

Norman wasted no time in crawling up to the ridge cap and, spotting the truck, joined Griggory, neither one realizing who it might be.

The green 1934 Ford pickup pulled into the yard, stopped and the driver's door opened.

"Good afternoon gentlemen. Fine day for roofing I would guess," said Dr. Decourcey.

Neither man wasted much time getting down from the roof and

Griggory lost the race to the ladder at the side of the house opposite the driveway.

"You fo… found us okay Doctor," stammered Norman.

"No problem at all Norman. Everyone in the area seems to know you. And, please, drop the Doctor thing. That's just for my students. My name is Helena Mae."

Just then Griggory joined the duo.

"Good to see you as well… Griggory, is it not?" inquired Helena Mae.

"Yes. That's correct. Good to see you again. Well, do you have any news for us," asked Griggory, gesturing for all to come inside the house.

"I'll put the kettle on for tea," said Norman, inviting them to be seated at the kitchen table.

Filling the kettle with water from the kitchen tap while Griggory stoked the stove with fresh wood from the wood box.

"I have news," started Helena Mae, "but I'm not sure if it's good news or useless."

Griggory sat in apprehensive excitement, hoping for the best but partially prepared for less than the best.

"The numbers were most intriguing: 461427665430. I took them apart and rearranged them in a multitude of combinations and came away empty handed," she explained. "It wasn't until late yesterday, while going over a geologic map of a site not far from here, that it hit me."

By this time, Norman, and especially Griggory were in full attention mode, leaning over the table as Helena Mae unfolded a map from her purse and spread it out on the table. It was a map that included the area on which the farm was located and a great deal of the surrounding region.

"I assume you know what longitude and latitude references are," asked Helena Mae.

"Yes of course," said Norman. "I was in the Merchant Marine Service for twenty years."

"Oh well then," said Helena Mae, "This will be a piece of cake to explain. The numbers could be longitude and latitude coordinates. 46 deg 14 min 27 sec north by 66 deg 54 min 30 sec west. If that's the case, then those coordinates point to a location right about... here," placing her finger on the map location.

"That's not far from here," said Norman. "Over on the ridge. I go there to do some hunt'n in the fall. I know where that is; just a big ol' empty field; used to be a farm back a few years; not much left of the old place now though. What's so special about that place,?"

"Well, it may be nothing at all Norman," answered Helena Mae, "and I have no idea if my assumption is correct, it's just a guess."

After a lot of discussion, Norman finally summoned up enough spirit to invite Helena Mae to stay for dinner.

"I really thank you for the kind invitation, Norman," she said, "but I'm expected at my parents home. Would Wednesday evening suit you? I have to be at the geologic site near here on Thursday morning. Would that be all right? You know, I love this place and the magnificent view you have of the valley. And besides, I hear that your cooking skills are almost legendary," she concluded.

Norman wasn't entirely certain of what she had just said but had a pretty reasonable idea that it was good.

"That would be fantastic. Roast beef and baked potatoes? Would that be okay?" replied Norman who couldn't believe that he was actually inviting a woman to join him for an evening meal.

"Sounds wonderful Norman," said Helena Mae, standing and shaking Normans hand. "About 6 or so?"

Both men watched and waved as she backed the pick up out of the driveway and headed for her parents home. Walking toward the house, Norman starred at Griggory.

"Don't say a word Greg! Not a word, you hear?" said Norman as Griggory stood at the shed door, arms folded across his chest, displaying his most annoying satirical smile.

SATURDAY, AUGUST 24, 1935

For both men, Saturday started out as a better than usual day, not just one in a long succession of days that tended to blend together into repetitive re-runs. Griggory well understood why and Norman steadfastly adhered to a not-know-why feeling. He had been reluctantly re-born. Both men talked on and off during the day, mostly about the longitude-latitude theory and, as the afternoon drew to a close, decided that they would at least visit the location in the morning since there was to be no church service. This would leave lots of time to complete the usual round of evening chores.

The only event of an otherwise 'standard' day was the sight of the black coupe that made two trips up and back on the main road but did not come up the hill to the farm. Both men wondered what was up but quickly dismissed any worry since it was a free country and they could do as they liked and there was nothing they could do about it anyway. The roofing project got finished, the chores done, meals eaten – and it was time for Hockey Night in Canada and Newfoundland, at least for Norman. For Griggory, it was an early turn-in.

NORTH TAY

SUNDAY, AUGUST 25, 1935

Both Norman and Griggory finished the morning chores in record time, had breakfast, and then Norman grabbed the old Winchester. After making sure that Sport was comfortable in his truck box dog house, he placed the rifle in the rack behind the seat and they were ready.

Looking around, he saw no one and that he took as a good sign that the jokesters were not waiting for him to leave. Along the way, he made a short stop to visit Clayton.

Griggory thought it best not to go in with him and remained in the truck, the subject of considerable attention from the three children playing in the yard.

Norman drove at normal speed down the dirt road to Taitsville with a slight exception at the Newton's Laws portion, careful not to become a centre of attention, but once he hit the main road north, care went the way of the wind!

The road to the site was narrow and poorly maintained and it took all Normans attention to make sure that they didn't skid off and into a tree or swamp. The automobile that took up a position about a half mile behind them escaped their attention for the first quarter hour. It was Griggory that first saw it when he turned to look out the rear window to check on Sport.

"Norman," said Griggory, "we've picked up a tail. I'm certain it's Kazamin and that other fellow."

"Wilsey; the other guys name is Wilsey, Don't worry about it. I think I can ditch them up ahead," answered Norman, without taking so much as a glance at the rear view mirror.

The dust that Normans truck was kicking up obliterated his view of the car from time to time but it was much closer than when Griggory first spotted it. Norman realized that this was not a good state of affairs. Letting the car go by was out of the question since he would lose all control of the situation, aside from the fact that the narrow road would make passing hazardous for both of them, especially for Norman and Griggory.

Norman was no race car driver but the advantage he figured he probably had was knowledge of the road and it was now up to him to use it. Ahead about a kilometre he knew there was a deceptively sharp turn to the right. He had taken the turn several times in the past at fairly high speed (necessitated by the fact that hunting was only allowed during hunting season and the local Game Warden took a dim view to violations of that law). The truck navigated the corner and came out moving predictably sideways, an easy position from which to recover.

Unfortunately for the driver of the Coupe, the corner proved too much for his skill level and the car took a detour, down a long bush covered embankment, ending up straddling a small brook.

"… where fishing at this time of the year is also illegal" laughed Norman.

Norman continued on, quite happy with himself and perhaps just a little complacent, both men neglected to notice a second vehicle had joined the pursuit; another black automobile.

Norman was quickly approaching his destination and only then saw the second vehicle in his rear view mirror. He felt certain that this was not just a driver out for a Sunday jaunt in the country, especially since this was a dead-end road. He knew he could not drive directly to the site without being followed but he had to do what he could to assure as best he could that the driver of the second vehicle would be unable to find the site or at least buy some time before he did stumble across it. The never ending twists and turns that characterized the road Norman knew to be to his advantage and not to his pursuer.

The "road" into the site was completely grown up with a healthy stand of alders. Plowing his truck through that would be difficult and, to say the least, time consuming. Time was something they didn't have. The plan was simple. Drive about a half kilometre beyond the "road", ditch the truck on the opposite side of the dirt road from the site entrance (but not to the extent that it could not be "un-ditched"), leave the truck and Sport (sound asleep in his comfortable quarters and completely oblivious to the goings-on), and as quick as they could, go straight into the woods on the site-side of the road until they could not be seen from the road, then turn northeast toward the site.

So, grabbing the rifle, and quickly explaining 'the plan' to Griggory, that's exactly what they did, and even Norman was surprised how well the maneuver came off. He could hear the second car coming to a rock grinding stop on the road, reversing, then two doors opening and slamming shut. This surprised both Norman and Griggory.

By the time the second car was vacated and the passengers decided on which side of the road they would enter the woods, Norman figured he was very near the clearing, perhaps another hundred meters or so. Sure enough, there was the open field, dead ahead. It was quite large, perhaps twenty hectares or more, and almost square.

He had been here a number of times in the past. Old rock fences divided the site into a number of smaller fields, the remnants of a cellar to his immediate right, even the hand pump was still in place, albeit covered in rust and the wooden pump handle had long since fallen off. An old apple orchard on the northeast side was ideal for deer hunting. But, there was nothing else of interest or out of place about the site. It was partially grown up in trees, mostly small spruce but that was about it.

Both Griggory and Norman were feeling a mix of emotions as they seated themselves on a piece of low rock wall and gazed around at the abandoned site. They had truly hoped that the trip here would result in at least a few answers but it was looking more and more like an elaborate hoax and he was the brunt of it. The realization raised even more questions.

Why would even a jokester send them out here on a wild goose chase? Who was it? wondered Norman.

Griggory rose from his perch and stared across the field, then to his left and to his right.

"Norman," he said, "They are here; right in front of us."

Norman looked at him with a puzzled expression.

"Who's here? What are you talking about?" asked Norman.

"The owners of the object I imagine. Can't you see it yet," said Griggory, pointing to the other side of the field.

Norman looked but clearly was not seeing what Griggory was seeing. He then stood up as well.

Then it came to him. The trees on the other side of the field appeared to be a little lighter green than those to his left and right.

"Whatever it is, is... invisible but apparently not to birds," said Griggory as a large crow landed on top of 'it" and seemed to be suspended in mid air.

"Good afternoon, Mr. MacLeod, Comrade Semjonov. If I didn't know better, I would think you are trying to avoid us... yes?"

Griggory and Norman, in total surprise, turned around. The man was tall, chunky build but not particularly muscular, well groomed although his suit was a bit dusty and holding a pistol pointed directly at Norman. Norman started to reach for his rifle but the other gentleman with him, who Norman recognized as Wilsey, got to it first.

"Well Comrade, don't you think introductions are in order? Where are your manners."

"Norman, this is Kazamin Barkov and I assume that lackey with him is Wilsey," said Griggory.

Norman recognized Wilsey

"I am not here to waste your time or mine, gentlemen. What I want is what I believe you have on your person…yes?" he concluded with a sardonic grin that spoke his comfort level with intimidation and treachery.

They both, of course, knew exactly what he was referring to.

"No more stalling, Mr. MacLeod," Kazamin continued.

"Give Mr. Wilsey what you have in your pocket and you may live to see another sunrise."

Norman reached into his pocket to get the pipe.

"Tell me", said Norman, "why do you want this thing?"

He held it up for Kazamin to see.

"Mr. MacLeod, that 'thing' as you call it, will make me a very rich man indeed, a situation I require to continue to live in this country in relative safety since there are those in my homeland who are very unhappy with me at present."

Wilsey became agitated and anger was clearly welling up inside him.

"What do you mean, 'me?' The deal, Barkov, my good friend," screamed Wilsey, whose anger shifted into high gear, "was that 'we' would split the profits, Do you think I have put myself through this just to be stuck in the middle of nowhere with Mr. Bumpkin here?"

He motioned toward Norman.

Norman was between the two of them, unarmed and the situation was deteriorating rapidly. Wilsey started to raise the rifle but Barkov cautioned him that that would not be a wise move and Wilsey slammed the rifle to the ground.

"You may stop playing the part of a lawyer now Mr. Wilsey and I have no longer any need of your services. In point of fact Mr. MacLeod, Comrade Semjonov, Mr. Wilsey is little more than a common crook, a thief, but a very good actor, yes?" stated Kazamin.

"Just a crook; something like you?" said Griggory.

Kazamin was so engrossed in his own drama, he didn't see the trail of small lights coming from the far right side of the invisible ship until the air in front of the four men was alive with rapidly circling brilliant white lights. More and more lights joined the mass until they almost obliterated the sky above. And then, they broke into four distinct circles, one over each of the four men and each was surrounded, head to foot, with white light in which no individual particles were distinguishable.

Once enveloped in the light, all trace of fear evaporated and each felt an overpowering sense of calm although none could move a muscle.

"We are not authorized to make direct contact."

The voice was mechanical, with no detectable emotion or

inflection.

"No harm will come to you. We merely wish to retrieve an object that is in your possession and to evaluate your understanding."

Norman was still holding onto the length of lead pipe. Suddenly, it began to disappear from his grip and, in a few seconds, was gone; completely.

Although he couldn't move, Normans brain was fully functioning and working overtime.

Evaluate my understanding, he wondered.

Suddenly, after what seemed like an hour, Norman felt weightless and surrounded by literally thousands of images. His home, only it had changed. The veranda was no longer falling away from the house and the whole place was sporting a new coat of white paint. Then his best friend Clayton, working in the vegetable garden to the side of his house, and Dr. Decourcey getting out of her truck in his driveway. It then stopped as quickly as it had started and then nothing; just the whiteness of his surroundings.

After some time (and Norman could not judge how long it was), the came voice again.

"We detect strongly hostile intentions in two that we cannot accommodate. We are requires to cede to a non-aggressive alternative. You may indicate your advice for our consideration." the voice informed.

This time Norman heard Griggory's voice loud and clear and they talked for a few moments before agreeing on a plan.

"Perhaps someday contact will be permitted," said the voice. "Please accept our token of appreciation of your efforts in retrieving the recorder from our destroyed ship."

In the blink of an eye, the light and the lights disappeared and there was no sign of the ship anywhere, nor was there any sign of Kazamin and Wilsey. Just Norman and Griggory standing in an empty field.

"Did you see anything while you were in that light thing," asked Norman.

"Yes. And it was wonderful. I saw Elsa, my wife and my parents and Yakov, my uncle and everybody is fine. I have never felt so good in my life. What about you Norman", asked Griggory and Norman quickly relayed his experience.

The field was not quite empty. About six meters in front of them was a small box sitting on the damp grass. Norman went over and picked up the box. It was clearly hand made with numerous symbols of a religious nature carved into the smooth well preserved wood.

"Here, have a look. What's this all about?" he said, handing it to Griggory.

Griggory opened the box and removed its contents. A book, opened it to the first page, then carefully closed it and gently replaced it in the box.

"Just a book. Generous of them, wouldn't you say," said Norman.

"Just a book? Just a book?" said Griggory almost screaming. "Norman, I believe sir, what you have in that box is not just a book. I have seen photos of such a book and there are only two in existence as far as I know. That book is a first edition Gutenberg Bible printed in 1456, the oldest printed item in existence. I'm not sure of its value but it's probably in the order of five million dollars, perhaps much, much more. Norman, you are a millionaire; a multi-millionaire. How do you feel now?"

"Go away with you Greg. It's just an old book, but I will say this, if it is what you think it is, we are millionaires, not just me. Without you, I would never have figured what those numbers meant." said Norman.

"Yes, well you should get it properly evaluated first. We can discuss sharing later on. Would that be well with you Norman?" asked Griggory as they began the walk toward the road and the parked vehicles.

"You know Norman," said Griggory, "it's going to be something of a problem telling how we inherited the book. I think we should spend some time discussing our game plan." Norman actually thought the same thing but no 'game plan' came to mind at the moment with the exception of the truth, figuring nobody would believe them anyway.

"Yeah, that's fine Greg. But tell me something. Did you hear an explanation of what that thing was? The thing in the lead pipe? I did but didn't understand much of it. You're the one with the schooling."

"I'm not all that certain. Norman," responded Griggory. "But I think the item in the pipe was some kind of recording devise that was on board the ship that exploded over Russia and they wanted it back so they could determine what went wrong."

"Okay, but what about the lights? What's the story with them?"

"They referred to them as Lumenots. I remember reading some of Dr. Oborski's notes and he mentioned that they could be very small machines. I mean really small. He couldn't distinguish them well with a microscope so he figured that you could line up a dozen of them on the diameter of a human hair. It seems that each of those things has a small bit of, shall we say, intelligence; not enough to do much of anything. But as a mass, say thousands, they are capable of carrying out some function that could be flying around and pin pointing a location or... burning numbers on a door."

"Right." said Norman. "Are you on medication of some kind, by any chance? By the way, you smell somethin' awful, again!. You really got to do something about that when we get back."

"Yes, well... Norman, your bathing facilities are, shall we say... limited. I used the puncheon in the barnyard one night. The water is very cold you know."

"Get used to it, Griggory – this is the country and we can't afford such luxuries as indoor plumbing. Besides, the wash tub was good enough when you decided to leave the barn" said Norman.

"Norman, you, my friend are a millionaire. You can afford anything, including plumbing" responded Griggory.

"Holy cow, we aren't even home yet and you're spending our money. How much is a ticket to Moscow these days" said Norman laughingly as they reached the truck.

Even though Griggory did not have a drivers permit, he drove Wilsey's Chev because Norman didn't want him "… stinking up the truck." The boys in the crashed car were on the road when Norman and Griggory drove by and were in added dismay, after they passed.

On the way back, Norman stopped off at Clayton's home. To his uncontrolled delight, his best friend was in the vegetable garden at the side of the house, working away.

"I can't explain it Norm," said Clayton, "but I got up this afternoon and not a sign of the disease. I feel as though I was 20 years younger. No cough, no trouble breathing and hungry as a horse. Can't explain it but I'll take it."

Norman also felt twenty years younger and could hardly wait to see his old house.

EPILOGUE

Even though it was August, it was cool. The gentle rain that was falling from the dark and murky sky added to the gloominess of the scene. Both men woke at the about the same instant, looking around and trying to put together what had happened to them. They both had headaches well beyond anything they had ever experienced. The last thing they recalled was standing in the field, completely surrounded by a white light and totally immobilized. They were in a wooded area for sure except that the area around them, and for as far as they could see in the mist, was short second growth and the ground littered with fallen trees that had met their violent end many years in the past. There were bent and rusted metal pots and pans, partially rotted bits of leather and canvas and a couple of empty vodka bottles. They could hear voices in the distance, farther down the shallow embankment on which they were sitting.

"Any idea where we are Mr. Barkov" asked Mr. Wilsey.

After a lengthy pause during which time Kazamin looked about the site.

"Unfortunately, I do. I am sure we are in the Tunguska Valley." said Kazamin.

"Don't kid with me you Russian piece of crap! Now, where are we?"

Kazamin said nothing, searching for his pistol without success, and that response, in itself, was sufficient confirmation for Wilsey.

"But we have nothing to worry about Mr. Wilsey. You will continue to play the part of the lawyer and we will get out of this mess, I promise you" said Kazamin.

"Oh really." said Wilsey. "Well Mr. Barkov, I've heard that line before and it seems your promises aren't worth a plugged nickel. And here's another piece of news for you, I am no longer in need of your services, sir."

Kazamin's face grimaced and he began screaming at Wilsey as he got up and was making his way down the slope.

"You need me Wilsey. You can't speak a word of Russian. You won't last a day without me!"

"I will probably outlast you, Barkov" said Wilsey. "You see, I'm an actor. I can be anyone I want. I'm also a Canadian citizen and that won't hurt me. But you Barkov, you are just a common, greed driven crook with nothing waiting for you except some rather nasty pals that would very much like you to explain where their money went and no 'object' to show for it. I'd love to be there when you try and explain that some men from Mars took it from you. I may have no reputation in Russia but you, Barkov, have and frankly I'm glad it's your reputation and not mine. Try and stay alive long enough to eat dinner, you jerk!"

And with that, Wilsey waved a good bye and continued on down the slope hoping to soon meet up with whoever was ahead of him and the relative safety they could provide, leaving Kazamin to contemplate his less than stellar future. Stopping, he turned around.

"Think about this Kazamin. You chased that thing half way around the world for years, ruined I don't know how many lives, just to satisfy your unsatisfiable greed and look where you are now; right back where it all started. Have a good day, *Comrade!*"

ABOUT THE AUTHOR

Norbert Stewart, with his wife Theresa, own and operate a print and graphics design business. He holds a B.Sc. Degree from Macdonald College of McGill University and an M.Sc. Degree from the University of Guelph. "The Luminots" is his first novel. He and his wife have two children and live in Charlottetown, PEI, Canada.

Also in the Griggory Semjonov series

The Amulet

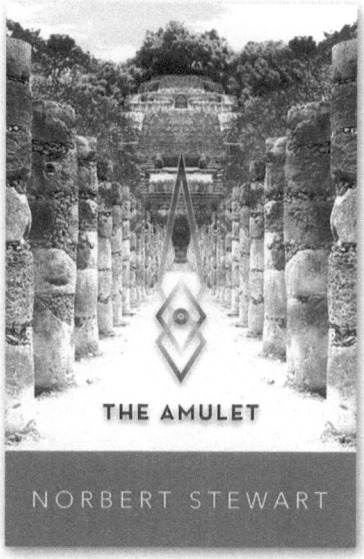

THE AMULET

NORBERT STEWART

Dr. Griggory Semjonov is back. When The Scholfield Group is asked to assist in translating and verifying inscriptions on a number of rune stones recently unearthed in Norway. The translation describes a 10th century Viking voyage to the south Atlantic, possibly the Caribbean area as well as a golden helmet long thought to have been merely a myth.

Tasked with validating the saga, the team soon learns there is far more to it than meets the eye. Their involvement sets in motion a series of deadly events that threatens their survival with the line between friend and foe plagued with uncertainty.

The search for truth takes the team on a dangerous and fast paced journey across western Europe, eastern Canada and the Caribbean as they separate fact from fiction and unweave the mystery surrounding the golden helmet and an ancient artifact.

LOWELL
STEWART
PUBLISHING

www.ingramcontent.com/pod-product-compliance
Lightning Source LLC
Chambersburg PA
CBHW030237200626
46816CB00002BA/406